DEREK LANDY

Skulduggery Pleasant

HarperCollins *Children's Books*

First published in hardback in Great Britain by HarperCollins *Children's Books* 2007
HarperCollins *Children's Books* is a division of
HarperCollins*Publishers* Ltd
77-85 Fulham Palace Road, Hammersmith, London W6 8JB

The HarperCollins *Children's Books* website address is
www.harpercollinschildrensbooks.co.uk

Skulduggery Pleasant rests his weary bones on the web at:
www.skulduggerypleasant.com

1

Illuminated letters by Tom Percival 2006

ISBN-13 978-0-00-725441-5
ISBN-10 0-00-725441-5

Printed and bound in England by
Clays Ltd, St Ives plc

This book is dedicated to my parents, John and Barbara.

Dad – this is for your bizarrely unwavering support and unflinching faith.

Barbs – this is for that look on your face when I told you the good news.

I owe you absolutely everything and, y'know, I suppose it's entirely possible that I feel some, like, degree of affection towards the two of you...

1

STEPHANIE

ordon Edgley's sudden death came as a shock to everyone – not least himself. One moment he was in his study, seven words into the twenty-fifth sentence of the final chapter of his new book *And The Darkness Rained Upon Them*, and the next he was dead. *A tragic loss*, his mind echoed numbly as he slipped away.

The funeral was attended by family and acquaintances but not many friends. Gordon hadn't been a well-liked figure in the publishing world, for although the books he wrote – tales of horror and magic and wonder – regularly reared their heads in the bestseller lists, he had the disquieting habit of insulting people without realising it, then laughing at their shock. It was at Gordon's funeral, however, that Stephanie Edgley first caught sight of the gentleman in the tan overcoat.

He was standing under the shade of a large tree, away from the crowd, the coat buttoned up all the way despite the warmth of the afternoon. A scarf was wrapped around the lower half of his face and even from her position on the far side of the grave, Stephanie could make out the wild and frizzy hair that escaped from the wide brimmed hat he wore low over his gigantic sunglasses. She watched him, intrigued by his appearance. And then, like he knew he was being observed, he turned and walked back through the rows of headstones, and disappeared from sight.

After the service, Stephanie and her parents travelled back to her dead uncle's house, over a humpbacked bridge and along a narrow road that carved its way through thick woodland. The gates were heavy and grand and stood open, welcoming them into the estate. The grounds were vast and the old house itself was ridiculously big.

There was an extra door in the living room, a door disguised as a bookcase, and when she was younger Stephanie liked to think that no one else knew about this door, not even Gordon himself. It was a secret passageway, like in the stories she'd read, and she'd make up adventures about haunted houses and smuggled treasure. This secret passageway would always be her escape route, and the imaginary villains in these adventures would be dumbfounded by her sudden and mysterious disappearance. But now this door, this secret passageway, stood open, and there was a steady stream of people through it, and she was saddened that this little piece of magic had been taken from her.

Tea was served and drinks were poured and little sandwiches were passed around on silver trays, and Stephanie watched the mourners casually appraise their surroundings. The major topic of hushed conversation was the will. Gordon wasn't a man who inspired, or even demonstrated, any great affection, so no one could predict who would inherit his substantial fortune. Stephanie could see the greed seep into the watery eyes of her father's other brother, a horrible little man called Fergus, as he nodded sadly and spoke sombrely and pocketed the silverware when he thought no one was looking.

Fergus's wife was a thoroughly dislikeable, sharp-featured woman named Beryl. She drifted through the crowd, deep in unconvincing grief, prying for gossip and digging for scandal. Her daughters did their best to ignore Stephanie. Carol and

Crystal were twins, fifteen years old, and as sour and vindictive as their parents. Whereas Stephanie was dark-haired, tall, slim and strong, they were bottle-blonde, stumpy and dressed in clothes that made them bulge in all the wrong places. Apart from their brown eyes, no one would guess that the twins were related to her. She liked that. It was the only thing about them she liked. She left them to their petty glares and snide whispers, and went for a walk.

The corridors of her uncle's house were long and lined with paintings. The floor beneath Stephanie's feet was wooden, polished to a gleam, and the house smelled of age. Not musty exactly but... experienced. These walls and these floors had seen a lot in their time, and Stephanie was nothing but a faint whisper to them. Here one instant, gone the next.

Gordon had been a good uncle. Arrogant and irresponsible, yes, but also childish and enormous fun, with a light in his eyes, a glint of mischief. When everyone else was taking him seriously, Stephanie was privy to the winks and the nods and the half-smiles that he would shoot her way when they weren't looking. Even as a child she felt she understood him better than most. She liked his intelligence and his wit, and the way he didn't care what people thought of him. He'd been a good uncle to have. He'd taught her a lot.

She knew that her mother and Gordon had briefly dated ("courted", her mother had called it), but when Gordon had introduced her to his younger brother, it was love at first sight. Gordon liked to grumble that he had never got more than a peck on the cheek, but he had stepped aside graciously, and had quite happily gone on to have numerous torrid affairs with numerous beautiful women. He used to say that it had almost been a fair trade, but that he suspected he had lost out.

Stephanie climbed the staircase, pushed open the door to Gordon's study and stepped inside. The walls were filled with the framed covers from his bestsellers and shared space with all manner of awards. One entire wall was made up of shelves, jammed with books. There were biographies and historical novels and science texts and psychology tomes, and there were battered little paperbacks stuck in between. A lower shelf had magazines, literary reviews and quarterlies.

Stephanie passed the shelves which housed the first editions of Gordon's novels and approached the desk. She looked at the chair where he'd died, trying to imagine him there, how he must have slumped. And then, a voice so smooth it could have been made of velvet:

"At least he died doing what he loved."

She turned, surprised, to see the man from the funeral in the overcoat and hat standing in the doorway. The scarf was still wrapped, the sunglasses still on, the fuzzy hair still poking out. His hands were gloved.

"Yes," Stephanie said, because she couldn't think of anything else to say. "At least there's that."

"You're one of his nieces then?" the man asked. "You're not stealing anything, you're not breaking anything, so I'd guess you're Stephanie." She nodded and took the opportunity to look at him more closely. She couldn't see even the tiniest bit of his face beneath the scarf and sunglasses.

"Were you a friend of his?" she asked. He was tall, this man, tall and thin, though his coat made it difficult to judge.

"I was," he answered with a move of his head. This slight movement made her realise that the rest of his body was unnaturally still. "I've known him for years, met him outside a bar in New York when I was over there, back when he had just published his first novel."

Stephanie couldn't see anything behind the sunglasses – they were black as pitch. "Are you a writer too?"

"Me? No, I wouldn't know where to start. But I got to live out my writer fantasies through Gordon."

"You had writer fantasies?"

"Doesn't everyone?"

"I don't know. I don't think so."

"Oh. Then that would make me seem kind of odd, wouldn't it?"

"Well," Stephanie answered. "It would *help*."

"Gordon used to talk about you all the time, boast about his little niece. He was an individual of character, your uncle. It seems that you are too."

"You say that like you know me."

"Strong-willed, intelligent, sharp-tongued, doesn't suffer fools gladly... remind you of anyone?"

"Yes. Gordon."

"Interesting," said the man. "Because those are the exact words he used to describe you." His gloved fingers dipped into his waistcoat and brought out an ornate pocket watch on a delicate gold chain.

"Good luck in whatever you decide to do with your life."

"Thank you," Stephanie said, a little dumbly. "You too."

She felt the man smile, though she could see no mouth, and he turned from the doorway and left her there. Stephanie found she couldn't take her eyes off where he had been. Who was he? She hadn't even got his name.

She crossed over to the door and stepped out, wondering how he had vanished from sight so quickly. She hurried down the stairs and reached the large hall without seeing him. She opened the front door just as a big black car turned out on to the road. She watched him drive away, stayed there for a few moments, then reluctantly rejoined her extended family in the living room, just in time to see Fergus slip a silver ashtray into his breast pocket.

2

THE WILL

ife in the Edgley household was fairly uneventful. Stephanie's mother worked in a bank and her father owned a construction company, and she had no brothers or sisters, so the routine they had settled into was one of amiable convenience. But even so, there was always the voice in the back of her mind telling her that there should be more to her life than *this*, more to her life than the small coastal town of Haggard. She just couldn't figure out what that something was.

Her first year of secondary school had just come to a close

and she was looking forward to the summer break. Stephanie didn't like school. She found it difficult to get along with her classmates – not because they weren't nice people, but simply because she had nothing in common with them. And she didn't like teachers. She didn't like the way they demanded respect they hadn't earned. Stephanie had no problem doing what she was told, just so long as she was given a good reason why she should.

She had spent the first few days of the summer helping out her father, answering phones and sorting through the files in his office. Gladys, his secretary of seven years, had decided she'd had enough of the construction business and wanted to try her hand as a performance artist. Stephanie found it vaguely discomfiting whenever she passed her on the street, this forty-three-year-old woman doing a modern dance interpretation of Faust. Gladys had made herself a costume to go with the act, a costume, she said, that symbolised the internal struggle Faust was going through, and apparently she refused to be seen in public without it. Stephanie did her best to avoid catching Gladys's eye.

If Stephanie wasn't helping out in the office, she was either down at the beach, swimming, or locked in her room listening to music. She was in her room, trying to find the charger for her mobile phone, when her mother knocked on the door and stepped in. She was still dressed in the sombre clothes she had worn to the funeral, though Stephanie had tied back her long dark hair and changed into her usual jeans and trainers within two minutes of returning to the house.

"We got a call from Gordon's solicitor," her mother said, sounding a little surprised. "They want us at the reading of the will."

"Oh," Stephanie responded. "What do you think he left you?"

"Well, we'll find out tomorrow. You too, because you're coming with us."

"I am?" Stephanie said with a slight frown.

"Your name's on the list, that's all I know. We're leaving at ten, OK?"

"I'm supposed to be helping Dad in the morning."

"He called Gladys, asked her to fill in for a few hours, as a favour. She said yes, as long as she could wear the peanut suit."

They left for the solicitor's at a quarter past ten the next morning, fifteen minutes later than planned thanks to Stephanie's father's casual disregard for punctuality. He ambled through the house, looking like there was something he'd forgotten and he was just waiting for it to occur to him again. He nodded and smiled whenever his wife told him to hurry up, said "Yes, absolutely," and just before he was due to join them in the car, he meandered off again, looking around with a dazed expression.

"He does this on purpose," Stephanie's mother said as they sat in the car, seatbelts on and ready to go. They watched him appear at the front door, shrug into his jacket, tuck in his shirt, go to step out, and then pause.

"He looks like he's about to sneeze," Stephanie remarked.

"No," her mother responded, "he's just thinking." She stuck her head out of the window. "Desmond, what's wrong now?"

He looked up, puzzled. "I think I'm forgetting something."

Stephanie leaned forward in the back seat, took a look at him and spoke to her mother, who nodded and stuck her head out again. "Where are your shoes, dear?"

He looked down at his socks – one brown, one navy – and his clouded expression cleared. He gave them the thumbs-up and disappeared from view.

"That man," her mother said, shaking her head. "Did you know he once lost a shopping centre?"

"He what?"

"I never told you that? It was the first big contract he got. His company did a wonderful job and he was driving his clients to see it, and he forgot where he put it. He drove around for almost an hour until he saw something he recognised. He may be a very talented engineer, but I swear, he's got the attention span of a goldfish. So unlike Gordon."

"They weren't very alike, were they?"

Her mother smiled. "It wasn't always that way. They used to do everything together. The three of them were inseparable."

"What, even Fergus?"

"Even Fergus. But when your grandmother died they all drifted apart. Gordon started mixing with a strange crowd after that."

"Strange in what way?"

"Ah, they probably just appeared strange to us," her mother said with a small laugh. "Your dad was getting started in the construction business and I was in college and we were what you might call normal. Gordon resisted being normal, and his friends, they kind of scared us. We never knew what they were into, but we knew it wasn't anything..."

"*Normal.*"

"Exactly. They scared your dad most of all though."

"Why?"

Stephanie's father walked out of the house, shoes on, and closed the front door after him.

"I think he was more like Gordon than he liked to let on," her mother said quietly, and then her dad got into the car.

"OK," he said proudly. "I'm ready."

They looked at him as he nodded, chuffed with himself. He strapped on his seatbelt and turned the key. The engine purred to life. Stephanie waved to Jasper, an eight-year-old boy with unfortunate ears, as her dad backed out on to the road, put the car in gear and they were off, narrowly missing their wheelie bin as they went.

The drive to the solicitor's office in the city took a little under an hour and they arrived twenty minutes late. They were led up a flight of creaky stairs to a small office, too warm to be comfortable, with a large window that offered a wonderful view of the brick wall across the street. Fergus and Beryl were there, and they showed their displeasure at having been kept waiting by looking at their watches and scowling. Stephanie's parents took the remaining chairs and Stephanie stood behind them as the solicitor peered at them through cracked spectacles.

"Now can we get started?" Beryl snapped.

The solicitor, a short man named Mr Fedgewick, with the girth and appearance of a sweaty bowling ball, tried smiling. "We still have one more person to wait on," he said and Fergus's eyes bulged.

20

"Who?" he demanded. "There can't be anyone else, we are the only siblings Gordon had. Who is it? It's not some charity, is it? I've never trusted charities. They always want something from you."

"It's, it's not a charity," Mr Fedgewick said. "He did say, however, that he might be a little late."

"Who said?" Stephanie's father asked, and the solicitor looked down at the file open before him.

"A most unusual name, this," he said. "It seems we are waiting on one Mr Skulduggery Pleasant."

"Well who on earth is that?" asked Beryl, irritated. "He sounds like a, he sounds like a... Fergus, what does he sound like?"

"He sounds like a weirdo," Fergus said, glaring at Fedgewick. "He's not a weirdo, is he?"

"I really couldn't say," Fedgewick answered, his paltry excuse for a smile failing miserably under the glares he was getting from Fergus and Beryl. "But I'm sure he'll be along soon."

Fergus frowned, narrowing his beady eyes as much as was possible. "How are you sure?"

Fedgewick faltered, unable to offer a reason, and then the door opened and the man in the tan overcoat entered the room.

"Sorry I'm late," he said, closing the door behind him. "It was unavoidable I'm afraid."

Everyone in the room stared at him, stared at the scarf and the gloves and the sunglasses and the wild fuzzy hair. It was a glorious day outside, certainly not the kind of weather to be wrapped up like this. Stephanie looked closer at the hair. From this distance, it didn't even seem real.

The solicitor cleared his throat. "Um, you are Skulduggery Pleasant?"

"At your service," the man said. Stephanie could listen to that voice all day. Her mother, uncertain as she was, had smiled her greetings, but her father was looking at him with an expression of wariness she had never seen on his face before. After a moment the expression left him and he nodded politely and looked back to Mr Fedgewick. Fergus and Beryl were still staring.

"Do you have something wrong with your face?" Beryl asked.

Fedgewick cleared his throat again. "OK then, let's get down to business, now that we're all here. Excellent. Good. This, of course, being the last will and testament of Gordon Edgley, revised last almost one year ago. Gordon has been a client of mine for the past twenty years, and in that time, I got to know him well, so let me pass on to you, his family and, and friend, my deepest, deepest—"

"Yes yes yes," Fergus interrupted, waving his hand in the air. "Can we just skip this part? We're already running behind schedule. Let's go to the part where we get stuff. Who gets the house? And who gets the villa?"

"Who gets the fortune?" Beryl asked, leaning forward in her seat.

"The royalties," Fergus said. "Who gets the royalties from the books?"

Stephanie glanced at Skulduggery Pleasant from the corner of her eye. He was standing back against the wall, hands in his pockets, looking at the solicitor. Well, he *seemed* to be looking at the solicitor; with those sunglasses he could have been looking anywhere. She returned her gaze to Fedgewick as he picked up a page from his desk and read from it.

"'To my brother Fergus and his beautiful wife Beryl,'" he read, and Stephanie did her best to hide a grin, "'I leave my car, and my boat, and a gift.'"

Fergus and Beryl blinked. "His car?" Fergus said. "His boat? Why would he leave me his boat?"

"You hate the water," Beryl said, anger rising in her voice. "You get seasick."

"I *do* get seasick," Fergus snapped, "and he knew that!"

"And we already have a car," Beryl said.

"And we already have a car!" Fergus repeated.

Beryl was sitting so far up on her chair that she was almost on the desk. "This gift," she said, her voice low and threatening, "is it the fortune?"

Mr Fedgewick coughed nervously, and took a small box from his desk drawer and slid it towards them. They looked at this box. They looked some more. They both reached for it at the same time, and Stephanie watched them slap at each other's hands until Beryl snatched it off the desk and tore the lid open.

"What is it?" Fergus asked in a small voice. "Is it a key to a safety deposit box? Is it, is it an account number? Is it, what is it? Wife, what is it?"

All colour had drained from Beryl's face and her hands were shaking. She blinked hard to keep the tears away, then she turned the box for everyone to see, and everyone saw the brooch, about the size of a drinks coaster, nestled in the plush cushion. Fergus stared at it.

"It doesn't even have any jewels on it," Beryl said, her voice strangled. Fergus opened his mouth wide like a startled fish and turned to Fedgewick.

"What else do we get?" he asked, panicking.

Mr Fedgewick tried another smile. "Your, uh, your brother's love?"

Stephanie heard a high-pitched whine, and it took her a moment to realise it was coming from Beryl. Fedgewick returned his attention to the will, trying to ignore the horrified looks he was getting from Fergus and his wife.

"'To my good friend and guide Skulduggery Pleasant I leave the following advice. Your path is your own, and I have no wish to sway you, but sometimes the greatest enemy we can face is ourselves, and the greatest battle is against the darkness within. There is a storm coming, and sometimes the key to safe harbour is hidden from us, and sometimes it is right before our eyes.'"

Stephanie joined in with everyone else as they stared at Mr Pleasant. She had known there was something different about him, she had known it the first moment she saw him – there was something exotic, something mysterious, something *dangerous*. For his part, his head dipped lower and that was the only reaction he gave. He offered no explanations as to what Gordon's message had meant.

Fergus patted his wife's knee. "See, Beryl? A car, a boat, a brooch, it's not that bad. He could have given us some stupid advice."

"Oh, shut up, would you?" Beryl snarled and Fergus recoiled in his chair.

Mr Fedgewick read on. "'To my other brother, Desmond, the lucky one of the family, I leave to you your wife. I think you might like her.'" Stephanie saw her parents clasp each other's hands and smile sadly. "'So now that you've successfully stolen my girlfriend, maybe you'd like to take her to my villa in France, which I am also leaving to you.'"

"They get the villa?" Beryl cried, jumping to her feet.

"Beryl," Fergus said, "please..."

"Do you know how much that villa is worth?" Beryl continued, looking like she might lunge at Stephanie's parents. "We get a brooch – they get a villa? There are only three of them! We've got Carol and Crystal! We have more! We could do with the extra space! Why do *they* deserve the villa?" She thrust the box towards them. "Swap!"

"Mrs Edgley, please retake your seat or we shall be unable to continue," Mr Fedgewick said, and eventually, after much bug-eyed glaring, Beryl sat down.

"Thank you," Fedgewick said, looking like he had had quite enough excitement for one day. He licked his lips, adjusted his glasses, and peered again at the will. "'If there is one regret that I have had in my life, it is that I have never fathered any children. There are times when I look at what Fergus and Beryl have produced and I consider myself fortunate, but there are also times when it breaks my heart. And so, finally, to my niece Stephanie.'"

Stephanie's eyes widened. What? *She* was getting something? Leaving the villa to her parents wasn't enough for Gordon?

Fedgewick continued reading. "'The world is bigger than you know and scarier than you might imagine. The only currency worth anything is being true to yourself, and the only goal worth seeking is finding out who you truly are.'"

She could feel Fergus and Beryl glaring at her and she did her best to ignore them.

"'Make your parents proud, and make them glad to have you living under their roof, because I leave to you my property and possessions, my assets and my royalties, to be inherited on the day you turn eighteen. I'd just like to take this opportunity to say that, in my own way, I love you all, even those I don't particularly like. That's you, Beryl.'"

Fedgewick took off his spectacles and looked up.

Stephanie became aware that everyone was staring at her and she hadn't a clue what she was supposed to say. Fergus was again doing his startled fish impression and Beryl was pointing one long bony finger at her, trying to speak but failing. Her parents were looking at her in stunned surprise. Only Skulduggery Pleasant moved, walking behind her and gently touching her arm.

"Congratulations," he said and moved on towards the door.

As soon as it clicked shut behind him, Beryl found her voice.

"HER?" she screamed. "HER?"

3

LITTLE GIRL, ALL ALONE

That afternoon Stephanie and her mother took the fifteen-minute drive from Haggard to Gordon's estate. Her mum opened the front door and stepped back.

"Owner of the house goes first," she said with a little smile and a bow, and Stephanie stepped inside. She wasn't thinking of this house as her property – the idea was too big, too silly. Even if her parents were, technically, the custodians until she turned eighteen, how could she own a house? How many other twelve-year-old kids owned houses?

No, it was too silly an idea. Too far-fetched. Too crazy. Exactly the kind of thing that Gordon would have thought made perfect sense.

The house was big and quiet and empty as they walked through it. Everything seemed new to her now, and Stephanie found herself reacting differently to the furniture and carpets and paintings. Did she like it? Did she agree with this colour or that fabric? One thing that had to be said for Gordon, he had a good eye. Stephanie's mother said there was very little she would change if she had to. Some of the paintings were a little too unnerving for her taste maybe, but on the whole the furnishings were elegant and understated, exuding an air of distinction that befitted a house of this stature.

They hadn't decided what they were going to do with the house. Any decision was left up to Stephanie, but her parents still had the villa to consider. Owning three houses between them seemed a bit much. Her father had suggested selling the villa but her mother hated the thought of letting go of a place so idyllic.

They had also talked about Stephanie's education, and she knew *that* conversation was far from over. The moment they had left Mr Fedgewick's office they warned her not to let all this go to her head. Recent events, they had said, should not mean she could stop studying, stop planning for college. She needed to be independent, they said, she needed to make it on her own.

Stephanie had let them talk, and nodded occasionally and muttered an agreement where an agreement was appropriate. She didn't bother to explain that she needed college, she needed to find her own way in the world because she knew that if she didn't, she'd never escape Haggard. She wasn't about to throw her future away simply because she had come into some money.

She and her mother spent so long looking around the ground floor that by the time they got to the bottom of the stairs, it was already five o'clock. With their exploring done for the day, they locked up and walked to the car. The first few drops of rain splattered against the windscreen as they got in. Stephanie clicked her seatbelt closed and her mother turned the key in the ignition.

The car spluttered a bit, groaned a little and then shut up altogether. Stephanie's mother looked at her.

"Uh oh." They both got out and opened the bonnet.

"Well," her mother said, looking at the engine, "at least that's still there."

"Do you know *anything* about engines?" Stephanie asked.

"That's why I have a husband, so I don't have to. Engines and shelves, that's why man was invented." Stephanie made a mental note to learn about engines before she turned eighteen.

She wasn't too fussed about the shelves.

Her mum dug her mobile phone out of her bag and called Stephanie's dad, but he was busy on site and there was no way he could get to them before nightfall. They went back inside the house and her mother called a mechanic, and they spent three quarters of an hour waiting for him to arrive.

The sky was grey and angry and the rain was falling hard by the time the truck appeared around the corner. It splashed through puddles on its way up the long drive, and Stephanie's mum pulled her jacket over her head and ran out to meet it. Stephanie could see a great big dog in the cab of the truck, looking on as the mechanic got out to examine their car. After a few minutes, her mother ran back inside, thoroughly drenched.

"He can't fix it here," she said, wringing out her jacket on the porch, "so he's going to tow it to the garage. It shouldn't take too long to fix."

"Will there be room for both of us in the truck?"

"You can sit on my knee."

"Mum!"

"Or I can sit on your knee, whatever works."

"Can I stay here?"

Her mother looked at her. "On your own?"

"Please? You just said it won't take long, and I'd like to have another look around, just on my own."

"I don't know, Steph..."

"Please? I've stayed on my own before. I won't break anything, I swear."

Her mother laughed. "OK fine. I shouldn't be any more than an hour, all right? An hour and a half at the most." Her mother gave her a quick kiss on the cheek. "Call me if you need anything."

She ran back outside and jumped in the cab next to the dog, who proceeded to slobber all over her face. Stephanie watched their car being towed off into the distance and then it vanished from sight.

She did a little more exploring, now that she was on her own. She climbed the stairs and went straight to Gordon's study.

His publisher, Seamus T. Steepe of Arc Light Books, had phoned them earlier that day, passing on his condolences and enquiring about the state of Gordon's last book. Her mother had told him that they'd find out if Gordon had completed it, and if he had, they'd send it on. Mr Steepe was very keen to get the book on the shelves, certain that it would crash on to the bestseller list and stay there for a long time. "Dead writers sell," he had said, like he approved of Gordon's clever marketing ploy.

Stephanie opened the desk drawer and found the

manuscript in a neat stack. She pulled it out carefully and laid it on the desktop, careful not to smudge the paper. The first page held the title, nothing more, in bold lettering:

And The Darkness Rained Upon Them.

The manuscript was thick and heavy, like all of Gordon's books. She'd read most of them, and the odd splash of pretension aside, had quite enjoyed his work. His stories tended to be about people who could do astonishing and wonderful things, and the strange and terrible events that invariably led up to their bizarre and horrible deaths. She noticed the way he would set up a strong and noble hero, and over the course of the book systematically subject this hero to brutal punishment in a bid to strip away all his arrogance and certainty so that by the end he was humbled and had learned a great lesson. And then Gordon killed him off, usually in the most undignified way possible. Stephanie could almost hear Gordon laughing with mischievous glee as she'd read.

She lifted the title page and carefully laid it face down on the desk beside the manuscript. She started reading. She didn't mean to spend long at it, but soon she was devouring every word, oblivious to the creaking old house and the rain outside.

Her mobile phone rang, making her jump. She had been reading for two hours. She pressed the answer button and held it to her ear.

"Hi, sweetie," came her mother's voice, "everything OK?"

"Yes," Stephanie answered. "Just reading."

"You're not reading one of Gordon's books, are you? Steph, he writes about horrible monsters and scary stuff and bad people doing worse things. It'll give you nightmares."

"No, Mum, I'm... I'm reading the dictionary."

Even the brief silence from the other end of the phone was sceptical. "The dictionary?" her mother said. "Really?"

"Yeah," Stephanie said. "Did you know that *popple* is a word?"

"You are stranger than your father, you know that?"

"I suspected as much... So is the car fixed yet?"

"No, and that's why I'm calling. They can't get it going and the road up to you is flooded. I'm going to get a taxi up as far as it'll go and then I'll see if I can find some way around on foot. It's going to be another two hours at least."

Stephanie sensed an opportunity. Ever since she was a child she had much preferred her own company to the company of others, and it occurred to her that she had never spent a whole night without her parents nearby. A small taste of freedom and it almost tingled on her tongue.

"Mum, it's fine, you don't have to. I'm OK here."

"There's no way I'm leaving you in a strange house by yourself."

"It's not a strange house; it's Gordon's and it's fine. There's no point in you trying to get here tonight – it's lashing rain."

"Sweetie, it won't take me long."

"It'll take you ages. Where's it flooded?"

Her mother paused. "At the bridge."

"The bridge? And you want to walk from the bridge to here?"

"If I speed-walk—"

"Mum, don't be silly. Get Dad to pick you up."

"Sweetheart, are you sure?"

"I like it here, really. OK?"

"Well, OK," her mother said reluctantly. "I'll be over first thing in the morning to pick you up, all right? And I saw some food in the cupboards, so if you're hungry you can make yourself something."

"OK. I'll see you tomorrow then."

"Call us if you need anything or if you just want some company."

"I will. Night Mum."

"I love you."

"I know."

Stephanie hung up and grinned. She slipped the phone back into her jacket and put her feet up on the desk, relaxing back into the chair, and went back to reading.

When she looked up again she was surprised to find that it was almost midnight and the rain had stopped. If she were home right now, she'd be in bed. She blinked, her eyes sore, stood up from the desk and went downstairs to the kitchen. For all his wealth and success and extravagant tastes, she was thankful that when it came to food, Gordon was a pretty standard guy. The bread was stale and the fruit was a bit too ripe, but there were biscuits and there was cereal, and the milk in the fridge was still good for one more day. Stephanie made herself a snack and wandered to the living room, where she flicked on the TV. She sat on the couch and was just getting comfy when the house phone rang.

She looked at it, resting there on the table at her elbow. Who would be calling? Anyone who knew Gordon had died wouldn't be calling because they'd know he had died, and she didn't really want to be the one to tell anyone who didn't know. It could be her parents, but then why didn't they just call her mobile?

Figuring that as the new owner of the house, it was her

responsibility to answer her own phone, Stephanie picked it up and held it to her ear. "Hello?"

Silence.

"Hello?" Stephanie repeated.

"Who is this?" came a man's voice.

"I'm sorry," Stephanie said, "who do you want to speak to?"

"Who is this?" responded the voice, more irritably this time.

"If you're looking for Gordon Edgley," Stephanie said, "I'm afraid that he's—"

"I know Edgley's dead," snapped the man. "Who are you? Your name?"

Stephanie hesitated. "Why do you want to know?" she asked.

"What are you doing in that house? Why are you in his house?"

"If you want to call back tomorrow—"

"I *don't* want to, all right? Listen to me, girlie, if you mess up my master's plans, he will be *very* displeased and he is *not* a man you want to displease, you got that? Now tell me who you are!"

Stephanie realised her hands were shaking. She forced herself to calm down and quickly found anger replacing her nervousness. "My name is none of your business," she said. "If you want to talk to someone, call back tomorrow at a reasonable hour."

"You don't talk to me like that," the man hissed.

"Goodnight," Stephanie said firmly.

"You do *not* talk to me like—"

But Stephanie was already putting the phone down. Suddenly the idea of spending the whole night here wasn't as appealing as it had first sounded. She considered calling her parents, then scolded herself for being so childish. *No need to worry them*, she thought to herself. *No need to worry them about something so*—

Someone pounded on the front door.

"Open up!" came the man's voice between the pounding. Stephanie got to her feet, staring through to the hall beyond the living room. She could see a dark shape behind the frosted glass around the front door. "Open the damn door!"

Stephanie backed up to the fireplace, her heart pounding in her chest. He knew she was in here, there was no use pretending that she wasn't, but maybe if she stayed really quiet he'd give up and go away. She heard him cursing, and the pounding grew so heavy that the front door rattled under the blows.

"Leave me alone!" Stephanie shouted.

"Open the door!"

"No!" she shouted back. She liked shouting – it disguised her fear. "I'm calling the police! I'm calling the police right now!"

The pounding stopped immediately and Stephanie saw the shape move away from the door. Was that it? Had she scared him away? She thought of the back door – was it locked? Of course it was locked... It had to be locked. But she wasn't sure, she wasn't certain. She grabbed a poker from the fireplace and was reaching for the phone when she heard a knock on the window beside her.

She cried out and jumped back. The curtains were open, and outside the window was pitch-black. She couldn't see a thing.

"Are you alone in there?" came the voice. It was teasing now, playing with her.

"Go away," she said loudly, holding up the poker so he could see it. She heard the man laugh.

"What are you going to do with that?" he asked.

"I'll break your head open with it!" Stephanie screamed at him, fear and fury bubbling inside her. She heard him laugh again.

"I just want to come in," he said. "Open the door for me, girlie. Let me come in."

"The police are on their way," she said.

"You're a liar."

Still she could see nothing beyond the glass and he could see everything. She moved to the phone, snatching it from its cradle.

"Don't do that," came the voice.

"I'm calling the police."

"The road's closed, girlie. You call them, I'll break down that door and kill you hours before they get here."

Fear became terror and Stephanie froze. She was going to cry. She could feel it, the tears welling up inside her. She hadn't cried in years. "What do you want?" she said to the darkness. "Why do you want to come in?"

"It's got nothing to do with *me*, girlie. I've just been sent to pick something up. Let me in. I'll look around, get what I came here for and leave. I won't harm a pretty little hair on your pretty little head, I *promise*. Now you just open that door right this second."

Stephanie gripped the poker in both hands and shook her head. She was crying now, tears rolling down her cheeks. "No," she said.

She screamed as a fist smashed through the window, showering the carpet with glass. She stumbled back as the man started climbing in, glaring at her with blazing eyes, unmindful of the glass that cut into him. The moment one foot touched the floor inside the house Stephanie was bolting out of the room, over to the front door, fumbling at the lock.

Strong hands grabbed her from behind. She screamed again as she was lifted off her feet and carried back. She kicked out, slamming a heel into his shin. The man grunted and let go and Stephanie twisted, trying to swing the poker into his face but he caught it and pulled it from her grasp. One hand went to her throat and Stephanie gagged, unable to breathe as the man forced her back into the living room.

He pushed her into an armchair and leaned over her and no matter how hard she tried she could not break his grip.

"Now then," the man said, his mouth contorting into a sneer, "why don't you just give me the key, little girlie?"

And that's when the front door was flung off its hinges and Skulduggery Pleasant burst into the house.

The man cursed and released Stephanie and swung the poker, but Skulduggery moved straight to him and hit him so hard Stephanie thought the man's head might come off. He hit the ground and tumbled backwards, but rolled to his feet as Skulduggery moved in again.

The man launched himself forward. They both collided and went backwards over the couch and Skulduggery lost his hat. Stephanie saw a flash of white above the scarf.

They got to their feet, grappling, and the man swung a punch that knocked Skulduggery's sunglasses to the other side of the room. Skulduggery responded by moving in low, grabbing the man around the waist and twisting his hip into him. The man was flipped to the floor, hard.

He cursed a little more, then remembered Stephanie and made for her. Stephanie leaped out of the chair, but before he could reach her, Skulduggery was there, kicking the man's legs out from under him. The man hit a small coffee table with his chin and howled in pain.

"You think you can stop me?" he screamed as he tried to stand. His knees seemed shaky. *"Do you know who I am?"*

"Haven't the foggiest," Skulduggery said.

The man spat blood and grinned defiantly. "Well, I know about *you*," he said. "My master told me all about *you*, detective, and you're going to have to do a lot more than that to stop me."

Skulduggery shrugged and Stephanie watched in amazement as a ball of fire flared up in his hand and he hurled it and the man was suddenly covered in flame. But instead of screaming, the man tilted his head back and roared with laughter. The fire may have engulfed him, but it wasn't burning him.

"More!" he laughed. "Give me more!"

"If you insist."

And then Skulduggery took an old-fashioned revolver from his jacket and fired, the gun bucking slightly with the recoil. The bullet hit the man in the shoulder and he screamed, then tried to run and tripped. He scrambled for the doorway, ducking and dodging lest he get shot again, the flames obstructing his vision so much that he hit a wall on his way out.

And then he was gone.

Stephanie stared at the door, trying to make sense of the impossible.

"Well," Skulduggery said, "that's something you don't see every day."

She turned. When his hat came off, his hair had come off too. In the confusion all she had seen was a chalk-white scalp, so she turned expecting to see a bald albino maybe. But no. With his sunglasses gone and his scarf hanging down, there was no denying the fact that he had no flesh, he had no skin, he had no eyes and he had no face.

All he had was a skull for a head.

4

THE SECRET WAR

Skulduggery put his gun away and walked out to the hall. He peered out into the night. Satisfied that there were no human fireballs lurking anywhere nearby, he came back inside and picked the door off the ground, grunting with the effort. He manoeuvred it back to where it belonged, leaving it leaning in the doorway, then he shrugged and came back into the living room, where Stephanie was still standing and staring at him.

"Sorry about the door," he said.

Stephanie stared.

"I'll pay to get it fixed."

Stephanie stared.

"It's still a good door, you know. Sturdy."

When he realised that Stephanie was in no condition to do anything but stare, he shrugged again and took off his coat, folded it neatly and draped it over the back of a chair. He went to the broken window and started picking up the shards of glass.

Now that he didn't have his coat on, Stephanie could truly appreciate how thin he really was. His suit, well-tailored though it was, hung off him, giving it a shapeless quality. She watched him collect the broken glass, and saw a flash of bone between his shirtsleeve and glove. He stood, looking back at her.

"Where should I put all this glass?"

"I don't know," Stephanie said in a quiet voice. "You're a skeleton."

"I am indeed," he said. "Gordon used to keep a wheelie bin out at the back door. Shall I put it in that?"

Stephanie nodded. "Yes OK," she said simply and watched Skulduggery carry the armful of glass shards out of the room. All her life she had longed for something else, for something to take her out of the humdrum world she knew – and now that it looked like it might actually happen, she didn't have one clue what to do. Questions were tripping over themselves in her head, each one vying to be the one that was asked first. So many of them.

Skulduggery came back in and she asked the first question. "Did you find it all right?"

"I did, yes. It was where he always kept it."

"OK then." If questions were people she felt that they'd all be staring at her now in disbelief. She struggled to form coherent thoughts.

"Did you tell him your name?" Skulduggery was asking.

"What?"

"Your name. Did you tell him?"

"Uh, no..."

"Good. You know something's true name, you have power over it. But even a given name, even Stephanie, that would have been enough to do it."

"To do what?"

"To give him some influence over you, to get you to do what he asked. If he had your name and he knew what to do with it, sometimes that's all it takes. That's a scary thought now, isn't it?"

"What's going on?" Stephanie asked. "Who was he? What did he want? Just who are you?"

"I'm me," Skulduggery said, picking up his hat and wig and placing them on a nearby table. "As for him, I don't know who he is, never seen him before in my life."

"You shot him."

"That's right."

"And you threw fire at him."

"Yes, I did."

Stephanie's legs felt weak and her head felt light.

"Mr Pleasant, you're a skeleton."

"Ah, yes, back to the crux of the matter. Yes. I am, as you say, a skeleton. I have been one for a few years now."

"Am I going mad?"

"I hope not."

"So you're real? You actually exist?"

"Presumably."

"You mean you're not sure if you exist or not?"

"I'm fairly certain. I mean, I could be wrong. I could be some ghastly hallucination, a figment of my imagination."

"You might be a figment of your own imagination?"

"Stranger things have happened. And do, with alarming regularity."

"This is too weird."

Skulduggery put his gloved hands in his pockets and cocked his head. He had no eyeballs so it was hard to tell if he was looking at her or not. "You know, I met your uncle under similar circumstances. Well, kind of similar. But he was drunk. And we were in a bar. And he had vomited on my shoes. So I suppose the actual circumstances aren't *overly* similar, but both events include a meeting, so... My point is, he was having some trouble and I was there to lend a hand, and we became good friends after that. Good, good friends." His head tilted. "You look like you might faint."

Stephanie nodded slowly. "I've never fainted before, but I think you might be right."

"Do you want me to catch you if you fall, or...?"

"If you wouldn't mind."

"No problem at all."

"Thank you."

Stephanie gave him a weak smile and then darkness clouded her vision and she felt herself falling and the last thing she saw was Skulduggery Pleasant darting across the room towards her.

Stephanie awoke on the couch with a blanket over her. The room was dark, lit only by two lamps in opposite corners. She looked over at the broken window, saw that it was now boarded up. She heard a hammering from the hall, and when she felt strong enough to stand, she slowly rose and walked out of the living room.

Skulduggery Pleasant was trying to hang the door back on its hinges. He had his shirtsleeve rolled up on his left forearm. *Ulna*, Stephanie corrected herself, proving that her first year of Biology class had not gone to waste. Or was it *radius*? Or both? She heard him mutter, then he noticed her and nodded brightly.

"Ah, you're up."

"You fixed the window."

"Well, covered it up. Gordon had a few pieces of timber out back, so I did what I could. Not having the same luck with the door though. I find it much easier to blast them off then put them back. How are you feeling?"

"I'm OK," Stephanie said.

"A cup of hot tea, that's what you need. Lots of sugar."

He abandoned the door and guided her to the kitchen. She sat at the table while he boiled the water.

"Hungry?" he asked when it had boiled, but she shook her head. "Milk?" She nodded. He added milk and spoonfuls of sugar, gave the tea a quick stir and put the cup on the table in front of her. She took a sip – it was hot, but nice.

"Thank you," Stephanie said, and he gave a little shrug. It was hard discerning some of his gestures without a face to go by, but she took the shrug to mean "think nothing of it".

"Was that magic? With the fire, and blasting the door?"

"Yes, it was."

She peered closer. "How can you talk?"

"Sorry?"

"How can you talk? You move your mouth when you speak, but you've got no tongue, you've got no lips, you've got no vocal cords. I mean, I know what skeletons look like, I've seen diagrams and models and stuff, and the only things that hold them together are flesh and skin and ligaments, so why don't you just fall apart?"

He gave another shrug, both shoulders this time. "Well, that's magic too."

She looked at him. "Magic's pretty handy."

"Yes, magic is."

"And what about, you know, nerve endings? Can you feel pain?"

"I can, but that's not a bad thing. Pain lets you know when you're alive, after all."

"And *are* you alive?"

"Well, *technically*, no, but..."

She peered into his empty eye sockets. "Do you have a brain?"

He laughed. "I don't have a brain, I don't have any organs, but I have a consciousness." He started clearing away the sugar and the milk. "To be honest with you, it's not even *my* head."

"What?"

"It's not. They ran away with my skull. I won this one in a poker game."

"That's not even yours? How does it feel?"

"It'll do. It'll do until I finally get around to getting my own head back. You look faintly disgusted."

"I just... Doesn't it feel weird? It'd be like wearing someone else's socks."

"You get used to it."

"What happened to you?" she asked. "Were you born like this?"

"No, I was born perfectly normal. Skin, organs, the whole shebang. Even had a face that wasn't too bad to look at, if I do say so myself."

"So what happened?"

Skulduggery leaned against the worktop, arms folded across his chest. "I got into magic. Back then – back when I was, for want of a better term, alive – there were some pretty nasty people around. The world was seeing a darkness it might never have recovered from. It was war, you see. A secret war, but war nonetheless. There was a sorcerer, Mevolent, worse then any of the others, and he had himself an army, and those of us who refused to fall in behind him found ourselves standing up against him.

"And we were winning. Eventually, after years of fighting this little war of ours, we were actually winning. His support was crumbling, his influence was fading, and he was staring defeat in the face. So he ordered one last, desperate strike against all the leaders on our side."

Stephanie stared at him, lost in his voice.

"I went up against his right-hand man who had laid out a wickedly exquisite trap. I didn't suspect a thing until it was too late.

"So I died. He killed me. The twenty-third of October it was, when my heart stopped beating. Once I was dead, they stuck my body up on a pike and burned it for all to see. They used me as a warning – they used the bodies of all the leaders they had killed as warnings – and, to my utter horror, it worked."

"What do you mean?"

"The tide turned. Our side starting losing ground. Mevolent got stronger. It was more than I could stand, so I came back."

"You just... *came back?*"

"It's... complicated. When I died, I never moved on. Something was holding me here, making me watch. I've never heard of it happening before that and I haven't heard of it happening since, but it happened to me. So when it got too much, I woke up, a bag of bones. Literally. They had gathered up my bones and put them in a bag and thrown the bag into a river. So that was a marvellous new experience right there."

"Then what happened?"

"I put myself back together, which was rather painful, then climbed out of the river and rejoined the fight, and in the end, we won. We finally won. So, with Mevolent defeated, I quit that whole scene and struck out on my own for the first time in a few hundred years."

Stephanie blinked. "Few *hundred*?"

"It was a long war."

"That man, he called you detective."

"He obviously knows me by reputation," Skulduggery said, standing a little straighter. "I solve mysteries now."

"Really?"

"Quite good at it too."

"So, what, you're tracking down your head?"

Skulduggery looked at her. If he'd had eyelids, he might well be blinking. "It'd be nice to have it back, sure, but..."

"So you don't need it, like, so you can rest in peace?"

"No. No, not really."

"Why did they take it? Was that another warning?"

"Oh, no," Skulduggery said with a little laugh. "No, *they* didn't take it. I was sleeping, about ten or fifteen years ago, and these little goblin things ran up and nicked it right off my spinal column. Didn't notice it was gone till the next morning."

Stephanie frowned. "And you didn't feel that?"

"Well, like I said, I was asleep. Meditating, I suppose you'd call it. I can't see, hear or feel anything when I'm meditating. Have you tried it?"

"No."

"It's very relaxing. I think you'd like it."

"I'm sorry, I'm still stuck on you losing your head."

"I didn't *lose* it," he said defensively. "It was stolen."

Stephanie was feeling stronger now. She couldn't believe that she'd fainted. *Fainted.* It was such an old woman thing to do. She glanced up at Skulduggery. "You've had a very unusual life, haven't you?"

"I suppose I have. Not over yet though. Well, *technically* it is, but..."

"Isn't there anything you miss?"

"About what?"

"About living."

"Compared to how long I've been like this, I was only technically alive for a blink of an eye. I can't really remember enough about having a beating heart in my chest to miss it."

"So there's nothing you miss?"

"I... I suppose I miss hair. I miss how it... was. And how it was there, on top of my head. I suppose I miss my hair." He took out his pocket watch and his head jerked back. "Wow, look at the time. I've got to go, Stephanie."

"Go? Go where?"

"Things to do, I'm afraid. Number one is finding out why that nice gentleman was sent here, and number two is finding out who sent him."

"You can't leave me alone," she said, following him into the living room.

"Yes," he corrected, "I can. You'll be perfectly safe."

"The front door's off!"

"Well, yes. You'll be perfectly safe as long as they don't come through the front door."

He pulled on his coat but she snatched his hat away.

"Are you taking my hat hostage?" he asked doubtfully.

"You're either staying here to make sure no one else attacks me or you're taking me with you."

Skulduggery froze. "That," he said eventually, "wouldn't be too safe for you."

"Neither would being left here on my own."

"But you can hide," he said, gesturing around the room. "There's so many places to hide. I'm sure there are plenty of good solid wardrobes your size. Even under a bed. You'd be surprised how many people don't check under beds these days."

"Mr Pleasant—"

"Skulduggery, please."

"Skulduggery, you saved my life tonight. Are you going to undo all that effort by leaving me here so someone else can come along and just kill me?"

"That's a very defeatist attitude you've got there. I once knew a fellow, a little older than you. He wanted to join me in my adventures, wanted to solve mysteries that beggared belief. He kept asking, kept on at me about it. He finally proved himself, after a long time, and we became partners."

"And did you go on to have lots of exciting adventures?"

"I did. He didn't. He died on our very first case together. Horrible death. Messy too. Lots of flailing around."

"Well, I don't plan on dying any time soon and I've got something he didn't."

"And that is...?"

"Your hat. Take me with you or I'll stand on it."

Skulduggery looked at her with his big hollow eye sockets, then held out his hand for his hat. "Don't say I didn't warn you."

5

MEETING CHINA SORROWS

Skulduggery Pleasant's car was a 1954 Bentley R-Type Continental, one of only 208 ever made, a car that housed a six-cylinder, 4.5-litre engine, and was retro-fitted with central locking, climate control, satellite navigation and a host of other modern conveniences. Skulduggery told Stephanie all of this when she asked. She'd have been happy with, "It's a Bentley."

They left Gordon's land via a back road at the rear of the estate to avoid the flooding, a road that Stephanie hadn't even noticed until they were on it. Skulduggery told her he was a regular visitor here, and knew all the little nooks and crannies. They passed a sign for Haggard and she thought about asking him to drop her home, but quickly banished that idea from her head. If she went home now she'd be turning her back on everything she'd just seen. She needed to know more. She needed to *see* more.

"Where are we going?" she asked as they drove on.

"Into the city. I've got a meeting with an old friend. She might be able to shed some light on recent events."

"Why were you at the house?"

"Sorry?"

"Tonight. Not that I'm not grateful, but how come you happened to be nearby?"

"Ah," he said, nodding. "Yes, I can see how that question would arise."

"So are you going to answer it?"

"That's unlikely."

"Well, why not?"

He glanced at her, or at least he turned his head a fraction. "The less you know about all this, the better. You're a perfectly normal young lady, and after tonight, you're going to return to your perfectly normal life. It wouldn't do for you to get too involved in this."

"But I am involved."

"But we can limit that involvement."

"But I don't want to limit that involvement."

"But it's what's best for you."

"But I don't want that!"

"But it might—"

"Don't start another sentence with 'but'."

"Right. Sorry."

"You can't expect me to forget about all of this. I've seen magic and fire and *you*, and I've learned about wars they don't tell us about in school. I've seen a world I never even knew *existed*."

"Don't you want to get back to that world? It's safer there."

"That's not where I belong."

Skulduggery turned his whole head to her and cocked it at an angle. "Funny. When I first met your uncle, that's what he said too."

"The things he wrote about," Stephanie said, the idea just dawning on her, "are they true?"

"His books? No, not a one."

"Oh."

"They're more *inspired* by true stories, really. He just changed them enough so he wouldn't insult anyone and get hunted down and killed. Your uncle was a good man, he really was. We solved many mysteries together."

"Really?"

"Oh, yes, you should be proud to have had an uncle like him. Of course, he got me into a hundred fights because I'd bring him somewhere, and he wouldn't stop pestering people, but... Fun times. Fun times."

They drove on until they saw the lights of the city looming ahead. Soon the darkness that surrounded the car was replaced with an orange haze that reflected off the wet roads. The city was quiet and still, the streets almost empty. They pulled into a small outdoor car park and Skulduggery switched off the engine and looked at Stephanie.

"OK then, you wait here."

"Right."

He got out. Two seconds passed, but Stephanie hadn't tagged along just to wait on the sidelines – she needed to see what other surprises the world had in store for her. She got out and Skulduggery looked at her.

"Stephanie, I'm not altogether sure you're respecting my authority."

"No, I'm not."

"I see. OK then." He put on his hat and wrapped his scarf

around his jaw, but did without the wig and the sunglasses. He clicked his keyring and the car beeped and the doors locked.

"That's it?"

He looked up. "Sorry?"

"Aren't you afraid it might get stolen? We're not exactly in a good part of town."

"It's got a car alarm."

"Don't you, like, cast a spell or something? To keep it safe?"

"No. It's a pretty good car alarm."

He started walking. She hurried to keep up.

"*Do* you cast spells then?"

"Sometimes. I try not to depend on magic these days, I try to get by on what's up here." He tapped his head.

"There's empty space up there."

"Well, yes," Skulduggery said irritably, "but you know what I mean."

"What else can you do?"

"Sorry?"

"With magic. Show me something."

If Skulduggery had had eyebrows, they would most likely be arched. "What, a living skeleton isn't enough for you? You want more?"

"Yes," Stephanie said. "Give me a tutorial."

He shrugged. "Well, I suppose it couldn't hurt. There are two types of mages, or sorcerers – Adepts practise one branch of magic, Elementals practise another. Adepts are more aggressive; their techniques are more immediately powerful. In contrast, an Elemental, such as myself, chooses the quieter course and works on mastering their command of the elements."

"Command of the elements?"

"Maybe that's a bit of an exaggeration. We don't command them as such, we manipulate them. We influence them."

"Like what? Like earth, wind—"

"Water and fire, yes."

"So show me."

Skulduggery tilted his head a little to the right and she could hear the good humour in his voice. "Very well," he said and held up his open hand in front of her. She frowned, feeling a little chilly, and then she became aware of a droplet of water running down her face. In an instant her hair was drenched, like she had just surfaced from a dive.

"How did you do that?" she asked, shaking her head, flinging drops of water away from her.

"You tell me," Skulduggery answered.

"I don't know. You did something to the moisture in the air?"

He looked down at her. "Very good," he said, impressed. "The first element, water. We can't part the Red Sea or anything, but we have a little influence with it."

"Show me fire again," Stephanie said eagerly.

Skulduggery snapped his gloved fingers and sparks flew, and he curled his hand and the sparks grew to flame, and he held that ball of flame in his palm as they walked. The flame intensified and Stephanie could feel her hair drying.

"Wow," she said.

"Wow indeed," Skulduggery responded and thrust his hand out, sending the ball of fire shooting through the air. It burned out as it arced in the night sky and faded to nothing.

"What about earth?" Stephanie asked, but Skulduggery shook his head.

"You don't want to see that, and hopefully you'll never have to. The earth power is purely defensive and purely for use as a last resort."

"So what's the most powerful? Is it fire?"

"That's the flashiest, that gets all the 'wows', but you'd be surprised what a little air can do if you displace it properly. Displaced air doesn't just disappear – it needs somewhere to be displaced *to*."

"Can I see?"

They reached the edge of the car park and passed the low wall that encircled it. Skulduggery flexed his fingers and suddenly splayed his hand, snapping his palm towards the wall. The air rippled and the bricks exploded outwards. Stephanie stared at the brand-new hole in the wall.

"*That*," she said, "is so cool."

They walked on, Stephanie glancing back at the wall every so often. "What about the Adepts then? What can they do?"

"I knew a fellow, a few years ago, who could read minds. I met this woman once who could change her shape, become anyone, right in front of your eyes."

"So who's stronger?" Stephanie asked. "An Elemental or an Adept?"

"Depends on the mage. An Adept could have so many tricks up his sleeve, so many different abilities, that he could prove himself stronger than even the most powerful Elemental. That's been known to happen."

"The sorcerer, the worst one of all, was he an Adept?"

"Actually, no. Mevolent was an Elemental. It's rare that you get an Elemental straying so far down the dark paths, but it happens."

There was a question Stephanie had been dying to ask, but

she didn't want to appear too eager. As casually as she could, thumbs hooked into the belt loops of her jeans, she said, as if she had just plucked this thought out of thin air, "So how do you know if you can do magic? Can anyone do it?"

"Not anyone. Relatively few actually. Those who can usually congregate in the same areas, so there are small pockets of communities, all over the world. In Ireland and the United Kingdom alone, there are eighteen different neighbourhoods populated solely by sorcerers."

"Can you be a sorcerer without realising it?"

"Oh, yes. Some people walk around every day, bored with their lives, having no idea that there's a world of wonder at their fingertips. And they'll live out their days, completely oblivious, and they'll die without knowing how great they could have been."

"That's really sad."

"Actually it's quite amusing."

"No, it's not, it's sad. How would you like it if you never discovered what you could do?"

"I wouldn't know any better," Skulduggery answered, stopping beside her. "We're here."

Stephanie looked up. They had arrived outside a crumbling old tenement building, its wall defaced with graffiti and its windows cracked and dirty. She followed him up the concrete steps and into the foyer, and together they ascended the sagging staircase.

The first floor was quiet and smelled of damp. On the second floor, splintered shards of light escaped through the cracks between door and doorway into the otherwise dark corridor. They could hear the sound of a TV from one of the apartments.

When they got to the third floor, Stephanie knew they had arrived. The third floor was clean, it didn't smell and it was well-lit. It was like an entirely different building. She followed Skulduggery to the middle of the corridor and noticed that none of the doors were numbered. She looked at the door Skulduggery knocked on, the door that had a plaque fastened to it: 'Library'.

While they waited there, Skulduggery said, "One more thing. No matter how much you might want to, do not tell her your name."

The door opened before she could ask any more questions and a thin man with large round spectacles peered out. His nose was hooked and his wiry hair was receding. He wore a checked suit with a bow tie. He glanced at Stephanie then nodded to Skulduggery and opened the door wide for them to come through.

Stephanie realised why none of the doors were numbered – it was because they all led into the same room. The walls between apartments had been taken away in order to accommodate the vast number of books on the shelves. Stacks and stacks of books, a labyrinth of bookshelves that stretched from one side of the building to the other. As they followed the bespectacled man through the maze she saw more people, their attention focused on their reading, people half-hidden in shadow, people who didn't look exactly *right*...

In the middle of the library was an open space, like a clearing in a forest, and in this open space stood the most beautiful woman Stephanie had ever seen. Her hair was black as raven wings, and her eyes were the palest blue. Her features were so delicate Stephanie feared they might break if she smiled, and then the lady smiled and Stephanie felt such warmth that for an instant she never wanted to be anywhere else but at this lady's side.

"Stop that," said Skulduggery.

The lady let her eyes move to him and her smile turned playful. Stephanie stared, enraptured. Her body felt so heavy, so clumsy; all she wanted to do with her life was just stand here, in this spot, and gaze at pure and true beauty.

"Stop that," Skulduggery said again, and the lady laughed and shrugged and looked back at Stephanie.

"Sorry about that," she said, and Stephanie felt a fog lift from her mind. She felt dizzy and staggered, but Skulduggery was there, a hand on the small of her back, supporting her.

"My apologies," the lady said, giving her a small bow. "I do forget the effect I have on people. First impressions and all that."

"Seems like every time you meet someone new, you forget that little fact," Skulduggery said.

"I'm a scatterbrain, what can I say?"

Skulduggery grunted and turned to Stephanie. "Don't feel self-conscious. The first time anyone sets eyes on China, they fall in love. Believe me, the effect lessens the more you get to know her."

"Lessens," the woman named China said, "but never entirely goes away, does it, Skulduggery?"

The detective took off his hat and looked at China, but ignored her question. China smiled at Stephanie and handed her a business card. It was eggshell white and bore a single telephone number, etched with delicate elegance.

"Feel free to call me if you ever stumble across a book or an item you think I might be interested in. Skulduggery used to. He doesn't any more. Too much water has flowed under that proverbial bridge, I'm afraid. Oh, where are my manners? My name is China Sorrows, my dear. And you are...?"

Stephanie was about to tell China her name when Skulduggery turned his head to her sharply, and she remembered what he had said. She frowned. The urge to tell this woman everything was almost overwhelming.

"You don't need to know her name," Skulduggery said. "All you need to know is that she witnessed someone breaking into Gordon Edgley's house. He was looking for something. What would Gordon have that someone might want?"

"You don't know who he was?"

"He wasn't anyone. His master, that's who I'm after."

"So who do you think his master is?"

Skulduggery didn't answer and China laughed. "Serpine *again*? My darling, you think Serpine is the culprit behind practically every crime."

"That's because he is."

"So why come to me?"

"You hear things."

"Do I?"

"People talk to you."

"I *am* very approachable."

"I was wondering if you'd heard anything: rumours, whispers, anything."

"Nothing that would help you."

"But you have heard *something*?"

"I've heard nonsense. I've heard something that doesn't even deserve to be *called* a rumour. Apparently Serpine has been making inquiries about the Sceptre of the Ancients."

"What about it?"

"He's looking for it."

"What do you mean? The Sceptre's a fairy tale."

"Like I said, it's nonsense."

Skulduggery fell silent for a moment, as if he was storing that piece of information away for further study. When he spoke again, it was with a new line of questioning. "So what would Gordon have that he – or anyone else – might want?"

"Probably quite a lot," China answered. "Dear Gordon was like me: he was a collector. But I don't think that's the question you should be asking."

Skulduggery thought for a moment. "Ah."

Stephanie looked at the two of them. "What? *What?*"

"The question," Skulduggery said, "is not what did Gordon have that someone might want to steal, but rather what did

Gordon have that someone had to wait until he was dead in order to steal it?"

Stephanie looked at him. "There's a difference?"

China answered her. "There are items that cannot be taken, possessions that cannot be stolen. In such a case, the owner must be dead before anyone else can take advantage of its powers."

"If you hear anything that might be of use," Skulduggery said, "will you let me know?"

"And what do I get in return?" China responded, that smile playing on her lips again.

"My appreciation?"

"Tempting. That is tempting."

"Then how about this?" Skulduggery said. "Do it as a favour, for a friend."

"A friend?" China said. "After all these years, after everything that's happened, are you saying that you're my friend again?"

"I was talking about Gordon."

China laughed and Stephanie followed Skulduggery as he walked back through the stacks. They left the library and travelled back the way they'd come.

When they were out on the street, Stephanie spoke up at last.

"So that was China Sorrows," she said.

"Yes, that was," Skulduggery responded. "A woman not to be trusted."

"Beautiful name, though."

"Like I said, names are power. There are three names for everyone. The name you're born with, the name you're given and the name you take. Everyone, no matter who they are, is born with a name. You were born with a name. Do you know what it is?"

"Is this a trick question?"

"Do you know what your name is?"

"Yes. Stephanie Edgley."

"No."

"No?"

"That's your given name. That's the name other people handed you. If a mage with any kind of knowledge wanted to, he could use that name to influence you, to attain some small degree of control – to make you stand, sit, speak, things like that."

"Like a dog."

"I suppose so."

"You're likening me to a dog?"

"No," he said, and then paused. "Well, yes."

"Oh, cheers."

"But you have another name, a real name, a true name. A name unique to you and you alone."

"What is it?"

"I don't know. You don't know it either, at least not consciously. This name gives you power, but it would also give other people absolute power over you. If someone knew it, they could command your loyalty, your love, everything about you. Your free will could be totally eradicated. Which is why we keep our true names hidden."

"So what's the third name?"

"The name you take. It can't be used against you, it can't be used to influence you and it's your first defence against a sorcerer's attack. Your taken name seals your given name, protects it, and that's why it's so important to get it right."

"So Skulduggery is the name you took?"

"It is."

"What about me? Should I have a third name?"

He hesitated for only a moment. "If you're going to be accompanying me on this, then yes, you probably should."

"And *am* I going to be accompanying you?"

"That depends. Do you need your parents' permission?"

Stephanie's parents wanted her to find her own way in life.

That's what they'd said countless times in the past. Of course, they'd been referring to school subjects and college applications and job prospects. Presumably, at no stage did they factor living skeletons and magic underworlds into their considerations. If they had, their advice would probably have been very different.

Stephanie shrugged. "No, not really."

"Well, that's good enough for me."

They reached the car and got in, and as they pulled out on to the road, she looked at him.

"So who's this Serpine you were talking about?"

"Nefarian Serpine is one of the bad guys. I suppose, now that Mevolent is gone, he'd be considered *the* bad guy."

"What's so bad about him?"

The purr of the engine was all that filled the car for a few moments. "Serpine is an Adept," Skulduggery said at last. "He was Mevolent's most trusted lieutenant. You heard what China was saying, about how she is a collector, how Gordon was a collector? Serpine is a collector too. He collects magic. He has tortured, maimed and killed in order to learn other people's secrets. He has committed untold atrocities in order to uncover obscure rituals, searching for the one ritual that he, and religious fanatics like him, have been seeking for generations. Back when the war broke out, he had this... weapon. These days he's full of surprises, but he still uses it because, quite frankly, there is no defence against it."

"What's the weapon?"

"To put it simply, agonising death."

"Agonising death... on its own? Not, like, fired from a gun or anything?"

"He just has to point his red right hand at you and... well, like I said, agonising death. It's a necromancy technique."

"Necromancy?"

"Death magic, a particularly dangerous Adept discipline. I don't know how he learned it, but learn it he did."

"And what does the Sceptre thing have to do with all this?"

"Nothing. It has nothing to do with anything."

"Well, what is it?"

"It's a weapon of unstoppable destructive power. Or it would be, if it actually existed. It's a rod, about the length of your thigh bone... Actually, I think I might have a picture of it..."

He pulled the car over and got out to open the Bentley's boot. Stephanie had never been to this part of town before. The streets were quiet and empty. She could see the bridge over the canal in the distance. Moments later Skulduggery was back behind the wheel, they were driving again and Stephanie had a leather bound book on her lap.

"What's this?" she asked, opening the clasp and flicking through the pages.

"Our most popular myths and legends," said Skulduggery. "You just passed the Sceptre."

She flicked back and came to a reproduction of a painting of a wide-eyed man reaching for a golden staff with a black crystal embedded in its hilt. The Sceptre was glowing and he was shielding his eyes. On the opposite page was another picture, this time of a man holding the Sceptre, surrounded by cowering figures, their heads turned away. "Who's this guy?"

"He's an Ancient. In the legends, they were the very first sorcerers, the first to wield the power of the elements, the first to use magic. They lived apart from the mortal world, had no interest in it. They had their own ways, their own customs and their own gods. Eventually, they decided that they wanted to have their own destinies too, so they rose up against their gods, rather nasty beings called the Faceless Ones, and battled them on the land, in the skies and in the oceans. The Faceless Ones, being immortal, won every battle, until the Ancients constructed a weapon powerful enough to drive them back – the Sceptre."

"You sound like you know the story well."

"Tales around the campfire might seem quaint now, but it's all we had before movies. The Faceless Ones were banished, forced back to wherever they came from."

"So what's happening here? He's killing his gods?"

"Yep. The Sceptre was fuelled by the Ancients' desire to be free. That was the most powerful force they had at their disposal."

"So it's a force for freedom?"

"Originally. However, once the Ancients no longer had the Faceless Ones to tell them what to do, they started fighting among themselves, and they turned the Sceptre on each other and fuelled it with hate."

The streetlights played on his skull as they passed in and out of darkness, flashing bone-white in a hypnotic rhythm.

"The last Ancient," he continued, "having driven his gods away, having killed all his friends and all his family, realised what he had done and hurled the Sceptre deep into the earth, where the ground swallowed it."

"What did he do then?"

"Probably went for a snooze. I don't know, it's a legend. It's an allegory. It didn't really happen."

"So why does Serpine think it's real?"

"Now that *is* puzzling. Like his master before him, he believes some of our darker myths, our more disturbing legends. He believes the world was a better place when the Faceless Ones were in charge. They didn't exactly approve of humanity, you see, and they demanded worship."

"The ritual that he's been looking for – is it to bring them back?"

"It is indeed."

"So he might think that the Sceptre, which drove them away, could somehow call them home, right?"

"People believe all kinds of things when it comes to their religion."

"Do you believe in any of it? The Ancients, Faceless Ones, any of it?"

"I believe in me, Stephanie, and that's enough for now."

"So could the Sceptre be real?"

"Highly unlikely."

"So what does any of this have to do with my uncle?"

"I don't know," Skulduggery admitted. "That's why they call it a mystery."

Light filled the car and suddenly the world was bucking, the only sounds a terrifying crash and the shriek of metal on metal. Stephanie lurched against her seatbelt and slammed her head against the window. The street outside tilted wildly and she realised the Bentley was flipping over. She heard Skulduggery curse beside her and for an instant she was weightless, and then the Bentley hit the ground again and jarred her against the dashboard.

It rocked back on to its tyres. Stephanie looked at her knees, her eyes wide but her brain too stunned to think. *Look up*, said a faint voice in her head. *Look up to see what's happening.* The Bentley was still, its engine cut out, but there was another engine. A car door opening and closing. *Look up.* Footsteps, running footsteps. *Look up now.* Skulduggery beside her, not moving. *Look up, there's someone coming for you. Look up NOW.*

A window exploded beside her for the second time that night, and the man from the house was grabbing her and hauling her out of the car.

6

A MAN APART

His clothes were ragged and charred but his skin had been untouched by the fireball that had enveloped him at Gordon's house. She glimpsed his face as she was dragged through the yellow light of the Bentley's headlamps, a face that was twisted in anger and hatred, and then she was lifted and slammed on to the bonnet of the car that had hit them. His hands had her collar bunched, his knuckles digging into her throat.

"You will die," he hissed, "right here and now if you do not give me that damned key."

Her hands were on his, trying to break his grip. Her head felt light, blood pounding in her temples. "Please," she whispered, trying to breathe.

"You're going to make me look bad," the man growled. "My master is going to think I'm a fool if I can't get one stupid little key off one stupid little girl!"

The street was empty around them. Shopfronts and businesses, closed for the night. No one was going to hear her. No one was coming to help her. Where was Skulduggery?

The man lifted her off the bonnet and slammed her down again… Stephanie cried out in pain and the man leaned in, his right forearm pressed beneath her chin. "I'll snap your scrawny neck," he hissed.

"I don't know anything about a key!" Stephanie gasped.

"If you don't know anything you're of no use to me and I'll kill you here."

She looked up at that horribly twisted face and stopped trying to pull his hands away. Instead she dug her thumb into the bullet hole in his shoulder. He screamed and let her go and staggered back, cursing, and Stephanie rolled off the car and ran to the Bentley. Skulduggery was pounding at the door but it had buckled under the impact, trapping his leg.

"Go!" he shouted at her through the broken window. "Get away!"

Stephanie glanced back, saw a figure loom up, and pushed herself away from the car. She slipped on the wet road but scrambled to her feet and ran, the man right behind her, clutching his injured shoulder.

He lunged and she ducked, caught a streetlight and swung herself from her course, and the man shot by her and sprawled on to the pavement. She took off the opposite way, passing the two cars and running on. The street was too long, too wide, and there was nowhere she could lose him. She turned off into a narrow lane and sprinted into the shadows.

She heard him behind her, heard the footsteps that seemed to be moving much more quickly then her own. She didn't dare look back – she didn't want the fear that was lending her speed to suddenly sabotage her escape. It was too dark to make out anything ahead of her: she couldn't see one arm's length ahead. She could be about to run smack into a wall and she wouldn't—

Wall.

Stephanie twisted at the last moment and got her hands up and hit the wall then pushed away, kicking off without losing too much momentum, continuing around the corner. The man couldn't see in the dark any better than she could and she heard him hit the wall and yell out a curse.

Up ahead was a break in the darkness. She saw a taxi pass. The man slipped and stumbled behind her – she was getting away. All she had to do was run up to the nearest person she could find and the man wouldn't dare follow her.

Stephanie plunged out of the shadows and screamed for help, but the taxi was gone and the street was empty. She screamed again, this time in desperation. The streetlights tinted everything orange and stretched her shadow out before her. Then there was another shadow moving up behind and she threw herself to one side as the man barrelled past, narrowly missing her.

The canal was ahead, the canal that flowed through the city. She ran for it, aware that the man was once again behind her and gaining fast.

She felt his fingers on her shoulder. The first touch was fleeting, but the second was a grip. His hand curled around her shoulder and tightened just as she reached the edge of the canal, and she managed to throw herself forward before he could drag her back. She heard a panicked shriek from behind and realised she had pulled him after her.

Then the freezing water enveloped them both.

The cold stunned her for a moment but Stephanie fought it and kicked out. She clutched at water and dragged it down to her sides, just like she had done countless times off the Haggard beach. Now she was moving up, up to where the lights were.

She broke the surface with a gasp and turned her head, saw the man struggling, flailing his arms in terror. For a moment she thought he couldn't swim, but it was more than that. The water was hurting him, working through him like acid, stripping pieces of him away. His cries became mere guttural sounds and Stephanie watched as he came apart and was silent and most dead.

She turned from the bits of him that floated to her and ploughed through the water. Her hands and feet were already numb with the cold, but she kept going until the bridge was far behind.

Shivering, Stephanie reached the edge of the canal and managed to haul herself out. Arms crossed over her chest, trainers squelching with every step and her hair plastered to her scalp, she hurried back to the Bentley.

When she got there, the Bentley was empty. Stephanie hung back, out of the light. A truck passed, slowing when it approached the crash. When the driver didn't see anyone, he drove on. Stephanie didn't move from her spot.

A few minutes later, Skulduggery emerged from the narrow lane she'd been chased down. He was walking quickly, looking up and down the street as he returned to his car. Stephanie stepped out of the shadows.

"Hey," she said.

"Stephanie!" Skulduggery exclaimed, rushing over to her. "You're all right!"

"I went for a swim," she said, trying to stop her teeth from chattering.

"What happened?" he asked. "Where is he?"

"Here and there." The light breeze was passing through her soaking garments. "The water kind of... took him apart."

Skulduggery nodded. "It happens."

He held out his hand and she felt herself drying and saw the water drifting off her, collecting as mist in the air over her head. "You're not surprised?" she asked.

He moved the cloud away and released it. A faint shower fell to the street. "Certain types of Adept magic don't come cheap. As we saw at Gordon's house, your attacker had made himself impervious to fire, and was probably very proud of himself for doing so. Unfortunately for him, the cost of that little spell was that a large amount of water would be lethal. Every big spell has a hidden snag."

He clicked his fingers and conjured fire, and Stephanie started to feel warm again.

"Neat trick," she said. "You'll have to teach me it some time."

With quite a bit of effort, Stephanie pulled open the car door. She wiped the broken glass from the seat and got in, buckling the seatbelt. Skulduggery went around the other side to his own broken window and climbed in behind the wheel. He twisted the key and the engine turned, complained and then came to life.

Her body was tired. Her mind was tired. Her limbs felt heavy and her eyes wanted to close. She dug her mobile phone out of her pocket – miraculously, the canal water hadn't ruined it. She pressed a button and the time flashed up and she groaned then looked outside as the first light of the morning started to seep into the sky.

"What's wrong?" Skulduggery asked. "Are you hurt?"

"No," she said, "but I will be if I don't get back to Gordon's house. Mum will be picking me up soon."

"You don't look too happy."

"Well, I don't want to go back to that world – a boring old

town with nosy neighbours and nasty aunts."

"You'd rather stay in a world where you get attacked twice in one night?"

"I know it sounds crazy, but yes. Things *happen* here."

"I'm going to see a friend later today, someone who might be able to help us out. You can come along if you want."

"Really?"

"I think you might have a real feel for this line of work."

Stephanie nodded and gave a little shrug, and when she spoke she fought hard to keep the sheer joy out of her voice. "And what about magic?"

"What about it?"

"Will you teach me?"

"You don't even know if you're *capable* of doing magic."

"How do I find out? Is there a test or something?"

"Yes, we cut off your head. If it grows back, you can do magic."

"You're being funny again, aren't you?"

"So glad you noticed."

"So will you teach me?"

"I'm not a teacher. I'm a detective. I already have a career."

"Oh, right. It's just, I'd really like to learn, and you know it all."

"Your flattery is subtle."

"But it's OK, if you don't want to teach me, that's OK. I suppose I could always ask China."

Skulduggery looked at her. "China won't teach you. She won't teach you because there is nothing that she does that is not for her own gain. You mightn't see it at first, you might think she's actually being nice to you, but you can never trust her."

"OK then."

"OK. So we're agreed?"

"We're agreed. No trusting China."

"Good. Glad we've got that sorted."

"So will you teach me magic?"

He sighed. "Dealing with you is going to be a trial, isn't it?"

"That's what my teachers at school say."

"This is going to be fun," Skulduggery said dryly. "I just know it."

Skulduggery dropped Stephanie off at Gordon's house, and half an hour later her mother's car splashed through huge puddles and Stephanie went outside to meet her. She managed to keep her mother's attention off the house, lest she notice that the front door was merely leaning against the doorframe.

"Good morning," her mother said as Stephanie got in the car. "Everything OK?"

Stephanie nodded. "Yeah, everything's fine."

"You're looking a little bedraggled."

"Oh, thanks Mum."

Her mother laughed as they drove back towards the gate. "Sorry. So tell me, how was your night?"

Stephanie hesitated, then shrugged. "Uneventful."

7

SERPINE

efarian Serpine had a visitor.

The Hollow Men bowed deeply as he strode through the corridors of his castle. They looked real from a distance, but up close they were nothing more than cheap imitations of life. Their papery skin was a mere expressionless shell, inflated from within by the foulest of gases. It was only their hands and feet that were solid and heavy – their feet clumped when they walked and their hands weighed down their arms, so they stood with a perpetual stoop.

Their number increased the closer he got to the main hall. They were simple creatures, but they did what they were told, and they hadn't known what to make of the visitor. Serpine entered the main hall, the crowd of Hollow Men parted and a man in a dark suit turned to him.

"Mr Bliss," Serpine said politely. "I thought you were dead."

"I heard that too," Bliss responded. He was an elegant man of muscle and mass, as tall as Serpine, but whereas Serpine had black hair and glittering emerald green eyes, Bliss was bald, with eyes of the palest blue. "In fact, it was a rumour I started. I thought it might make people leave me alone in my retirement."

"And has it?"

"Unfortunately, no."

Serpine motioned for the Hollow Men to leave them and then led his guest into the drawing room.

"Can I get you a drink?" Serpine asked, heading to the liquor cabinet. "Or is it too early in the day?"

"I'm here on business," Bliss said. "Elder business."

Serpine turned, gave him a smile. "And how are the Elders?"

"Worried."

"When are they not?"

Serpine went to the armchair by the window, watched the sun as it struggled to rise then settled into the chair, crossed his legs and waited for Bliss to continue. The last time they had been in the same room together they had been trying to kill each other while a hurricane tore the place down around them. The very fact that Bliss remained standing right now told Serpine that he was thinking the same thing. Bliss was wary of him.

"The Elders called me in because, five days ago, two of their people went missing – Clement Gale and Alexander Slake."

"How very unfortunate, but I don't believe I've ever had the pleasure of meeting either of them."

"They were assigned to... observe you, from time to time."

"Spies?"

"Not at all. Merely observers. The Elders thought it prudent to keep tabs on a few of Mevolent's followers, to make sure no one strayed from the terms of the Truce. You were always at the top of that list."

Serpine smiled. "And you think I had something to do with their disappearance? I'm a man of peace these days, not war. I seek only knowledge."

"You seek secrets."

"You make that sound so sinister, Mr Bliss. As for the missing 'observers', maybe they'll turn up safe and well, and the Elders can apologise for dragging you out of your retirement."

"They turned up yesterday."

"Oh?"

"Dead."

"How terrible for them."

"Not a mark on their bodies. No indication at all as to how they died. Sound familiar?"

Serpine thought for a moment then arched an eyebrow and held up his gloved right hand. *"You think* this *did it? You think* I *killed those men? I haven't used this power in years. When I first learned it, I thought it was a wonderful thing, but now I look on it as a curse, and a reminder to me of my many mistakes and transgressions in my servitude to Mevolent. I don't mind telling you, Mr Bliss, that I am deeply ashamed of what I have done with my life."*

Bliss stood there and Serpine almost spoiled it all by laughing, but he managed to retain his look of mocking innocence.

"Thank you for your co-operation," Bliss said, turning to leave. "I shall be in touch if I need to ask you more questions."

Serpine waited until Bliss was at the door before speaking again. "They must be scared."

Bliss stopped. "What makes you say that?"

"They sent you, didn't they? Why didn't they send the detective, I wonder?"

"Skulduggery Pleasant is busy with another investigation."

"Is that so? Or maybe they thought I would be intimidated by you."

"They thought you'd listen to me. This Truce will hold only for as long as both sides want it to. The Elders want it to hold."

"That must be nice for them."

Mr Bliss looked at him like he was trying to read his thoughts. "Be careful, Nefarian. You might not like what's at the end of this road you're on."

Serpine smiled. *"You're sure you won't join me for a drink?"*

"I have a plane to catch."

"Going somewhere nice?"

"I have a meeting in London."

"I hope that goes well for you. We'll have a drink some other time then."

"Perhaps."

Mr Bliss inclined his head in a small bow, and left.

8

GHASTLY

tephanie went to bed as soon as she got home and woke at a few minutes past two in the afternoon. She padded to the bathroom and showered, her body aching as she stood under the spray. Her knees were scraped and cut from when she'd been dragged along the road. Her skin was mottled with deep bruises. Her neck was stiff.

She turned off the water and stepped out of the shower, dried herself off and pulled on fresh jeans and a T-shirt. Barefoot, she took her old clothes downstairs and threw them in the washing machine, added the powder and turned it on. It was only after she'd had something to eat that she allowed herself to think about the previous night.

Well, she said to herself, *so that happened.*

She pulled on her shoes and went out, the sunshine warm on her face. At the end of her road, she passed the old pier and started towards Main Street. Normality. Kids playing football, riding bikes and laughing, dogs running about, tails wagging, neighbours talking to neighbours and the world being as she'd always thought it was. No living skeletons. No magic. No men trying to kill her.

A crazy laugh escaped her lips when she reflected on how much her life had changed in the space of a day. She had gone from being a perfectly ordinary girl in a perfectly ordinary world to becoming a target for water-soluble weirdos and a partner for a skeleton detective out to solve her uncle's murder.

Stephanie faltered. Her uncle's *murder?* Where had she got that from? Gordon had died of natural causes: the doctors had said so. She frowned. But these were doctors who lived in a world without walking, talking skeletons. But still, why assume he'd been murdered? What on earth had made her think that?

"There are items that cannot be taken," China had said, "possessions that cannot be stolen. In such a case, the owner must be dead before anyone else can take advantage of its powers."

Her attacker, and whoever had sent him, wanted something. They wanted something badly enough to kill her to get it. And if they wanted it that badly, would they really have waited for her uncle to die of natural causes before they went looking for it?

Stephanie felt cold. Gordon had been murdered. Someone had killed him and no one was doing anything about it. No one was asking the questions, no one was trying to figure out who did it.

Except for Skulduggery.

She narrowed her eyes. He must have known Gordon was murdered. If he hadn't already suspected it when they first met, he must have worked it out in the library. China probably knew as well, but neither of them had told her. They didn't think she could handle it, maybe. Or maybe they didn't think it was any of her business. It had to do with their world after all, not hers. But Gordon was still her uncle.

A car pulled up behind her. People stared. She looked back and saw the Bentley.

The driver's side was still badly buckled from where the car had rammed it, and the windscreen was cracked. Three of the windows were without glass and the bonnet had a series of ugly dents running up its left side. The usual purr of the engine was replaced by a worrying rattle that cut out abruptly when the engine turned off. Skulduggery – in hat, scarf and sunglasses – went to get out, but the door wouldn't open.

"Oh, boy," Stephanie muttered.

She watched him lean away from the door and raise his knee, and then he kicked it open and got out, adjusting his coat as he walked over.

"Good afternoon," he said brightly. "Wonderful weather we're having, isn't it?"

"People are staring," Stephanie whispered as he neared.

"Are they really? Oh, so they are. Good for them. So, are we ready to go?"

"That depends," she answered, speaking softly and keeping a smile on her face. "When were you going to tell me that my uncle was murdered?"

There was a slight hesitation. "Ah. You worked that out, then?"

Stephanie turned down a narrow lane between two buildings, moving away from the prying eyes of Haggard's gossip mongers. Skulduggery hesitated a moment, then caught up to her, walking fast.

"I had a very good reason for not telling you."

"I don't care." Now that no one could see her, she dropped the smile. "Gordon was *murdered*, Skulduggery. How could you not have told me?"

"This is a dangerous business. It's a dangerous world that I'm part of."

She stopped suddenly. Skulduggery kept walking, realised she wasn't beside him any more and turned on his heel. She crossed her arms. "If you don't think I can handle it—"

"No, you've certainly proved yourself capable." She heard the tone of his voice change slightly. "I knew from the moment I met you that you're just the type of person who would *never* walk away from danger, simply out of stubbornness. I wanted to keep you out of it as much as I could. You've got to understand – Gordon was my friend. I thought I owed it to him to try and keep his favourite niece out of harm's way."

"Well, I'm *in* harm's way, so it's not your decision any more."

"No, apparently it isn't."

"So you won't keep anything from me again?"

He put his hand to his chest. "Cross my heart and hope to die."

"OK."

He nodded and led the way back to the Bentley.

"Though you don't actually have a heart," she said.

"I know."

"And technically, you've already died."

"I know that too."

"Just so we're clear."

"What's he like?" Stephanie asked as they drove.

"What's who like?"

"This guy we're going to see. What's his name?"

"Ghastly Bespoke."

She looked at Skulduggery to make sure he wasn't joking, then realised there was no way she could tell. "Why would anyone call themselves Ghastly?"

"All manner of names suit all manner of people. Ghastly is my tailor and also happens to be one of my closest friends. He first taught me how to box."

"So what's he like?"

"Decent. Honourable. Honest. But more fun than I'm making him sound, I swear. Also, he's not magic's biggest fan..."

"He doesn't like magic? How could he not like magic?"

"He just doesn't find it interesting. He prefers the world he reads about in books and sees on TV, the world with cops and robbers and dramas and sports. If he had to choose, I expect he'd live in the world without magic. That way, he could have gone to school and got a job and been... normal. Of course, he's never been given the choice. I suppose, for him, there could never really *be* a choice. Not really."

"Why not?"

Skulduggery hesitated for only a moment, as if he was choosing how best to say it, then told her that Ghastly was born ugly.

"Not just unattractive," he said, "not merely unappealing, but really, honestly ugly. His mother was jinxed when she was pregnant with him and now his face is ridged with scars. They tried everything to fix it – spells, potions, charms, glamours, various and sundry creams, but nothing worked."

He explained that, as a child, Ghastly had always told his friends that he got his love of boxing from his father and his love of sewing from his mother. The truth was, his father was the one who was constantly making alterations to hemlines and such, and his mother was a bare-knuckle boxing champ, who boasted twenty-two consecutive wins. Skulduggery had seen her fight once. She had a right hook that could take a head clean off. And according to legend, it *had* once too.

Regardless, Ghastly was brought up in these two separate disciplines and, figuring he was ugly enough already, decided to try a career as a tailor, rather then a boxer.

"And I for one am glad he did," Skulduggery said. "He makes extraordinary suits."

"So we're going to see him because you need a new suit?"

"Not quite. You see, his family has amassed a unique collection of artwork, paintings and literature about the Ancients, from all over the world. Included are a couple of rare volumes that could be very useful indeed. All anyone knows about the Sceptre is based on half-forgotten myths. Those books, and whatever else is in Ghastly's collection, will hold a far more detailed description of the legends, about what the Sceptre does and, in theory, how one would go about defending oneself against it."

They parked and got out. The neighbourhood was dirty and run down, and people hurried by without even glancing at the battered car in their midst. A little old lady shuffled past, nodding to Skulduggery as she went.

"Is this one of those secret communities you were telling me about?" Stephanie asked.

"Indeed it is. We try to keep the streets as uninviting as possible so no casual passer-by will stop and have a look around."

"Well, you've succeeded."

"You should be realising by now that looks are, more often than not, deceiving. A neighbourhood like this, with its graffiti and litter and squalor, is the safest neighbourhood you could possibly visit. Open the door to any one of these houses around us and you walk into a veritable palace. Surface is nothing, Stephanie."

"I'll try to remember that," she said as she followed him to a little shop perched on the corner. She looked around for a sign. "Is this the tailor's?"

"Bespoke tailor's, yes."

"But there's no sign. There aren't any clothes in the window. How would anyone know it's even open?"

"Ghastly doesn't need to advertise. He has a very specific clientele, and he can't really afford to let ordinary people wander in when he's measuring out a new suit for an eight-armed octopus-man."

"Are you serious? There's an eight-armed octopus-man?"

"There's a whole colony of octopus people," Skulduggery said as they approached the door.

"Really?"

"Good God, Stephanie, of course not. That would be far too silly."

He walked on before she could even *try* to hit him. The shop door was unlocked and he led the way in. Stephanie was surprised by how clean and bright and ordinary-looking it was. She didn't know what she was expecting – mannequins that came alive and tried to eat you, perhaps. There was a nice smell in here too. Comforting.

Ghastly Bespoke walked out from the backroom and when he saw them he smiled. He shook Skulduggery's hand warmly. He was broad-shouldered and his scars covered his whole head. When Skulduggery turned to introduce Stephanie, and he saw the way she was staring at Ghastly, he shrugged.

"Don't mind her," he said. "She stares. That's what she does when she meets new people."

"I'm quite used to it," Ghastly said, still smiling. "Do you want to shake hands, Miss, or start off with something easy, like waving?"

Stephanie felt herself blush and she stuck out her hand quickly. His hand was normal, no scars, but tough and strong.

"Do you have a name?" he asked.

"Not yet," she admitted.

"Better make sure that you really want one before you think any more about it. This life isn't for everyone."

She nodded slowly, not sure what he was getting at. He took a moment, looking her up and down.

"There's been some trouble?"

"Some," answered Skulduggery.

"Then the proper attire is probably called for." Ghastly took out a small pad, started jotting down notes. "Do you have a favourite colour?" he asked her.

"I'm sorry?"

"To wear. Any preference?"

"I'm not sure I understand..."

"Not all of the clothes I make are merely examples of exquisite tailoring. Sometimes, if the situation arises, special requirements are catered for."

"Such as keeping you safe until this whole thing is over," Skulduggery said. "Ghastly can make you a suit, nothing too formal, which could very possibly save your life."

"Fashion," said Ghastly with a shrug. "It's life or death." His pen was at the ready. "So, once more, do you have a favourite colour to wear?"

"I... I'm not sure I could afford it..."

Ghastly shrugged. "I'll put it on Skulduggery's tab. Go nuts."

Stephanie blinked. To go from her mother buying most of her clothes to *this* was a step she hadn't been expecting. "I don't know, I'm not sure... Black?"

Ghastly nodded and scribbled in his notebook. "Can't go wrong with black." He looked up at Skulduggery. "Just let me lock up," he said, "then we can talk properly."

While they waited for him to do so, Skulduggery and Stephanie wandered into the back of the shop. Material and fabrics of all types and textures were arranged very neatly in massive shelves that lined the walls. There was a single workplace in the centre of the room and another doorway leading further back.

"He's going to make me clothes?" Stephanie whispered.

"Yes, he is."

"Doesn't he need to take measurements or something?"

"One glance, that's all he needs."

They passed through into a small living room, and moments later Ghastly joined them. Stephanie and Skulduggery sat on the narrow sofa and Ghastly sat in the armchair opposite, both feet flat on the ground and fingers steepled.

"So what's all this about?" he asked.

"We're investigating Gordon Edgley's murder," Skulduggery said.

"Murder?" Ghastly said after a short pause.

"Indeed."

"Who would want to kill Gordon?"

"We think Serpine did it. We think he was looking for something."

"Skul," Ghastly said, frowning, "usually when you want my help you just call and we go off and you get me into a fight. You've never explained what's going on before, so why are you doing it now?"

"This is a different type of help I need."

"So you don't need me to hit anyone?"

"We'd just like your help in finding out what Serpine is after."

"I see," Ghastly said, nodding his head.

"You don't see, do you?"

"No," Ghastly said immediately. "I really don't know what you want me to do."

"We think Serpine is after the Sceptre of the Ancients," Stephanie said and she felt Skulduggery sink lower into the cushion beside her.

"The what?" Ghastly said, his smile reappearing. "You're not serious, are you? Listen, I don't know what my dear friend here has been saying, but the Sceptre isn't real."

"Serpine thinks it's real. We think that has something to do with my uncle's death."

"I'm sorry for your loss," Ghastly said, "I really am. I

respected Gordon. He knew there was magic in the world and he wasn't seduced by it. He just wanted to observe and to write about it. That takes a strength that I hope has been passed on to you."

Stephanie didn't answer. Skulduggery didn't look at her.

"But," Ghastly continued, "to say that his death has something to do with a legend that has been passed down from generation to generation, and that has changed with each telling, is just nonsense. He had a heart attack. He was mortal. He died. That's what mortals do. Let him have his death."

"I think my uncle knew where the Sceptre is, or he had it and Serpine killed him, and now Serpine knows where it is and that's why he wants the key."

"What key?"

"The key to get the Sceptre maybe. We're not sure. What we do know is that he tried to kill me twice to get it."

Ghastly shook his head. "This isn't your world."

"I'm a part of it now."

"You've just stepped into it. You've seen magic and sorcerers and a living skeleton and I bet you're having great fun – but you haven't the slightest idea what's at stake."

Skulduggery didn't say anything. Stephanie got to her feet.

"You know what?" she said. "For me, this *is* an adventure.

That's what you're saying, isn't it? Well, you're right. I do look at all this as a big adventure, and I'm fascinated and excited and thrilled by it all. I've seen amazing people do amazing things, and I've been amazed." Her eyes hardened. "But don't you dare, for one second, think that this is just a game to me. My uncle left me a fortune: he left me everything I could ever want. He did all that for me, but he's dead now. So now I'm going to do something for *him*. I'm going to find out who killed him, and I'm going to do what I can to make sure they don't just walk away from it. He's got to have *someone* on his side."

"This is insane!" Ghastly said, leaning forward in his chair. "The Sceptre's a fairy tale!"

"I believe it exists."

"Of course *you* believe it exists! You've been dragged into a world where you think anything can happen, but that's not how it works. Your uncle involved himself in this and if what you say is true, he got killed for it. Are you so eager to do the same? You're playing with fire."

"Everyone plays with fire around here."

"This hasn't gone the way I was expecting," Skulduggery said.

"There are rules for things like this," Ghastly said, ignoring her and speaking to Skulduggery. "There's a reason we don't tell everyone we're out there. She is a prime example of *why*."

Stephanie's anger flared and she knew she couldn't talk now without her voice cracking and betraying her, so she dashed past Ghastly. She walked through the shop, unlocked the door and walked out on to the street. She could feel the anger twisting in her insides, making her fingers curl. She hated not being treated as an equal, she hated being talked down to and she hated the feeling of being protected. She didn't much like to be ignored either.

Skulduggery emerged from the shop a few minutes later, hat back on. He walked up to her as she leaned against the Bentley, arms crossed and staring at a crack in the pavement.

"So that went well," he said eventually. When she didn't answer, he nodded and said, "Did I tell you how I first met Ghastly?"

"I don't want to know."

"Ah. All right then." Silence drifted down like smog. "It's not very interesting anyway. But it has pirates in it."

"I couldn't care less," Stephanie said. "Is he going to help us or not?"

"Well, he doesn't think it's a great idea to have, you know, to have you with me on this one."

"Oh, really?" Stephanie responded bitterly.

"He seems to think I'm being irresponsible."

"And what do you think?"

"I have been known to be irresponsible in the past. It's entirely plausible that it's happening again."

"Do you think I'm in danger?"

"Oh, yes. Serpine still believes you are in possession of whatever key he's looking for. The moment he learns who you are or where you are, he'll send someone else. You're in – and I don't think I'm exaggerating here – especially *grave* danger."

"Then let's be absolutely clear on this, OK? I can't leave this. I can't go back to my dull, boring, ordinary life, even if I wanted to. I've seen too much. I'm involved here. It's *my* uncle who was murdered, it's *my* life that was in danger and I am not about to just walk away. That's all there is to it."

"Well, I'm convinced."

"So why are we standing around?"

"My question exactly," Skulduggery said, unlocking the Bentley. They got in and the Bentley rattled to life at the turn of the key. Skulduggery checked the rear-view, then the wing mirrors, then remembered that he didn't have any wing mirrors any more, and pulled out on to the road.

"So we don't get to look at his family's collection?"

Stephanie asked as they drove.

"Ghastly is a good man, and a good friend, and precisely the kind of person you want on your side, but he is also one of the most stubborn people I know. In four days, once he has had time to think, he will change his mind, and he will quite happily let us see what we need to see, but until then we don't have a hope."

"Wouldn't the books be in China's library too?"

Skulduggery made a noise halfway between a laugh and a grunt. "China has been after those books for years, but they're locked away where even she can't reach them."

"You know where they are?"

"In the Vault."

"In a vault? So what?"

"Not *a* vault, *the* Vault. It's a series of chambers housed beneath the Dublin Municipal Art Gallery, very well protected, where they don't take kindly to trespassers."

Stephanie took a moment then spoke. "Ghastly will change his mind in four days?"

"That's how long it usually takes, yes."

"But we don't have four days, do we?"

"No, we don't."

"So you know what we have to do, right?"

"Unfortunately, yes."

"We *need* to look at that collection."

Skulduggery looked at her. "I knew you'd be good at this. The moment I saw you, I knew you had an instinct for this job."

"So we break into the Vault?"

He nodded reluctantly. "We break into the Vault."

The Dublin Municipal Art Gallery was situated in one of the more affluent parts of the city. A gleaming triumph of steel and glass, it stood alone and proud, its lush gardens keeping the other buildings at a respectable distance.

Stephanie and Skulduggery parked across the road as part of what Skulduggery was calling a *preliminary stake-out*. They weren't going to break into the Vault *yet*, he assured her; they were just here to get some idea of what they were up against. They had just seen the gallery staff and a half-dozen security guards leave the building, their shift over for the day. Two people, a man and a woman, dressed in blue overalls, passed them on the steps and entered the gallery, locking the doors behind them.

"Ah," Skulduggery said from beneath his scarf. "We may have a problem."

"What problem?" Stephanie asked. "Them? Who are they?"

"The night shift."

"Two people? That's all?"

"They're not exactly people."

"So who are they?"

"It's not so much *who* as *what*."

"I swear, Skulduggery, you either give me a straight answer or I'm finding the biggest dog you've ever seen and I'm going to make him dig a hole and bury you in it."

"Oh that's charming, that is," Skulduggery said, then made a sound like he was clearing his throat, though there was nothing to clear and no actual throat to clear it from. "Did you notice the way they moved?"

"Very, I don't know... gracefully. What about it? Are they dancers? The Vault has ballerina security guards?"

"They're vampires," Skulduggery said. "The Vault has *vampire* security guards."

Stephanie made a show of poking her head out of the window and looking up at the sky. "The sun's still out, Skulduggery. It's still bright."

"Doesn't matter to them."

She frowned. "Doesn't sunlight kill them? Doesn't it turn

them to dust, or make them burst into flames or something?"

"Nope. Vampires tan, just like you and me. Well, just like you. I tend to bleach."

"So sunlight has no effect on them?"

"It binds them. It dampens their powers. During the day, they are for all intents and purposes mortal, but when the sun goes down, their powers flare up."

"I didn't know that."

"And the Vault employs two of them as their nightshift. The ultimate guard dogs."

"If sunlight doesn't hurt them, I don't suppose crosses will scare them off?"

"The best way to stop a vampire is with a whole lot of bullets, and since we don't want to hurt anyone, this is that problem I was telling you about."

"There must be a way to get by them. We could disguise ourselves as cleaning staff or something."

"No one works when vampires are around – vampires don't make a distinction between allies and prey. They can't resist the bloodlust any more than a moth can resist a big bright light. They're killers: the most efficient, deadly killers on the face of the planet."

"Scary."

"Yes, well, vampires aren't known for being cute."

"Well then, we're going to have to come up with something really really clever."

Skulduggery paused then shrugged. "I suppose I *am* good at that."

9

THE TROLL BENEATH WESTMINSTER BRIDGE

Skulduggery took Stephanie home, and as she was lying in bed that night, finally drifting off to sleep, a young woman in London was hunkering down and peering into the darkness.

"Hello?" she said. "Anyone down there?"

The Thames was dark and rushing beneath her, but no one answered. She glanced at her watch then looked around. It was seven minutes to midnight and Westminster Bridge was empty except for her. Perfect.

"Hello?" she said again. "I need to talk to you."

A voice answered: "There's no one down here."

"I think there is," she said.

"No," came the voice. "No one."

"I think there's a troll down there," the young woman said. "And I need to talk to him."

A face rose up out of the shadows, small and wrinkled, with large ears and a shock of spiky black hair. Huge eyes blinked at her.

"What do you want?" the troll asked.

"I want to talk to you," the young woman answered. "I'm Tanith Low. What's your name?"

The troll shook his head. "No no, not telling. Not telling that."

"Oh yes," Tanith said, "trolls only have one name, isn't that right?"

"Yes yes, one name. No telling."

"But I can guess, isn't that how it goes? If I guess your name correctly, what happens then?"

The troll grinned, showing lots of sharp yellow teeth. "You get to live," he said.

"And if I get it wrong?"

The troll giggled. "You get eaten!"

"That sounds like a fun game," Tanith said with a smile.

"What time do you usually play?"

"Midnight, stroke of midnight, yes yes yes. When I'm *strong*."

"And you pop out from under there at whoever's passing, don't you?"

"Three chances," the troll said, nodding. "Three chances is what they get. Guess the name, don't get eaten; get it wrong, come along."

"Do you want to play it with me?"

The grin faded on the troll's face. "Not strong yet. Need to wait, yes yes. Stroke of midnight."

"*We* don't have to wait, do we?" Tanith said with a pout. "I want to play *now*. I bet I can guess your name."

"No, you can't."

"Bet I can."

"No, you can't!" the troll said, giggling again.

"Come on up out of there, we'll see."

"Yes yes, play the game."

Tanith glanced at her watch and stepped back as the troll scampered up. Two minutes to midnight. He was small, up to her waist, with thin arms and legs and a bloated belly. His fingernails were hardened and pointed and he was grinning in anticipation, though keeping his distance.

She let her coat fall open a little and smiled at him. "You're a handsome little fellow, aren't you? Are you the only troll in London?"

"Only one," he said proudly. "Now we play! Guess the name, don't get eaten; get it wrong, come along. Guess guess guess."

"Let's see," she said, taking a step closer. The troll narrowed its eyes and stepped back, towards the edge of the bridge. She stopped moving. "Is your name Bollohollow?"

The troll roared with laughter. "No no, not Bollohollow! Two guesses left, only two!"

"This is harder than I thought," said Tanith. "You're really good at this, aren't you?"

"Best! Very best!"

"Not many people have guessed your name, huh?"

"*No one*," the troll cackled. "Guess guess!"

"Is it... Ferninabop Caprookie?"

The troll whooped and hollered and danced, and Tanith moved a little closer.

"Not Ferninabop!" he laughed. "Not Caprookie!"

"Wow," Tanith said, looking worried. "I'm not doing too well here, am I?"

"Gonna get eaten!"

"You eat a lot of passers-by?"

"Yes yes, yum yum."

"You gobble them all up, don't you? They scream and cry and run away—"

"But I catch them!" the troll giggled. "Stroke of midnight, I'm big and strong and fast, gobble them up, gobble them all up! They struggle and wriggle and tickle inside me!"

"I'd better get my last guess right then, eh?" said Tanith. "Is it... Rumplestilskin?"

The troll laughed so hard he fell on to his back. "No no!" he managed to say between gales of laughter. "They always say that! Always get it wrong!"

Tanith took one more step, and dropped her smile. The sword flashed from her coat but the troll saw it just in time and squealed and rolled.

Tanith cursed and swiped again, but the troll dodged beneath her and she spun and kicked out, sending him sprawling. He scrambled to his feet, hissing and spitting at her as she advanced, and then, in the warm London night, the sound of Big Ben. Midnight.

Tanith lunged but it was too late. The troll skipped back as his shoulders hunched and he snarled and started to grow.

"Nuts," Tanith whispered to herself.

Muscles bulged in his arms and legs, stretching the skin so

tight it looked like it might split. She moved forward again but he flipped back through the air, and when he landed he was as tall as she was. His chest broadened and his neck thickened and still he grew, and still he snarled. His bones popped and he finished growing. He was now almost twice her size.

Facing down a fully-grown troll was not what she had planned. She held the sword down by her leg and circled the creature.

"You cheated," the troll said, his voice deep and guttural now.

"You've been a very naughty boy," she said.

"Gobble you up. Gobble you all up, yes yes."

Tanith shot him a smile. "Come and have a go if you think you're hard enough..."

The troll roared and lunged, moving fast despite his size, but Tanith was ready. She slipped to the side and then past him, her sword opening up his thigh. He hissed in pain and swung a massive fist that slammed into her back. She hit the ground hard. He went to stamp on her but she rolled, coming up on one knee and bringing the sword from her side to her shoulder and the blade found his arm.

The troll stumbled back and she got to her feet.

"Gonna bite you," the troll growled, "gonna bite you into little pieces, yes yes."

"The game's not so much fun when you're playing with someone who can fight back, is it?"

"*My* bridge," he snarled. "*My* game."

She smiled at him. "My rules."

Another roar and he dived straight at her and she stood her ground. One swipe of the sword took the fingers on his left hand and he howled in pain and staggered back and she jumped. She planted her feet on his chest and swung, the blade flashing in the bridge's lights as it took his head. The troll's body stumbled back and she jumped off. The body hit the barrier and tipped backwards into the river.

Tanith stooped to pick up the head and moved to the barrier. She turned as a man walked up. She had never met him before but she knew who he was. He was tall and bald, and his face was lined and his eyes were a startling blue, the palest eyes she had ever seen. His name was Mr Bliss.

Mr Bliss nodded to the head in her hand. "Risky."

"I've fought trolls before," she said respectfully.

"I meant the risk you took with being seen."

"It had to be done. This troll has killed many innocent people."

"But that's what trolls do. You can't blame him for doing what nature intended." She didn't know how to respond. Mr Bliss smiled.

"I'm not berating you," he said. "You've done a noble and selfless thing. That is to be admired."

"Thank you."

"You puzzle me, however. I have been keeping an eye on your progress over the last few years. It is unusual to find a mage, even an Adept like you, focusing as heavily on physical conflict as you have done. Yet you don't seek power."

"I just want to help people."

"And that is what puzzles me."

"My mother used to tell me stories about the war," she said. "I think you may be forgetting some selfless acts of your own."

Mr Bliss smiled softly. "There is no heroism in war – there are simply things that need to be done. The heroes come later. But I am not here to discuss philosophies."

He looked at her with his startling blue eyes. "A storm is brewing, Miss Low. Coming events will threaten to turn the tide of power in this world, and so I have left my place of solitude and come here, searching for you. I have a need for someone of your ability and your outlook."

"I'm not sure I understand."

"The sorcerer Serpine is about to break the Truce. If I fail in my endeavours, we will once again slip into war. I need you on our side."

"It would be an honour," Tanith said.

"We have much to learn from each other," Mr Bliss responded, bowing. "Make your way to Ireland," he said, "and I will be in touch with you soon."

She nodded and he walked away. Tanith threw the troll's head into the Thames and, hiding her sword under her coat, walked off in the other direction.

10

THE GAL IN BLACK

tephanie was woken the next morning by the stereo playing very loudly indeed. Her dad had been trying to tune into a news station and the volume knob had snapped off, so instead of a quiet little traffic report they were treated to Wagner's *The Ride of the Valkyries* at full blast. He had lost the remote control down the back of the sofa and hadn't the first clue how to turn the stereo off. The music reverberated through the floor and in the walls. There was no escaping its sheer power. By the time her mother had yanked the plug out of the socket, Stephanie was wide awake.

Her mother poked her head in to say goodbye, and as her parents went off to work Stephanie threw on a pair of jeans and a T-shirt. While she waited for Skulduggery to arrive, she thought about what would be a good name for her to take. Skulduggery had explained how the actual taking of a new name casts a seal around the old one – so if Stephanie took the name Crystal Hammer (she didn't plan on it) then the name Stephanie Edgley would be instantly immune to any controlling spells. But while she only went by her given name, she was vulnerable.

If she were to have a new name, it would have to be a name she wouldn't be embarrassed about in years to come. It would have to be something classy and also something she felt comfortable with. Skulduggery had told her about people who'd taken names like Razor and Phoenix, and how he wouldn't advise anyone to take a name that seemed cool. He'd once been introduced to a woman who had put on a little weight over the years, and her hair had been a bit windswept and she had spinach in her teeth, and he was told her name was Jet. Jet did not suit this woman, the same way Razor did not suit the short fat man who took that as a name.

Stephanie looked up from her desk as Skulduggery

knocked on the window. She opened it.

"I thought girls were supposed to be tidy," he said as he peered in.

Stephanie kicked some underwear under her bed and ignored the comment. "You OK out there?"

"I've been perched on worse roofs, believe me."

"My parents have gone to work, you know. You could have used the door."

"Doors are for people with no imagination."

"Are you sure no one saw you? The last thing I need is for a neighbour to be passing and see you climbing up the side of the house."

"I was careful, don't you worry. And I have something for you." He gave her a short piece of chalk.

"Uh, thank you," she said slowly.

"Go to your mirror."

"I'm sorry?"

"Go to your mirror and draw this symbol on it." He handed her a small card that showed an eye in a circle with a wavy line through it.

"What's this for?"

"It's to help you. Go on."

She frowned, then went to the mirror.

"No," Skulduggery said, "a full length mirror. Do you have one?"

"Yeah," Stephanie said. Still with no clue why she was doing this, she opened her wardrobe and used the chalk to copy the symbol on to the mirror on the other side of the door. When she was done, she handed the card and the chalk back to Skulduggery. He thanked her, put them away and then looked at the mirror.

"Surface speak, surface feel, surface think, surface real." He looked at her again. "Could you wipe the symbol off now, please?"

"What is going on? What are you doing? Did you just cast a spell on my mirror?"

"Yes. Could you wipe the symbol off?"

"Well what does the spell *do*?" she asked as she used her sleeve to erase the chalk.

"You'll see," he answered. "Are you wearing a watch?"

"My watch broke. I wore it swimming. I thought it was waterproof."

"Was it?"

"As it turned out, no. Why do you need to know the time?"

"Oh, I don't. Touch the mirror."

She narrowed her eyes. "Why?"

"Touch it."

Stephanie hesitated, then did as he said and reached out, touching her fingers lightly against the mirror. But when she pulled back, her reflection did not. She watched in amazement as her reflection blinked, as if awakening from a trance, then dropped its arm to its side and looked around. Then, very slowly, it stepped out through the mirror.

"Oh my God..." Stephanie said, moving back as the reflection joined her in the room. "Oh my God," she said again, because she couldn't think of anything else to say.

Skulduggery looked on from the window. "It will carry on with your life while you're away, so you won't be missed."

Stephanie stared. "She's me."

"Not she, *it*. And it isn't you, it's a surface copy. It walks like you, talks like you, behaves like you, and it should be enough to fool your parents and anyone else it comes into contact with. When you return, it goes back into the mirror and the experiences and the memories it has made transfer to you."

"So... so I can be in two places at once?"

"Precisely. It can't spend too long in other people's company or they'll start to notice that things aren't quite right, and it would never fool a mage, but it is ideal for your needs."

"Wow." Stephanie peered closer at the reflection. "Say something."

The reflection looked back at her. "What do you want me to say?"

Stephanie laughed suddenly, then clapped a hand over her mouth. "You sound just like me," she said through her fingers.

"I know."

"Do you have a name?"

"My name is Stephanie."

"No, a name of your own."

Skulduggery shook his head. "Remember, it's not a real person. It has no thoughts or feelings of its own: they're all imitations of yours. It's your reflection – that's all it is. Operating instructions are as follows: it cannot change out of the clothes you're wearing when you cast it, so make sure you're not wearing anything with a logo or insignia. They'll come out backwards. Make sure you're not wearing a watch or a ring – they'll appear on the opposite hand. Apart from that, it's pretty simple."

"Wow."

"We should go."

She turned to him, frowning. "Are you sure they won't realise it's not me?"

"It'll stay out of other people's way for most of the time and try to avoid any long conversations. Even if your parents corner it and bombard it with questions, they'll just think you're acting strange."

Stephanie chewed her lip then shrugged. "I suppose jumping to the conclusion that it's my reflection come to life is a *bit* unlikely."

"You'd be surprised by how many things we get away with that fall into the category of 'unlikely'. You ready to go?"

"I suppose I am."

"Do you want to leave by door or window?"

"Doors are for people with no imagination," Stephanie grinned and joined Skulduggery on the window sill. She took one look back. The reflection was standing in the middle of the room, perfectly still.

"Bye," Stephanie said.

"Bye," the reflection responded and tried a smile for the first time. It looked kind of eerie.

Stephanie climbed out and hung on to Skulduggery as he jumped, displacing the air beneath them to act as a cushion. They landed gently and made it to the end of the road without any neighbours seeing them, but when they reached the pier, Stephanie's face fell. She stared in horror as Skulduggery marched onwards.

"What the hell is *that*?" she demanded.

"It's my car," Skulduggery answered, leaning against it with his arms folded. The sea breeze ruffled his wig beneath his hat.

She stared at him, at the car, and then at him again.

"What happened to the Bentley?" she asked.

His head tilted. "I don't know if you noticed, but it was ever-so-slightly dinged."

"And where is it now?"

"It's getting fixed."

"Right. That's a good answer. Fixed is a good answer. But I don't know, I'm kind of drawn back to my original question. What the *hell* is *that*?"

Skulduggery was leaning against a canary yellow hatchback with lime-green seat covers.

"It's my replacement car," he said proudly.

"It's hideous!"

"I don't mind it actually."

"Well, you're wearing a disguise, so no one will recognise you anyway!"

"That may have something to do with it..."

"When will the Bentley be fixed?"

"That's the nice thing about living in a world of magic and

wonder, even our most extreme car repairs happen in less than a week."

Stephanie glared at him. "*A week?*"

"Not a week," he said quickly. "Six days. Sometimes five. Definitely four. I'll call him, tell him I'll pay the extra..." She was still glaring.

"Day after tomorrow," he said quietly.

Her shoulders sagged. "Do we really have to ride around in this?"

"Think of it as an adventure," he said brightly.

"Why should I do that?"

"Because if you don't you'll just become really really depressed. Trust me. Now hop in!"

Skulduggery hopped in. Stephanie dragged her feet around to the other side and more kind of *fell* in. She squirmed down in the lime-green seat as much as she could as they drove through Haggard. There was a parcel in the back seat, wrapped in brown paper and tied with string. Beside that was a black bag.

"Is that the gear for breaking into the Vault?" she asked. "Is that where we're going?"

"Well, to answer your first question first, yes. That bag contains all the equipment needed for a beautifully executed break-in. To answer your second question, no, that is not where we're going. Before I get to introduce you to a life of crime, I get to introduce you to the Elder Mages."

"Crime sounds more fun."

"As indeed it is, though I would never condone crime in any of its forms. Except when *I* do it, naturally."

"Naturally. So why are we delaying the fun? What do these Elder Mages want?"

"They've heard that I've been dragging a perfectly nice young lady into all manner of trouble and they want to admonish me for it."

"Tell them it's none of their business."

"Well, while I do admire your moxie..."

"What's moxie?"

"...I'm afraid that won't work too well with these fellows. One thing you have to remember about the Elder Mages is that they're—"

"Really old sorcerers?"

"Well, yes."

"Worked that out all by myself."

"You must be so proud."

"Why do you have to report to them? Do you work for them?"

"In a way. The Elders pass the laws, and they have people

who enforce the laws, but there are only a few of us who actually investigate the *breaking* of those laws – murders, robberies, a couple of kidnappings, the usual. And while I may be freelance, most of my work, and my money, comes from the Elders."

"So if they want to wag their fingers at you..."

"I have to stand there and be wagged at."

"So why do they want me to be there? Aren't I the innocent young girl being led astray?"

"See, I don't really want them to view you as the innocent young girl. I want them to view you as the rebellious, insubordinate, troublesome tearaway who has made herself my partner. Then maybe they'll take pity on me."

"Wait, do they even know I'm coming with you?"

"No. But they like surprises. Almost always."

"Maybe I should wait in the car."

"In *this* car?"

"Ah, good point."

"Stephanie, we both know something serious is going on, but as yet the Elders have refused to consider that their precious Truce might be in jeopardy."

"And why would they believe me and not you?"

"Because I go to them loaded with baggage. I have a history and, some might say, an agenda. Besides, tales of horror are always more effective coming from a lady."

"I'm no lady."

He shrugged. "You're the closest I've got."

Skulduggery had another surprise for her as they drove. He pulled into a fast-food place and nodded to the parcel in the back seat.

"What's that?" she asked.

"What do you think it is?"

"It looks like a parcel."

"Then that's what it is."

"But what's inside it?"

"If I tell you, I deprive the parcel of its whole reason to be."

She sighed. "And what *is* its reason to be?"

"To be opened, of course, and to reveal what it's holding."

"You are so annoying," Stephanie muttered, reaching back and taking the parcel. It was soft to the touch. She looked at Skulduggery. "The clothes?"

"I'm saying nothing."

"Ghastly made the clothes already? I didn't think he was going to make them *at all*, not after, you know... the argument."

Skulduggery shrugged and started humming. Stephanie sighed, then took the parcel. She got out of the yellow car and walked into the fast food restaurant, making her way to the toilets at the back. Once secured inside a cubicle, she pulled open the string and the parcel unfolded before her. It was the clothes. They were the deepest black, made of a material she had never seen before.

She got changed quickly, noting how perfectly everything fitted, and stepped out of the cubicle to admire herself in the mirror. The trousers and the tunic, a sleeveless garment with silver clasps, were pretty good by themselves, and the boots fitted as though she'd been wearing them for years. But it was the coat that completed the picture. Three-quarter length, shaped especially for her, made of a material so black it nearly shimmered. She resisted the temptation to leave her other clothes in the toilet, and instead wrapped them in the brown paper and left the restaurant.

"Surprise!" Skulduggery said when she was back in the Canary Car. "It's the clothes!"

She looked at him. "You are so weird."

Twenty minutes later they were walking into the Waxworks Museum. The building was old, in dire need of repair, and the street wasn't much better. Stephanie didn't say a word as they paid and went wandering through the dark corridors, surrounded on both sides by imitation celebrities and fictional characters. She had been here two or three times as part of school trips when she was younger, but couldn't see the point of visiting *now*. They hung back from a small group of tourists until they were certain they were alone, and only then did Stephanie say anything.

"What are we doing here?"

"We're here to visit the Elders' Sanctuary," Skulduggery replied.

"And are the Elders made of wax?"

"I like coming here," he said, taking off his sunglasses and ignoring her question. "It's very liberating."

He took off his hat and wig and pulled the scarf from his neck. Stephanie looked around nervously.

"Aren't you afraid someone might see?"

"Not in the slightest."

"Well, maybe we should go and talk to the Elders then."

"Good idea."

Skulduggery moved to one side of the corridor and traced his hand over the wall. "Where is it?" he muttered. "Bloody idiots keep changing it..."

The tourists came back around the corner and Stephanie went to drag Skulduggery out of sight but it was too late – they had already seen him. A small American boy left his parents' side and walked right up to him. Skulduggery was frozen to the spot.

"Who's that meant to be?" the boy asked, frowning slightly.

Stephanie hesitated. Now the entire tour was looking at her, including the tour guide. "This is," Stephanie said, racking her brains for a likely-sounding explanation, "this is Sammy Skeleton, the world's worst detective."

"Never heard of him," the boy said, giving Skulduggery's arm a poke. He shrugged and lost interest, and Stephanie watched the tourists carry on. When they were out of sight, Skulduggery swivelled his head to her.

"'World's worst detective'?" he asked.

She shrugged and hid her grin, and Skulduggery *harumphed* good-naturedly and went back to running his hand along the wall. He found what he was looking for and pressed inwards. A section of the wall slid open to reveal a hidden passage.

"Wow," Stephanie said. "The Sanctuary is *here*? I used to come here when I was little..."

"Never knowing that beneath your feet was a world of magic and wonder?"

"Exactly."

He tilted his head slightly. "Better get used to that feeling."

She followed him in and the wall sealed shut behind them.

The stairway downwards was lit by torches that flickered in their brackets, but the closer they got to wherever it was they were going, the brighter it became.

They emerged into the gleaming foyer of the Sanctuary. It would have reminded Stephanie of the lobby to a high tech company building – all marble and varnished wood panelling – were it not for the lack of windows. Two men stood guard against the far wall, hands clasped behind them. Dressed entirely in grey, with long coats and some sort of helmet with a visor that covered their entire faces, they each had a scythe, a wicked-looking blade on a one-and-a-half-metre staff, strapped to their backs. A slight man in a suit came out to greet them.

"Detective," he said, "you are early. The Council is not ready to convene. I could show you to the waiting area, if you wish."

"Actually, I might take the opportunity to show our guest around, if that's all right."

The man blinked. "I'm afraid access is strictly limited, as well you know."

"I was just going to show my friend the Repository," Skulduggery said. "The Book, in fact."

"I see. Well, as Administrator of the Sanctuary, I would have to accompany you, naturally."

"Wouldn't have it any other way."

The Administrator bowed and spun on his heel, and led them down an adjoining corridor. They passed more people in grey uniforms as they walked. Stephanie was getting used to dealing with people with no eyes and no expressions, but there was something about them that unnerved her. Skulduggery, living skeleton though he was, was still fundamentally human, and yet these people, who merely wore helmets to hide their faces, seemed to her much more sinister.

"Who are they?" Stephanie whispered as they walked.

"Cleavers," Skulduggery replied in a low voice. "Security guards, enforcers and army, rolled into one. Dangerous individuals. Be glad they're on our side."

She did her best not to look at them as they passed. "Where are we going?" she asked, trying to change the subject.

"I'm taking you to see the Book of Names," Skulduggery said. "Some say it was created by the Ancients, but the truth is no one knows who really made it or how it was made. It lists the names of every person living on this earth: the given name, the taken name – when and if a name is taken – and the true name. Every time a baby is born, a new name appears in its pages. Every time someone dies, their name fades away."

Stephanie looked at him. "So my true name is in that Book?"

"As is mine. As is everyone's."

"Isn't that dangerous? If someone got their hands on that, they'd be able to rule the world." She let a few moments pass. "And I felt ridiculous even saying that."

The Administrator glanced over his shoulder as he walked. "Not even the Elders open the Book. It is too powerful – it can corrupt too easily. But they can't find a way to destroy it – it can't be torn; it can't be burnt; it can't be damaged by any means we have at our disposal. If the legends are true and the Book *was* created by the Ancients, then it stands to reason that only the Ancients could destroy it. The Elders, for their part, see it as their responsibility to protect it, to keep it away from prying eyes."

They reached a set of double doors. The Administrator waved his hand and the heavy doors swung slowly open. They walked into the Repository – a large room with marble pillars – which, as Skulduggery explained, housed some of the rarest and most unusual magical artefacts in existence. They passed row upon row of shelves and tables, on which lay items so bizarre they defied description. The Administrator pointed out one of the strangest of these – a two-dimensional box that held wonders to sate the most jaded of appetites, but which only existed if approached from a right angle. In contrast to this clutter, however, was the centre of the room, which was empty save for a pedestal, and on that pedestal, a book.

"That's the Book of Names?" Stephanie asked.

"Yes, it is," the Administrator answered.

"I thought it'd be bigger."

"It's as big as it needs to be, no more, no less."

"And it's OK to leave it out in the open like that?"

"It's not as vulnerable as you might think. When it was placed here, the security arrangements did cause the Elders some concern. How would it be protected? Guards can be overcome. A locked door can be unlocked. A wall can be broken. A shield can be pierced."

"So, what? They decided not to bother?"

"Actually, they came up with a most ingenious defence. Willpower."

"Sorry?"

"The Book is protected by the Will of the Elders." Stephanie wasn't sure if he was joking or not.

"See for yourself," the Administrator said. "Take the Book."

"Me?"

"You. You won't be harmed."

Stephanie glanced at Skulduggery, but he gave no indication as to what she should do. Finally, she just turned and started walking towards it.

Her eyes darted from one side of the room to the next. She thought about trapdoors and immediately started examining the floor she walked on. What form did willpower take? She hoped it wasn't bullets or anything painful like that. She was mildly annoyed that she was even doing this, walking right into whatever trap the Elders had set up, and doing so willingly. For what? To prove a point that wasn't even hers? She didn't even *want* to take the Book. This whole thing was ridiculous.

She glanced back, saw the Administrator standing there with a placid expression on his face, obviously anticipating whatever was about to happen, whatever was going to pop out in front of her to stop her from taking their precious Book. She stopped walking. If he wanted the Book, he could get it himself. She turned and walked right back again. The Administrator peered at her.

"You didn't take it," he said.

Stephanie forced herself to remain polite. "No, I didn't. But I'll take your word for it that it's well protected."

"When you started walking, you wanted to take the Book, yes?"

"I suppose so."

"And why didn't you?"

"Because I changed my mind."

"Because you didn't want to take it any more."

"Well, yes. So?"

"That is the Will of the Elders. No matter how badly you want that Book in your hands, the closer you get, the less you want it. It doesn't matter if you want it for yourself, if you want it because you were ordered to take it or because your very life depends on it. With every step you take, your indifference towards the Book increases, no matter who you may be or what power you may have. Even Meritorious himself couldn't get close to it."

Stephanie looked at him, taking it all in. Finally, she had to say it, there was no way she couldn't: "That's very impressive."

"It is, isn't it?" The Administrator turned his head a little, as if hearing something. "The Council is ready for you now. Please come this way."

They walked into an oval-shaped room and stood facing a large door. There was only one light source, from somewhere overhead, and the edges of the room remained in relative darkness.

"The Elders will be but a moment," the Administrator said and walked quietly away.

"They always do this," Skulduggery said. "Keep people waiting."

"My headmaster does the same thing whenever someone's called to his office. He thinks it makes him look important."

"Does it work?"

"It makes him look late."

The door ahead opened and an old man entered. He had short white hair and a tightly cropped beard, and he was tall, taller than Skulduggery. He wore a suit the colour of granite, and as he walked, Stephanie became aware of the shadows to his right. They seemed to shift and stretch alongside him, and she watched as more of them reached over from the corners of the room to join the mass. The shadows suddenly rose up from the floor and melted into an elderly woman in black. She fell into step beside the tall man and their footsteps slowed as they neared. A third person faded up from nothing, materialised right out of thin air on the other side of the tall man. He looked a little younger than the others and he wore a sky-blue suit, the jacket of which was struggling to contain his hefty paunch.

Stephanie looked at the Elder Mages and the Elder Mages looked at Stephanie.

"Skulduggery," the tall man said eventually, his voice deep and resonant, "trouble follows in your wake, doesn't it?"

"I wouldn't say follows," Skulduggery answered. "It more kind of sits around and waits for me to get there."

The man shook his head. "This is your new partner then?"

"Indeed it is," Skulduggery answered.

"No taken name?"

"No."

"That's something, at least." The man shifted his focus to Stephanie. "I am Eachan Meritorious, Grand Mage of this Council. Beside me are Morwenna Crow and Sagacious Tome. Can I assume, because you have not yet picked a name, that you do not intend to involve yourself in our affairs for very much longer?"

Stephanie's throat was dry. "I'm not sure."

"See?" Skulduggery said. "Insubordinate."

"You have been placed in dangerous situations," Meritorious continued. "Surely you would prefer to go back to the safety of your normal life?"

"What's so safe about it?"

"Ah," Skulduggery chimed in. "Rebellious."

"I mean," Stephanie continued, "I could get knocked down crossing the road tomorrow. I could get mugged tonight. I could get sick next week. It's not safe anywhere."

Meritorious raised an eyebrow. "While this is true, in your normal life you never had to deal with sorcerers and murder attempts."

The Elders were gazing at her with interest. "Maybe," she admitted. "But I don't think I can just forget about all this."

Skulduggery shook his head sadly. "Troublesome."

The woman, Morwenna Crow, took over. "Detective, you have petitioned the Council on numerous occasions concerning a supposed threat to the Truce."

"I have."

"And as yet you have failed to produce evidence."

"This girl standing beside me is my evidence," Skulduggery said. "Twice she has been attacked and twice her attacker has been after a key."

"What key?" asked Sagacious Tome. Skulduggery hesitated.

"Mr Pleasant?"

"I believe the attacker's master to be Serpine."

"What key, detective?"

"If Serpine is ordering attacks on civilians, this is a clear breach of the Truce and the Council has no choice but to—"

"The key, Mr Pleasant, what does it open?"

Stephanie glanced at Skulduggery's inscrutable visage and

thought she could detect hints of frustration in the small movements he was making.

"I believe the key will lead Serpine to the recovery of the Sceptre of the Ancients."

"I never know when you're joking, Skulduggery," Meritorious said, starting to smile.

"I hear that a lot."

"You are aware that the Sceptre is a fable?"

"I am aware that it is *thought* to be, yes. But I am also aware that Serpine has been working on tracking it down, and I believe Gordon Edgley may have had it."

"Nefarian Serpine is now an ally," said Sagacious Tome. "We live in a time of peace."

"We live in a time of fear," Skulduggery said, "where we're too scared of upsetting the status quo to ask the questions we need to be asking."

"Skulduggery," Meritorious said, "we all know what Serpine did; we all know the atrocities he has committed in the name of his master Mevolent, and for his own gains. But for as long as the Truce holds, we cannot act against him without good cause."

"He has ordered the attacks on my companion."

"You have no proof."

"He murdered Gordon Edgley!"

"But you have no proof."

"He is after the Sceptre!"

"Which doesn't even *exist*." Meritorious shook his head sadly. "I am sorry, Skulduggery. There is nothing we can do."

"As for the girl," said Morwenna, "we had hoped her involvement in all this would be minimal."

"She's not going to tell anyone," Skulduggery said quietly.

"Maybe so, but if she takes one more step deeper into our world, it may be impossible for her to step out again. We want you to consider this carefully, detective. Consider what it would mean."

Skulduggery gave a slight nod of acknowledgement but said nothing.

"Thank you for agreeing to meet us," Meritorious said. "You may leave." Skulduggery turned and walked out, Stephanie right behind him. The Administrator hurried over.

"I know the way out," Skulduggery growled and the Administrator backed off. They passed the Cleavers, standing as still as the wax models above them, and climbed the staircase out of the Sanctuary. Skulduggery donned his disguise and they walked back to the Canary Car in silence. They had almost reached it when he stopped and turned his head.

"What's wrong?" Stephanie asked.

He didn't answer. She couldn't see anything beneath his disguise. Stephanie looked around, paranoid. It appeared to be a normal street, populated by normal people doing normal things. Granted, the street had potholes and the people were scruffy, but there was nothing out of the ordinary. And then she saw him, a tall man, broad and bald, his age impossible to gauge. He walked towards them like he had all the time in the world, and Stephanie stood by Skulduggery and waited.

"Mr Pleasant," the man said when he had reached them.

"Mr Bliss," Skulduggery responded.

Stephanie looked at this man. He radiated power. His pale blue eyes settled on her.

"And you must be the girl who attracts all sorts of attention."

Stephanie couldn't speak. She didn't know what she would have said, but she did know that her voice would have been thin and reedy if she tried. There was something about Mr Bliss that made her want to curl up and cry.

"I haven't seen you in a while," Skulduggery said. "I heard you'd retired."

There was something peaceful about Mr Bliss's eyes, but it wasn't the calming kind of peaceful. It wasn't a peaceful that comforted you and made you feel safe. It was another kind of peaceful, the kind that promised you no more pain, no more joy, no more anything. Looking at him was like looking into a void with no beginning and no ending. Oblivion.

"The Elders asked me to return," Mr Bliss said. "These are troubling times, after all."

"Is that so?"

"The two men who had Serpine under surveillance were found dead a few days ago. He is up to something, something he doesn't want the Elders to know about."

Skulduggery paused. "Why didn't Meritorious tell me this?"

"The Truce is a house of cards, Mr Pleasant. If it is disturbed, it will all come down. And you are known for your disturbances. The Elders hoped my involvement would be enough of a deterrent, but I fear they have underestimated Serpine's ambition. They refuse to believe that anyone would benefit from war. And, of course, they still think the Sceptre of the Ancients is a fairy tale."

Skulduggery's voice changed, but only slightly. "You think the Sceptre's real?"

"Oh, I know it is. Whether it can do everything the legends claim, that I do not know, but as an object, the Sceptre is quite real. It was uncovered during a recent archaeological dig. As I understand it, Gordon Edgley had been searching for the Sceptre for some time, as part of his research for a book about the Faceless Ones, and he paid a substantial amount of money to gain possession of it. I imagine he worked to verify its authenticity, and once he had done so, he realised he couldn't keep it. Nor could he pass it on. Gordon Edgley, for all his faults, was a good man, and if there was a chance that it did have the destructive capabilities we've all heard about, he would have felt that the Sceptre was too powerful for anyone to possess."

"Do you know what he did with it?" Stephanie asked, finding her voice at last.

"I don't."

"But you think Serpine's willing to risk war?" Skulduggery asked.

Mr Bliss nodded. "I think he views the Truce as having outlived its usefulness, yes. I imagine he has been waiting for this moment for quite some time, when he can seize all the power and plunder every secret, and invite the Faceless Ones back into the world."

"*You* believe in the Faceless Ones?" Stephanie asked.

"I do. I grew up with those teachings and I have carried my faith through to this day. Some dismiss them; some view them as morality tales; some view them as stories to tell children at night. But I believe. I believe that once we were ruled by beings so evil, even their own shadows shied away from them. And I believe they have been waiting to come back, to punish us for our transgressions."

Skulduggery cocked his head. "The Elders would listen to you."

"They are bound by their rules. I have learned what I can, and I have passed it on to the only person who would know what to do with it. What you do next is up to you."

"With you on our side," Skulduggery said, "things would be a lot easier."

A small smile appeared on Mr Bliss's face. "If I have to act, I will."

Without even a "Good day", Mr Bliss turned and walked away. They stayed where they were for a few moments then got in the Canary Car and Skulduggery pulled away from the curb. They drove for a bit before Stephanie spoke.

"He's kind of scary."

"That happens when you rarely smile. Mr Bliss is, physically, the most powerful individual on the face of the planet. His strength is beyond legendary."

"So he *is* scary?"

"Oh, yes, very much so."

He drove on, and settled into silence. Stephanie let a few moments drift by.

"What are you thinking?"

Skulduggery gave a small shrug. "Lots of clever little things."

"So do you believe that the Sceptre is real?"

"It certainly looks that way."

"I suppose this is a big deal for you, huh? Finding out that your gods really existed?"

"Ah, but we don't know that. If the Sceptre *is* real, its true history could have been mixed up with the legends. Its existence does not prove that it was used to drive away the Faceless Ones."

"Funny. I wouldn't have thought that a living skeleton would be such a sceptic. So what's our next move?"

Skulduggery was silent for a bit. "Right, well, we've got to work out what we need. We've got to work out what we need, how we get it and what we need to get to get what we need."

"I think I actually understood that," Stephanie said slowly. The car went over a bump. "No, it's gone again."

"We need the Elders to take action, so we need proof that Serpine has broken the Truce. We need to find the Sceptre and we also need to find out how to destroy the Sceptre."

"OK, so how do we do the first one?"

"We'll get the proof once we find the Sceptre."

"And how do we find the Sceptre?"

"We find the key."

"And how do we destroy the Sceptre?"

"Ah," he said. "That'll be the little bit of crime that we'll have to embark on."

"Crime," Stephanie said with a smile. "Finally."

11

THE LITTLE BIT OF CRIME

From their vantage point, parked across the road, they watched the vampires, once again in their blue overalls, walk up the steps and enter the gleaming art gallery. They were chatting and didn't look intimidating at all. A few minutes later the staff and day shift security started to trickle out of the building. When every one of them was accounted for, Skulduggery reached into the back seat and pulled the black bag into his lap.

"We're going now?" Stephanie asked, looking up into the evening sky. "But it's still bright."

"And that's precisely why we're going now," he said. "Twenty minutes from now, there'll be two fully-fledged vampires prowling around in there. I want to get in, find out how to destroy the Sceptre and get out before that happens."

"Ah. Probably wise."

"Very probably."

They got out of the horrible Canary Car and crossed the street, left the pavement and moved through the garden area to a tall tree behind the gallery. Making sure they wouldn't be seen, Skulduggery put the bag over his shoulder and started to climb. Stephanie jumped for the lowest branch, grabbed it and started climbing up after him. She hadn't done anything like this in years, but climbing a tree was like falling out of one – easy. The tree's limbs were long and strong, and they quickly came adjacent to the gallery's roof, which was ridged with a dozen skylights. Stephanie hoisted herself up on a branch and sat there, regarding the large gap between building and tree with curiosity. It looked too far to jump.

"You sure I can't come with you?" Stephanie asked.

"I need you out here in case something goes terribly, terribly wrong."

"Like what?"

"Oh, any one of a number of things."

"Fills me with confidence, that," she muttered.

Skulduggery manoeuvred himself on to the longest branch and then walked along it, bent-legged and stooped over. His balance was unnatural. But there was still that gap. Without pausing he sprang forward, off the branch. He brought his arms up by his sides and out in front, and a tremendous gust of wind buffeted him over to the rooftop.

Stephanie promised herself that, one day, she'd get him to teach her how to do that.

Skulduggery looked back. "The gallery is outfitted with the most elaborate security systems," he said as he opened the bag. "But because of the vampires, the alarms on the outer corridors are never set, so once I get by the main hall, it should be plain sailing, as they say."

"As who say?"

"I don't know. People who sail presumably." He opened the bag and took out a harness that he started to strap himself into. He looked up at her. "Where was I?"

"I have no idea."

"Oh, yes, my cunning plan. I need to access a control panel on the east wall. From there, I can disable everything. The floor is pressure sensitive, so I'm going to have to stay off it, but that shouldn't be a problem for someone of my natural grace and agility."

"You're very impressed with yourself, aren't you?"

"Exceedingly so." He secured a thin wire on to a ventilation duct, looped it through his harness and led it back to one of the skylights.

Stephanie frowned. "You're going to lower yourself down from here?"

"Yes. That's the fun bit."

"Right. But you're going to have to *open* the skylight, yes? Won't *that* set off an alarm?"

"Only a small one," Skulduggery said with confidence.

She stared at him. "And wouldn't that be enough?"

"It's a silent little thing, hooked up to the nearby police station. Or it *was* hooked up. I passed by their transformer box before I collected you this morning. Oddly enough, it happened to short out at the exact same time. Something to do with a large amount of water mysteriously manifesting inside. I think they're baffled. They certainly *looked* baffled..."

"And your entire plan hinges on the hope that they haven't restored electricity yet?"

"Well, yes," he said, after a slight hesitation. "But anyway." He looked over at the setting sun then back at Stephanie.

"If you hear any screaming," he said, "that'll be me."

He passed his hand over the lock and it broke apart, then opened up one of the halves of the skylight and climbed over the side. She watched him disappear into it, and then heard a slight whirring as he used the hand-held control to lower himself down in the harness.

Stephanie sat back against the tree trunk, keeping an eye out for... whatever she was supposed to be keeping an eye out for. Anything unusual. She frowned to herself, not entirely certain of what constituted "unusual" any more, and then she heard an unsettling scraping noise. She looked up.

The wire Skulduggery had attached to the ventilation duct was slipping.

She watched in horror as it slipped again, getting closer to the edge, closer to slipping off entirely. She thought of the pressure-sensitive floor, thought about Skulduggery crashing down and setting off every alarm in the place and the vampires running in and catching him. Although he didn't have any blood for them to drink, she was sure they'd be able to find some other ways to punish the trespass.

The wire slipped again and Stephanie knew she didn't have a choice. She crawled along the same branch Skulduggery had jumped from and it groaned beneath her weight. Skulduggery was nothing but bones, she reminded herself, in an effort not to feel fat.

The gap was gaping. It was a gaping gap.

Stephanie shook her head – she couldn't make it. There was no way she could jump that. With a decent run at it, she might have had a chance, but from crouching on the end of an unsteady branch? She closed her eyes, forcing the doubts from her mind. It wasn't a choice, she reminded herself. It wasn't a question of whether she *could* jump, or *would* jump. Skulduggery needed her help, and he needed it now, so it was a question of when she *did* jump, what would happen then?

So she jumped.

She stretched out and the ground moved far beneath her and the edge of the building rushed at her and then she started to dip. Her right hand thudded against the edge and her fingers gripped. The rest of her body slammed into the side of the building and she almost fell, but she shot her left hand up to join her right and held on. She pulled herself up, little by little, until she could get an arm over the edge and soon she was safe. She had made it.

The wire slipped again. It was about to snap from the duct and then it'd all be over. Stephanie ran to it, got her fingers around the wire and tried to tug it down again but it was no use. She stood, put the sole of her boot against the wire and used all her weight to try and push it down, but she didn't make the slightest bit of difference. She looked around for something to use, saw the bag and snatched it up. Nothing inside but more wire.

She grabbed the wire and dropped to her knees, tying a new piece to the wire already attached to the harness. Her father had taught her all about knots when she was little, and although she couldn't remember the names of most of them, she knew which knot suited this occasion.

With the new length of wire added, she looked around for something to secure it to. There was another skylight right in front of her. She ran to it, wrapping the wire around the entire concrete base and getting it tied off just as the first piece of wire shot off the duct. There was a sudden snap as the wire went taut again, but it stayed secure.

Stephanie hurried over to the open skylight and looked down. Skulduggery was hovering right above the floor, trying to stay horizontal after the sudden drop. The motion control for the harness was still in his hand, but both arms were outstretched for maximum balance and he couldn't move himself back up.

There was a second control on the roof beside Stephanie, attached to the harness with a lead that twisted down through the skylight around the wire. Stephanie grabbed the control, jammed her finger against the UP button and Skulduggery started whirring upwards.

When he was safe he raised his head, saw her and gave her the thumbs up. He took over the controls, positioning himself next to the wall, by the panel that he had already opened. Stephanie watched him flick a few switches, and then he spun himself gently. His feet touched the floor. No alarms went off.

He undid the clasp on the harness and stepped out of it, then looked up. A moment passed and he motioned for her to come down. Grinning, Stephanie recalled the harness, strapped herself in, climbed over the edge, and lowered herself down. Skulduggery helped her unclip it.

"I suppose I *could* do with some back-up," he whispered and she smiled.

The gallery was big and spacious and white. There were huge glass sections in the walls. The main hall was full of paintings and sculptures, artfully arranged so it was neither cluttered nor sparse.

They moved to the double doors and listened intently. Skulduggery opened one of the doors, checked outside, nodded to Stephanie. They crept out, closing the door behind them. She followed him through the white corridors, around turns and through archways. She caught him glancing out of the windows as they passed. Night was coming.

They got to a small alcove, away from the main hub of the gallery. Within this alcove was a heavy wooden door, criss-crossed by a grid of bolted steel. Skulduggery whispered for her to keep watch and then hurried to the door, taking something from his pocket.

Stephanie crouched where she was, peering into the ever-increasing gloom. She glanced back at Skulduggery as he worked at picking the lock. There was a window next to her. The sun had gone down.

She heard footsteps and shrank back. The man in the blue overalls had appeared around the corner on the far side of the corridor opposite. He was walking slowly, like any security guard she'd seen in a mall. Casual, disinterested, bored. She felt Skulduggery sneak up behind her, but he didn't say anything.

The man's hand went to his belly and then he doubled over in pain. Stephanie wished she was closer. If he sprouted fangs she'd hardly be able to see them from here. The man straightened up and arched his spine, and the sounds of his bones cracking echoed through the corridor. Then he reached up and grabbed his hair and pulled his skin off.

Stephanie stifled a gasp. In one fluid movement he had pulled it all off – hair, skin, clothes – and he was pale underneath, and bald, and his eyes were big and black. He moved like a cat, kicking off the remnants of his human form. She didn't have to be closer to see his fangs, they were big and jagged and hideous, and now she was quite content to be viewing them from a distance. These weren't the vampires she'd seen on TV; these weren't sexy people in long coats and sunglasses. These were animals.

She felt Skulduggery's hand on her shoulder and he pulled her back a fraction, very gently, just before the vampire looked over. It moved away from them, down the corridor, in search of prey.

Stephanie followed Skulduggery to the door, and they passed through and closed it behind them. Skulduggery wasn't creeping any more, but Stephanie didn't dare make a sound. He led the way down beneath the gallery, a flame in his hand lighting the steps. It was cold down here. They were in an old corridor now with heavy doors on either side, and they walked until they came to a door with a crest etched into it – a shield and a bear. Skulduggery raised both hands and lowered his head and didn't move for almost a minute. Then the door clicked and they stepped in.

12

VAMPIRES

Skulduggery clicked his fingers and candles flared up all around the chamber. There were books piled on books, and artefacts and statues, and paintings and wood carvings, and there was even a suit of armour to one side.

"This is all to do with the Sceptre?" Stephanie asked in a whisper.

"It's all to do with the Ancients," Skulduggery answered, "so I'm sure there must be something about the Sceptre in all this. I honestly didn't expect there to be this much. You don't have to whisper by the way."

"There are vampires above us."

"These chambers are sealed. I broke the locking seal, but the sound seal is still in place. Did you know locking seals have to be dismantled every single time you want to go through, and then crafted again once you leave? I don't see what's wrong with a good old-fashioned key. That would certainly keep someone like me out. Well, until I knocked the door down."

"What's a sound seal?" Stephanie whispered.

"Hmm? Oh. Even if they were standing outside the door and you were shouting at the top of your voice, they wouldn't hear you."

"Ah," she said, "OK then." But she still kept her voice low.

They started searching. Some of the books were about the legends of the Ancients, some took a more practical and analytical viewpoint and some were written in a language Stephanie didn't recognise. A few of the books held nothing but blank pages, yet Skulduggery seemed able to read them, although he said they contained nothing of immediate interest.

She started rooting through a collection of paintings, stacked in frames against the wall. A lot of them showed people holding the Sceptre aloft and looking heroic. The paintings toppled over and she stooped to push them back up. She looked at the painting in front of her, recognising it from the book she had seen in Skulduggery's car – a man shielding his eyes from a glowing Sceptre as he reached for it. This was the full painting, not the truncated little rectangle on a page. Skulduggery glanced over as Stephanie put the pictures back as she had found them. She approached the suit of armour, noting the shield and bear etched into the breastplate.

"Family crest?" she asked.

"Sorry?" Skulduggery said, looking up. "Oh, yes. We don't have family names that we can keep, so crests serve as our only link to our ancestors."

"Do you have a crest?"

He hesitated. "I used to. I don't any more."

She turned. "Why not?"

"I abandoned it actually."

"Why?"

"You ask an awful lot of questions."

"When I grow up I want to be a detective just like you."

He looked over and saw her grinning. He laughed. "I suppose you do share my penchant for raising Cain."

"Raising what now?"

"It's an old expression. It means to make trouble."

"Well why can't you say 'make trouble'? Why do you always have to use these words that I don't know?"

"You should read more."

"I read enough. I should get out more."

Skulduggery held a small box up to the light, turning it over in his hands and examining it from every angle.

"What's that?" she asked.

"It's a puzzle box."

"Can't you play with it some other time?"

"The purpose of a puzzle box, its whole *raison d'être*, is to be solved."

"What kind of raisin?"

"*Raison d'être*. It's French for *reason to be*."

"There you go again. Why didn't you just say *reason to be*? Why do you have to complicate things?"

"My point is, leaving a puzzle box unsolved is like leaving a song unsung. It may as well cease to exist."

"There's a crossword in the paper my dad gets every single day. He starts it, ends up making up nonsensical words to fill in the blanks, and abandons it. I'll give you every paper we have lying about the house if you put that down and get back to searching."

"I've given up searching."

She stared at him. "And they say my generation has a short attention span."

"That painting you were looking at, notice anything strange about it?"

"There were a lot of paintings."

"The man reaching for the Sceptre."

"What about it?"

"Did you notice anything unusual about it?"

Stephanie went over to the wall again, moved the frames one by one till she came to the painting he was talking about.

"OK, unusual like how?"

"Describe it to me."

She moved the others out of the way so she could take a better look. "There's this man, he's reaching for the Sceptre, it's glowing... and that's it."

"Nothing strange about him?"

"No, not really..." She frowned. "Well..."

"Yes?"

"The Sceptre's really bright and he's got one hand shielding his eyes, but both eyes are wide open."

"So?"

"So if it's really that bright, you'd kind of expect him to be squinting at least. Even if it *is* just a picture."

"Anything else strike you as a little off?"

She scanned the painting. "The shadows."

"What about them?"

"He's got two of them."

"So? The Sceptre *is* magical, remember. It could be casting two shadows as easy as one, for whatever bizarre magical reason."

"But the Sceptre isn't casting these shadows. The angles are wrong."

"So what would cause that?"

"Two different light sources."

"And what is the primary source of light?"

"The sun?"

"If it *is* the sun, what time of day would it be?"

"Well, the shadow at his feet would make it noon, when the sun is directly overhead, but the shadow behind him would make it either morning or evening."

"Which one?"

"How should I know? It's behind him, so it might be morning."

"So what you're looking at is a painting of a man reaching for the Sceptre, seeing everything, at a time when it is both the past and the present?"

"I suppose so. What does this have to do with the puzzle box?"

"Who painted it?"

Stephanie peered at the bottom corner. "There's no name, only a crest. A leopard and crossed swords."

Skulduggery raised the puzzle box for her to see what was carved into its base – a leopard and crossed swords.

"Right," she said, standing, "guessing games are over."

"That painting tells us that the painter, or the painter's family, can offer us a glimpse into the past, and that is what we in the profession call a *clue*. A clue is part of a mystery, a mystery is a puzzle. I hold in my hands a puzzle box."

Skulduggery's fingers played over the surface of the box and Stephanie saw his head tilt. He pressed his hands against opposite sides, making subtle rotations until something clicked. There was a noise, like the whirring of a motorised part, and the top of the box opened to reveal a blue gemstone.

"Ah," Skulduggery said.

Stephanie peered closer. The gem was a little bigger than a golf ball. "What? What is it?"

"It's an Echo Stone," he said. "Very rare. Generally, it's used by people who are dying. They sleep with the stone close by for three nights, and in doing so they imprint it with their memories and personality. It's given to loved ones to help comfort them through their grief, or to answer any lingering questions they might have, things like that."

"How does it work?"

"I'm not entirely sure," he said. "I've never seen one up close." He pressed a fingertip to the Stone and it immediately started to glow. His head tilted again and he sounded very pleased with himself. "Would you look at that? I'm such a genius."

"You just *touched* it."

"Still a genius, Stephanie." She sighed.

A moment slipped by and then an old man faded up from nothing before them. Stephanie stepped back.

"Don't be alarmed," the old man said, smiling. He was wearing a robe and he had kind eyes. "I'm not going to hurt you, young lady. I am here to answer questions and provide whatever information I can to assist you in your..." His voice trailed off. He was looking at Skulduggery. "My, oh my. You're a skeleton."

"I am."

"As I live and breathe... figuratively speaking, of course, as I neither live nor breathe. But a *skeleton*, and a *talking* skeleton at that!"

"I *am* very impressive," Skulduggery said. "Who are you?"

"My name is Oisin and I am here to answer whatever questions you may have."

"Well that's good news, because we're looking for a few answers."

"How did you manage that then?" Oisin asked.

"I'm sorry?"

"Becoming a skeleton. That's a new one on me."

"Well, it's a long story."

Oisin waved his hand. "Better not tell me. This Stone will only work for a short while before it needs to be charged. I don't have a lot of time to give you the answers you seek."

"Then we'd better start."

"Yes, we had better. Was it painful, though? Losing your flesh?"

"I, uh, I don't mean to be rude, Oisin, but aren't you the one supposed to be *answering* questions? Not asking them?"

Oisin laughed. "I admit, I'm a little too curious for my own good. On the other hand, I do have an in-depth knowledge of the Stories of the Ancients, so in many ways, I'm the ideal candidate. Better suited to this than my colleagues, believe me. Before we get started, could I ask what century this is?"

"The twenty-first," Stephanie said.

"Twenty-first?" he repeated, laughing with delight. "Oh, my! So this is what the future looks like, eh? Kind of... gloomy and cluttered. I always thought it'd be *brighter*, you know? So what's been happening in the world?"

"You... you want us to tell you everything you missed?"

"Well, not *everything*. Just the high points. What language am I speaking, by the way?"

Stephanie frowned. "English."

"English, eh? Marvellous. I've never spoken English before. How does it sound?"

"Uh, fine, I suppose. Does the stone translate what you're saying?"

"Yes, it does. I could have used something like this on my travels, I'll tell you that much. It would have really impressed the ladies!" He started to chuckle, then stopped. "Not that I travelled far. Or at all. I don't trust boats, you see. If nature had intended us to travel across water, we would have been provided with fins."

"Can we ask you a question?" Skulduggery asked. "Again, I don't want to be rude, but if the Stone runs out of power before we learn what we need..."

The old man clapped his hands and rubbed them together. "Of course, my boy! Say no more! Ask me your first question!"

"You're an expert on the Ancients?"

"Yes, I am. I'm the one charged with the task of documenting their existence. It's a great honour, even if it does leave me with precious little time to travel. Not that I would, even if I could. But it'd be nice to have options, you know?"

"Yes... Anyway, we need to know about the Sceptre. We need to know its power."

Oisin nodded. "The Sceptre of the Ancients was created to destroy and destroy it does. There is nothing that will not crumble to dust under its glare."

"Is there any kind of defence against it?"

Oisin shook his head. "No shield, no spell, no barrier. It can't be stopped and it can't be destroyed."

"What about its power source?" Stephanie asked.

"A single crystal, a black crystal, embedded in its hilt, capable of channelling the energy that's poured into it."

"And can the *crystal* be destroyed?"

Oisin gave a little frown. "I've thought about this, actually. I know more about the Sceptre than anyone else since the time of the Ancients, certainly more than any of my colleagues, and while there is no record of a weakness, we have translations of texts that suggest the crystal can be destroyed from within."

"How?" Stephanie asked.

"I, um... I don't really know."

"Who created the Sceptre?" Skulduggery asked.

Oisin puffed out his chest. "'The Sceptre was created by the

Ancients as a weapon to be used against their gods. For one year they toiled, out of sight and in darkness, so that the gods could not see what they were creating.'"

His chest deflated and he smiled. "That's a direct quote from one of the first texts we found. I found it, actually. The others were so jealous. That's probably why they didn't want me to be the one to answer your questions."

Stephanie frowned. "You're not supposed to be here?"

"We had a vote. I voted for me. No one else did. They're just jealous. They said I'd waste time, talk too much. So I stole the stone and went away for a few days to imprint it with my consciousness. They can't imprint anything over it, you see. And now here I am." He beamed, then his whole body faded, became suddenly transparent, and his beaming smile vanished. "Ah. Time seems to be running out. If you have any more questions..."

"Who created the crystal?" Skulduggery asked quickly.

"Well, if you'll allow me to quote from the text that I discovered: 'The Faceless Ones created the crystal and the crystal sang to the Faceless Ones when an enemy neared. But when the Ancients approached the crystal was silent, and it did not sing to the Faceless Ones, and the Faceless Ones did not know it was taken.'"

"So their security system had a blind spot," Stephanie said.

"It looks that way," Oisin said, nodding. His image grew even fainter, and he held up a hand and gazed through it. "This is sort of unnerving."

"The Sceptre has returned," Skulduggery said.

Oisin looked up. "What?"

"It was uncovered recently, then hidden again. We need to know how to find it."

"Oh my," Oisin said. "If the wrong sort of person takes possession of the Sceptre..."

"It'll be bad, we know. Oisin, how do we find it?"

The old man vanished for a moment, then flickered back into sight. "I don't know, dear boy. Who hid it?"

"My uncle," Stephanie said. "He realised it was too powerful for anyone to own."

"A wise man, it seems. Of course, a truly wise man would return it to the place he found it. Failing that, somewhere similar."

Skulduggery straightened. "Of course."

A smile popped up on Oisin's face. "Have I helped you?"

"You have. I know where it is. Thank you, Oisin."

Oisin nodded proudly. "I knew I could do this. I knew I could answer questions and not talk too much. That's what I told them, right before they called for a vote, I said, listen, I can—"

And he vanished and the Echo Stone stopped glowing.

Stephanie looked at Skulduggery. "Well?"

"Gordon followed the example of the Last of the Ancients, and buried the Sceptre deep within the earth. It's in the caves."

"What caves?"

"Beneath Gordon's land is a network of caves and tunnels, stretching for miles in each direction. It's a death trap, even for the most powerful sorcerer."

"Why?"

"There are creatures in those caves who feed off magic. It would be the safest place to hide the Sceptre. I should have thought of it sooner."

Beneath Gordon's house, a world of magic and wonder Stephanie never knew was there. Bit by bit, she was seeing how close magic had been to her when she was growing up, if only she had known where to look. It was such a strange sensation – but what had Skulduggery told her when they were about to enter the Sanctuary? *Better get used to that feeling.*

Skulduggery closed his hand over the puzzle box and the top slid over, hiding the Echo Stone once again.

"Maybe Oisin has more information," Stephanie said. "How long does it take to recharge the stone?"

"About a year."

She blinked. "Ah. Well... OK then, that's probably a little too long. Still, who knows what else he could help people with? I'm sure it'll be invaluable to, you know, folks who are interested in history. Historians, like."

"Actually, we can't tell anyone we were here."

"You could tell Ghastly. I'm sure he'd forgive the little trespass if you told him what we'd found."

"Not really. See, this is his family's chamber. It's a sacred thing. Us being here is inexcusable."

"What? You said this was just like a storage shed. You didn't say anything about it being *sacred*."

"Now you know why I have difficulty keeping friends."

Skulduggery put the box back where he had found it. Stephanie was still staring at him.

"Is this disrespectful?" she asked. "Is this like dancing on someone's grave?"

"A little worse then that," he admitted. "It's like digging up that grave, taking out the body, rifling through its pockets and *then* dancing on the whole thing. It's a little more than disrespectful."

"Then yes," she said as he walked over, "I can see why you have difficulty keeping friends."

Skulduggery waved his hand and every candle in the chamber flickered out. They were plunged into darkness. Stephanie opened the door and peeked out. The corridor was long and silent and empty. She stepped out and Skulduggery followed, closing the door behind them.

They crept along the corridor, up the stone steps and out of the wood and iron door. They moved quickly through the gallery. The corners were the worst, as they were always expecting a vampire to round them just as they approached. They were nearing the main hall when Skulduggery held up his hand.

Ahead of them, crouching in the middle of the corridor, was a vampire.

Stephanie stopped breathing. Its back was to them, so they moved backwards, careful not to make a sound. They were just turning when Stephanie saw something out of the corner of her eye. She clutched Skulduggery's arm.

The other vampire was approaching from the opposite direction.

They sank behind a marble pillar, trapped. Across from them was an archway leading into another section of the gallery, but Stephanie was pretty sure that even if they made it through without being seen, they'd be cut off. Their only way out was back in the main hall, with the harness, but their chances of making it without being torn to pieces were getting slimmer with every moment. Skulduggery had his powers, and he had his gun, but she knew he didn't hold out much hope that he'd be able to fend off *one* of those creatures, let alone two.

He turned to her, hand raised. One finger, pointing at her, then pointing at the ground. *Stay.* That finger, pointing at himself, then pointing at the arch. *Go.*

Stephanie's eyes widened and she shook her head but now that finger was pressed to his mouth. If he'd had lips, she knew his finger would be on them. She didn't want to, she didn't want to agree to this, but she knew she had no choice.

Skulduggery took his gun from his jacket and passed it to her, and gave her a nod, and then immediately sprang up and lunged for the arch.

The vampire approaching from behind saw him and broke into a run. The vampire up ahead turned and sprang off its haunches, and Stephanie shrank back as it passed the pillar and took off through the archway, joining the hunt for the intruder.

The gun was surprisingly heavy in her hand as Stephanie crept out and started running for the main hall. Her footsteps echoed loudly in the dark corridors but she didn't care – the only thing going through her mind was the fact that she needed to get out. She took each corner quickly, knowing the threat was behind her, and every time she took a corner she let herself glance back.

Empty corridor. Nothing coming for her. Not yet.

She was approaching the Main Hall. Just a few more turns and she'd be there. She tucked the gun into her coat – she'd need both hands to strap herself into the harness. She turned the next corner and skidded to a stop.

No. No, this couldn't be right.

She looked up at the blank wall, her eyes wide. This couldn't be right. This wall should not have been here.

She'd taken a wrong turn. She'd taken a wrong turn in this stupid gallery and now she didn't know where she was. She was lost.

She turned away from the dead end, wanting to scream at herself in frustration. She hurried back the way she had come, glancing through every arch and doorway she passed, looking for something she recognised. Everything looked the same in the gloom. Why weren't there any signs? Where were the signs?

There was an intersecting corridor up ahead. Could that be it? Stephanie tried remembering their trail from the hall to the iron door and mentally reversing it. Had they turned at an intersecting corridor? She cursed herself for not paying attention, cursed herself for relying on Skulduggery to lead the way. They must have come from there. Every turn behind her seemed to lead to the dead end, so they *must* have come from there.

She was ten paces from the intersecting corridor when the vampire emerged from a small hall up ahead. It saw her instantly. She didn't even have time to duck down.

The corridor was ten paces away. The vampire was about thirty paces beyond that. She couldn't go back. If she went back she'd be cut off. She had to go forward. She didn't have a choice.

Stephanie bolted. The vampire kicked off and bounded towards her. It was going to cover the thirty paces faster than she would cover the ten. They ran straight at each other and the vampire leaped. Stephanie dropped and slid beneath it and she felt the rushing air as it passed overhead. She came out of the slide on her feet and twisted her body, then sprinted down the intersecting corridor. This was it.

She recognised the statue. Only a few more turns.

She heard the vampire behind her. Every corner she turned cost her precious moments, but the vampire just leaped to the outer wall and sprang diagonally to the wall beyond the corner.

It was closing the distance between them.

Stephanie burst through the doors to the main hall and Skulduggery was there, launching himself at the vampire as it reached for her. They crashed backwards and tumbled.

"Get out of here!" Skulduggery shouted, kicking the vampire away and scrambling to his feet.

Stephanie grabbed the harness and hit the button. Her arms were almost jerked out of their sockets as the harness withdrew. She rose to the skylight too fast, and when the harness hit the top she lost her grip. She managed to get one hand around the edge of the skylight as her body swung wildly.

Her other hand clawed on and she gritted her teeth and pulled herself up. Her head and shoulders emerged into the night air, and she hauled herself up the rest of the way to tumble out on to the roof. Fighting to catch her breath, she immediately went back to the skylight and looked down, just in time to see the vampire leap.

She cried out and fell backwards as the vampire burst through the closed section of the skylight, showering her with glass. It hit the roof in a crouch. Stephanie didn't even have time to get to her feet before it dived at her.

She turned away and its claws raked across her coat but didn't penetrate the material, although the impact slammed her to the roof again. The vampire overshot but spun as soon as it landed, snarling. Its fangs dripped with saliva and its eyes locked on to hers.

For a moment neither of them made a move, then Stephanie slowly got to her hands and knees. The vampire hissed, but she didn't break eye contact. She tucked her feet beneath her and squatted. The vampire was waiting for her to make a sudden move. The gun was in her pocket but she didn't go for it.

Stephanie moved slowly. She kept her eyes open, didn't blink, didn't do anything that might give it an excuse to resume its attack. Her knees straightened, though she stayed bent over. She took her first step, to her left. The vampire moved with her.

Its eyes blazed with sheer animal ferocity. All it wanted to do was rip her apart. All it wanted was her complete and utter annihilation. She forced herself to keep calm.

"Easy, boy," she said softly and the vampire snapped at the air. Its claws clicked against themselves. Even though they hadn't pierced her coat, her back was throbbing in pain. She knew that if it hadn't been for whatever material this coat was made from, that single swipe would have killed her.

The vampire began moving towards her. Stephanie started to back away but the moment she tried moving her foot behind her, the vampire's hackles rose. She froze. If it leaped from that distance it would be on her before she knew what was happening. It kept coming, moving slowly, stalking its prey.

The second skylight exploded and then everything was happening too fast.

The vampire broke its eye-lock and lunged but Stephanie was already moving, twisting to the side as the claws lacerated the space where she had just been. The other vampire was on the roof and closing in, and Stephanie sprinted for the edge of the building and she jumped.

Her legs hit branches and she flipped over and was crashing headlong into the tree and falling. She smacked from one branch to the next, each impact spinning her and making her cry out. She hit a branch with her ribs and the breath rushed out of her and still she fell, then there were no more branches and for a moment it was just her and the sound of rushing air, and then the ground slammed into her from behind.

Stephanie lay on the grass, trying to breathe. She could see the tree; she could see the gallery; she could see the sky. Something was falling towards her. Two things, two figures, dropping from the edge of the building. The vampires hit the ground and came at her.

The window to her left shattered and the security alarm pierced the night. Skulduggery landed in front of her. He thrust his hand out and the air shimmered and he caught one of the vampires, sending it hurtling back. The second one kept coming and Skulduggery threw fire at it but it leaped, cleared the flame and landed with both feet on Skulduggery's chest. They went down and Stephanie's body started obeying her again. She got up, still struggling to breathe. The vampire swiped and Skulduggery's shirt parted and he cried out in pain.

Stephanie wrapped both arms around the vampire's neck and pulled back. It hissed and flailed and Stephanie stumbled back to avoid its claws. Skulduggery sat up and he pressed his hand against the vampire. The vampire shot backwards like it had been fired from a cannon. It hit the wall of the building with a sickening thwack and fell to the ground and didn't get up. Stephanie grabbed Skulduggery's arm and dragged him to his feet, and they ran for the car.

13

THE RED RIGHT HAND

"How are you?"

Stephanie shrugged and managed not to wince. Her entire body ached. "I'm good," she lied.

Skulduggery glanced at her as he drove. "Are you hurt? Are you injured?"

"No, just a bruise or two. I'm fine, really. You don't have to worry about me."

"Stephanie, you jumped off a building."

"Yes, but the branches broke my fall. Every one of them."

"And how *were* the branches?"

"A lot unlike pillows."

"You could have been killed."

"But I wasn't."

"But you could have been."

"But I wasn't."

"I'm not denying that you make a good point, but the fact is you could have been. I've already lost a dear friend to all this and I don't want that to happen again."

She looked at him. "Are you saying you'd be very upset if I died?"

"'Very' is such a strong word..."

"Well, if you teach me some magic, maybe I won't get hurt as bad next time."

"You said you weren't hurt."

"Are you kidding? I jumped off a building, of course I'm hurt."

"Stephanie—"

"Yes, Skulduggery?"

"You can be really annoying at times."

"I know. So where are we going?"

"We're going to at least *find* the doorway to the caves. Then we'll concentrate on finding the key to open it."

Half an hour later they were driving into Gordon's estate.

Stephanie climbed stiffly out of the Canary Car and followed Skulduggery inside.

The cellar was chilly and dark, and the single bulb hanging amid cobwebs wasn't doing its job very well. Countless years' worth of junk was collecting dust down here, and from somewhere in the dark corners came the occasional scuffle of rats. Stephanie wasn't scared of rats as a rule, but she wasn't too keen on them either, so she stayed away from the corners.

Skulduggery had no such qualms. He examined the walls, scanning their surface as he moved sideways along them. Now and then he'd tap the wall, mutter to himself and move on.

"Is this the same as the way into the Sanctuary?" Stephanie asked. "Are you looking for a secret passageway?"

"You watch too many haunted-house movies," he said.

"But *are* you looking for a secret passageway?"

"Yes," he admitted. "But that's just a coincidence."

She pulled up the sleeve of her coat, revealing an ugly bruise on her arm, and covered it up again before Skulduggery glanced over.

"Did Gordon build the passage?" she asked.

"No, it was included in the original designs. A few hundred years ago, this was a sorcerer's house."

"And he built a secret passageway to the caves? I thought you said the caves were a death trap for sorcerers."

"I did say that, yes."

"So why did he build himself a short cut? Was he a stupid sorcerer?"

"No, he just wasn't a very nice one. He used to drag his enemies down there and leave them to whatever creatures were hungriest."

"What a charming history. I can see why my uncle bought the place."

"*Aha.*"

Stephanie moved closer. Skulduggery's hand was flat against the wall. He moved it and she could see a slight indentation, almost invisible to the naked eye.

"That's the lock?"

"Yes, this is one of those good old-fashioned key-required locks – the kind a spell won't open. Damn it."

"Can you break it?"

"I *could* break it, but then it wouldn't work and we couldn't get the door open."

"I meant break *through* it."

"That would work if the door was in the same place as the lock, but things are rarely that straightforward."

"So we need the key."

"We need the key."

"I don't suppose we'll find it on one of Gordon's keyrings."

"Indeed. This is not a regular key we're looking for."

"We don't have to solve a puzzle to get to it, do we?"

"We may."

Stephanie groaned. "How come nothing's ever simple?"

"Every solution to every problem is simple. It's the distance between the two wherein the mystery lies."

They turned off the light and climbed the stairs out of the dank mustiness of the cellar. They walked into the living room and a man in a suit, a suit that looked almost Victorian in design, turned to them.

He had black hair and thin lips and his right hand, which was skinless, glistened with blood and wet muscle, and before Stephanie could even register surprise Skulduggery was pulling the gun from his jacket. The man moved as gunshots filled the room, stepping to one side and waving his right hand.

She didn't know what he did but it worked, and no bullets hit him.

"Run!" Skulduggery said, pushing her out of the room.

She stumbled and something moved beside her and she turned as another man came at her. There was something wrong with him – something wrong with his skin, with his features – they didn't look real: they looked almost papery. She tried to hit it, but it was like hitting a bag of air. A fist swung at her, but unlike its body the fist was heavy and solid, and it snapped her head back. She staggered and it reached for her, but then Skulduggery was there, hurling it away.

Three more of them came through the front door. Stephanie ran to the stairs, Skulduggery covering her escape. Halfway up she looked back as the man in the suit strolled into the hall. She shouted a warning and Skulduggery turned to face him but it was too late. Purple vapour gathered in the man's left palm and he released it in a stream that flowed into Skulduggery and arced out behind him and above, flowing back into the man's other hand, forming a circle. Skulduggery dropped to his knees, tried to raise the gun but couldn't hold it, and it fell to the floor.

"Take him," the man said, cutting off the purple stream. Skulduggery sagged and three of the paper men grabbed him, started dragging him out of the house. The man motioned to the fourth. "You, kill the girl."

And he walked out.

Stephanie sprinted to the landing, the papery thing clumping up the stairs behind her. She ran to Gordon's dark study, slammed the door and pushed over one of the bookcases. It toppled and crashed and books spilled across the floor.

The door opened a fraction and hit the bookcase. Heavy fists started to pound on it from the other side.

She went to the window, opened it and looked down. Even if she made the drop without breaking her legs, she'd land right in front of the man with the red hand. She backed off, looked around for a weapon.

The bookcase slowly scraped across the floor. The door opened wider. Stephanie turned, moved behind the desk and hid. The pounding continued. She peered out. She could see a papery arm now, reaching around. Then a shoulder, and a head. She ducked back into hiding.

One last heave and the door was open wide enough for the thing to step over the fallen bookcase. Stephanie stopped breathing. She peeked out. It crossed to the window and leaned out, hands on the sill.

Stephanie rose and launched herself forward. It heard her and tried to turn but she slammed into it. Its heavy hands slipped off the window sill and dragged it through, and Stephanie reached down, grabbed its lower leg and hauled. The thing tried to reach back through the window but it was too late, and out it went with a faint rustle of paper.

It landed in a heap and she saw the man in the suit glare up at her. He waved his arm and she threw herself away from the window as the air turned purple and the window exploded. Glass shards rained down on her back, but they didn't tear through the coat.

She lay where she was, hands over her head, until she heard a car start up. Then she got up, glass and splinters of wood falling from her, and reached the window just in time to see the silver car leave the estate. They'd left her, obviously deciding it wasn't worth the effort to make sure she was dead.

Stephanie pulled the crumpled business card from her pocket, got out her phone and dialled the number. The call was picked up almost immediately. She spoke urgently.

"I need help. They've taken Skulduggery."

"Tell me where you are," China Sorrows said. "I'll send someone to pick you up."

14

ELEMENTAL MAGIC

hina Sorrows was very still. She sat with her legs crossed, hands flat on the arms of the chair. The sounds of the city at night did not seep into her apartment – they were alone in here, the only two people left on the face of the earth. Stephanie watched her and waited.

The apartment was vast, occupying the space across the hall from her library. Stephanie had leaped out of the car China had sent, run up the stairs and had been directed in here by the man in the bow tie. No time had been lost.

Skulduggery was in danger and they needed to get him back *now*.

China spoke at last. "How can you be sure it was Serpine?"

"What?" Stephanie said, exasperated. "Of course it was Serpine! Who else could it have been?"

A delicate shrug of delicate shoulders. "We have to be sure, that's all."

"I *am* sure, OK?"

China looked at her, and Stephanie felt ashamed of her impatience. She lowered her eyes and closed her mouth. She was so sore, her body was so sore, but it was all right now because she was safe, and China would know what to do. Everything would be OK. Stephanie would wait for her to make a decision, no matter how long she deliberated, and she felt sure that Skulduggery would be safe and well. Even if he wasn't, what did it matter? China knew what was best, and if she wanted to wait, then Stephanie would be happy to wait with her.

No, she said to herself, *that's the spell, that's China's spell working on me*. She dragged her eyes up, met China's gaze and thought she saw a flicker of surprise.

"What are you going to do?" Stephanie asked.

China rose from the chair in one graceful movement. "I will see to it," she said. "You should go home, dear: you look dreadful."

Stephanie felt herself blush. "I'd rather stay," she said.

"It could take some time before plans are in place. Wouldn't you be more comfortable in familiar surroundings?"

Stephanie didn't like disagreeing with China but she couldn't go home, not while Skulduggery was in trouble. "I'd rather stay," she repeated softly.

"Very well," China said with a small smile. "I must leave, but I'll return when I have news."

"Can I come with you?"

"I'm afraid not, child." Stephanie nodded, hiding her disappointment.

China left the building, accompanied by the man in the bow tie. Stephanie stayed in the apartment for a while, but despite the fact that it was almost three in the morning, she couldn't relax. There was no TV and the only book in a language she could understand was a leather-bound address book on a small table.

She crossed the hall and stepped into the library. She passed a man in a porcelain mask, too engrossed in his reading to notice her. She walked slowly, reading the titles on the spines of the books, trying to keep her mind occupied. If she could find something here, a book that had what she needed, then maybe she wouldn't be so helpless next time she went up against

Serpine, or anyone else. If she'd had even the slightest bit of power, she might have been able to help Skulduggery.

Stephanie followed one shelf to its end then chose another one, wandering deeper into the labyrinth. She couldn't work out the system – the books weren't arranged alphabetically, or by author, or even by topic. It all seemed completely random.

"You look lost."

She turned. The young woman who had addressed her slipped a book back into its place. She had tousled blonde hair and she was pretty, but her eyes were hard and she wore a sleeveless tunic that showed her strong arms. She spoke with an English accent.

"I'm looking for a book," Stephanie said, unsure.

"This would seem to be the place for that."

"Are there any books here on magic?"

"They're *all* books on magic," the young woman replied.

"I mean learning magic. I just need something. *Anything.*"

"You have no one to teach you?"

"Not yet. I don't know how to find anything in here."

For a moment, Stephanie felt like she was being studied. Finally the young woman spoke again. "My name is Tanith Low."

"Oh, hi. I'm afraid I can't tell you my name. No offence."

"None taken. The books are arranged in terms of experience. These are far too advanced for someone without instruction. Two rows over, you might find what you need."

Stephanie thanked her and Tanith walked away, disappearing in the maze of shelves. Stephanie found the section she was referring to and started scanning the titles. *An Introductory Guide to Monster Hunting, The Sorcery Doctrines, A History So Far, Three Names...*

Stephanie took the *Three Names* book from the shelf, and flicked through it. She came to the part on Taken Names, a chunk of the book that went on for roughly 200 pages, and scanned the headings in bold print. She turned pages, skimmed paragraphs, looking for anything that stood out. The best advice it had for taking a name was this: *"The name you take should fit you, define you, and already be known to you."*

She put the book back, unimpressed, and scanned a few more titles before she found it: *Elemental Magic*. She took it down, opened it and started reading. This was it. This was what she was looking for. She found an old chair in one corner and sat, bringing her legs up under her.

Her mobile phone was perched on the arm of the chair.

Stephanie held one hand closed, trying to think of the space between her hand and the phone as a series of interlocking objects. Moving one would move another, which would move another, which would move the phone. She focused, opened her hand slowly and then snapped open her palm, like she had seen Skulduggery do.

Nothing happened.

She made a fist, then tried again. The phone stayed where it was. Just like it had done the previous fifty times she'd tried.

"How's it going?" She looked up as Tanith Low approached.

"You're starting off too big," Tanith said. "A phone's too heavy. A paper clip would be enough."

"I don't have a paper clip," Stephanie said.

Tanith took the book from her, opened it and balanced it on the arm of the chair. "Use that," she said.

Stephanie frowned. "But that's even heavier than the phone."

"Not the book. Just the page."

"Oh," Stephanie said. She concentrated again, flexed her fingers and splayed her hand. The page didn't turn. It didn't even lift.

"It takes time," Tanith said. "And patience."

"I don't have time," Stephanie said bitterly. "And I've never had patience."

Tanith shrugged. "There's always the possibility that you just can't do magic. It's one thing to know it exists – it's quite another to be able to do it yourself."

"I suppose," Stephanie said.

"That's some bruise you've got there."

Stephanie glanced at her arm, to where her sleeve was pulled back. "I had a bit of trouble," she said.

"So I see. Did you give as good as you got?"

"Not really," Stephanie admitted. "But most of the bruising was done by a tree anyway, so..."

"I've fought just about every type of opponent you could name," Tanith said, "but I've never been attacked by a tree. Well done."

"Thank you."

Tanith dug into her pocket and brought out a piece of yellow porous rock. "Run a bath, let this dissolve. A few minutes in there, the bruises will be gone."

Stephanie took the rock. "Thank you," she said, and Tanith shrugged.

"I don't want to scare you, but this mightn't be the best time for someone to start learning magic. Bad things are happening."

Stephanie didn't say anything. She didn't know anything about Tanith, and she didn't know how many sides there were in the coming conflict. She wasn't about to start trusting perfect strangers.

"Thanks for the rock," she said.

"Not a problem," Tanith responded. "Us warriors have to look out for one another."

Stephanie saw movement through the stacks – the man in the bow tie was back. Which meant China had returned.

"I have to go," she said at once, getting up off the chair.

She found China in the apartment, her back to Stephanie as she approached.

"Have you told the Elders?" Stephanie asked.

"Word has been sent," China said without turning.

"You sent *word*? That's it?"

"Do not presume to question me, child."

Stephanie glared at her. "I really wish you wouldn't call me child."

China turned. "And I really wish you would pick a name, so I wouldn't have to."

"Why aren't we going to the rescue?"

"Going to the rescue?" China said with a laugh. "On our horses, is that right? With bugles sounding and flags flying? You think that's how it works?"

"Skulduggery has come to my rescue."

"Well, they don't make them like him any more, do they?"

"Sending word isn't good enough. Meritorious has to be told. Tell him that we need Skulduggery to get the Sceptre; tell him that without Skulduggery, Serpine will destroy everything. Tell him whatever you want, but we *have* to make the Elders act!"

"And then what? They call the Cleavers to action, they call their allies together, and then we all go merrily along to war? Child, you know nothing about war. You think it's big and it's loud and it's good versus evil. It's not. War is a delicate thing: it requires precision. It requires timing."

"We don't have time."

"Not so. Time is in short supply, but we still have it."

"So you're *delaying*? Why?"

"I cannot have chaos erupting around me until I am prepared for it. I am a collector. I am an observer. I don't participate. My resources, and my standing, must be secure before I can allow the uncertainty of war to crash down upon us."

"And what about Skulduggery? While you're waiting for the right moment to tell everyone Serpine is the bad guy, Skulduggery might be killed!"

The hesitation that flickered across China's face was barely noticeable. "There are casualties in every conflict."

Stephanie hated her. She turned and stormed back to the open door.

"Where are you going?" China called after her.

"I'm going to do what you're too scared to do yourself!"

"No, you're not."

The door slammed shut before Stephanie reached it and she spun around. China was walking towards her, her exquisite face perfectly calm.

"You have no right," China said softly, "to plunge us all into war. Who are you to decide when we fight? Why should you decide when we die?"

"I just want to help my friend," Stephanie said, taking a step back.

"Skulduggery is not your friend."

She narrowed her eyes. "You don't know what you're talking about."

"And you don't know *him*, child. He has anger in him like you have never seen. He has hatred in him that you would never dream about. There is not one place he would rather be than where he is right now."

"You're crazy."

"He told you how he died then?"

"Yes," Stephanie said. "He was killed by one of Mevolent's men."

"Nefarian Serpine killed him," China said. "He tortured him first, purely for fun. He ridiculed him and he stripped him of his powers. And then he pointed at him. Did you know that's all it takes, with that red right hand of his? For him to *point* and then it's all over?"

Agonising death, Skulduggery had said. Stephanie hadn't realised he had felt it himself. She shook her head defiantly. "That doesn't change anything."

"When he came back, he fought Mevolent's forces with a single-minded determination – not to defeat evil, but to have his revenge on Mevolent's lackey. Mevolent himself fell, but just as Skulduggery was in a position to claim his vengeance..."

"There was the Truce," Stephanie said slowly.

"And suddenly his enemy was now a protected citizen. Skulduggery has been waiting a long time to get his revenge, and he will risk anyone and anything in order to get it."

Stephanie stood up straighter. "Even if you're right, that doesn't change the fact that he has been the only one investigating my uncle's murder, or that he seems to be the only one around here who cares about what is really going on, or that he has saved my life."

"And put it at risk. Every good thing he has done *for* you has been cancelled out by every bad thing he has done *to* you. You don't owe him anything."

"I'm not going to abandon him."

"It is hardly your choice."

"What are you going to do?" Stephanie challenged.

"I am simply going to ask you to do what I say."

"Then the answer's no."

"My dear Stephanie..."

Stephanie froze. China looked at her. "I've known your name since before I met you, child. Your uncle spoke of you often."

Stephanie lunged for the door but it was no use.

"Stephanie," China said softly. Stephanie's hands dropped to her sides and she turned. "Tell no one of this."

Stephanie felt it inside her and knew she would obey, knew no matter how much she raged against it, she would obey. She had no choice. So she nodded as tears stung her eyes and China smiled that beautiful smile of hers.

15

THE TORTURE ROOM

The moon was out and the stars were twinkling and it really was a beautiful night for pain.

Serpine descended into the castle's cold, dank depths and strode through the stone corridors. Already, he was beginning to smile. He came to the heavy wooden door and paused with his hand over the latch, savouring the deliciousness of the moment.

The latch lifted and Serpine stepped in. "Here we are again," he said.

Skulduggery Pleasant raised his head, practically the only part of his body he could move. Serpine had placed a binding spell on the shackles that secured him to the chair and so, unable to use magic, the detective could only watch as Serpine closed the door behind him.

"Life is a cycle, isn't it, Skulduggery? We are all destined to repeat ourselves, over and over. You, at my mercy. Me, merciless."

"You, talking," the detective said. "I thought you'd have grown out of the whole villainy thing by now, Nefarian."

Serpine smiled as he sat in the wooden chair opposite. The room was small, with stone walls and a single light bulb hanging from the ceiling. "Being a respectable citizen wasn't for me, but then you knew that, didn't you? You warned them about me, but they didn't listen. That must have been annoying, for the Elders not to even respect you enough to take you seriously."

"I think it's because I'm always smiling."

"Perhaps you're right. Oh, Skulduggery, what am I going to do with you?"

"Untie me?"

Serpine laughed. "Maybe later. We always seem to be at each other's throats, don't we?"

"Let me ask you a question. Let's pretend, just for a moment, that we live in your world, where things are crazy and the Faceless Ones are real. When you call them, what do you hope to gain? A pat on the head?"

"How my lords and masters will reward me for my servitude is up to them. I would never presume to guess."

"The door is closed, Nefarian. Just us two guys in here, chatting. What's in it for you?"

Serpine leaned in. "I get to be by their side when they raze this world, when they expunge the stain of humanity. And when it's over, I get to bask in their terrible glory."

Skulduggery nodded. "Yeah, I haven't a clue what you just said." Serpine laughed.

"You're going to fall," Skulduggery continued.

"Really?"

"You're going to fall hard and I'm going to be there. I'll be the one pushing you."

"Big talk from the man tied to the chair. Or are you even a man? A thing, perhaps? An oddity?"

"They'll come for you."

"Who will? The Elders? Meritorious and his lot? Please. They're too busy worrying about being rude to me."

"Not after this. They're probably at your doorstep as we speak."

Serpine stood, walked behind his captive. "Somehow I don't think they would be able to marshal their forces so quickly. Or so efficiently. No, my old enemy, I think for the moment anyway, we're all alone. And you have something I want."

"A winning sense of style?"

"The key," Serpine said as he walked back into the detective's line of sight.

"Don't know what you're talking about."

Serpine was moving his left hand slightly, like he was conducting music. "Obviously you're not going to just offer up the information, so I think a spot of torture is required."

"Ah," the detective said. "Old times."

"I remember those dark autumn days that I'd while away, cutting you, making you cry out."

"Fun for the whole family."

"You may think my options would be limited as far as torture is concerned, especially now that you don't have skin to cut. But I've picked up a few new tricks that I think you'll enjoy."

Serpine moved his fingers in a wave motion, directing it at the chair he had just been sitting on. The wood creaked and groaned as it expanded and contracted, like it was breathing. The detective couldn't avoid looking at it.

"If I can do that to the chair," Serpine said, enjoying the moment, "think what I can do to bone." There was a loud crack as the chair splintered.

Serpine hunkered down in front of him. "Well, Skulduggery? Where is that tired old defiance – the taunting, the goading? Where are the endless heroic clichés? Aren't you going to look me in the eye and tell me to do my worst?"

"Actually, I was going to ask that you go easy on me. I'm feeling kind of tender today."

Serpine stood, opened his left hand in front of the detective. "This is your one chance. Tell me where the key is."

"OK."

Serpine raised an eyebrow. "Really?"

"No, only joking. Do your worst."

Serpine laughed and his fingers started moving and the detective started screaming.

16

WHAT'S IN A NAME?

Stephanie soaked her elbow in the sink. She had broken off a piece of the rock Tanith Low had given her and dissolved it in the water, filling the sink with bubbles and the Library's restroom with a pungent odour. Whatever the rock was, it was doing its job. The bruises on her arms were fading.

She dried herself with a spotless white towel, let the water gurgle into the drain and allowed herself to sag against the wall.

Her body may have been tired but her mind was alert and racing, surging with anger. She was still furious at herself for being unable to disobey China's instruction. How could China have done that to her, to Skulduggery? After he had trusted her?

No, she reminded herself. He hadn't trusted her. That had been *Stephanie's* mistake, not his. And because she went to China before the Elders, or even Ghastly, now it could be too late to do anything. And it was all her fault.

What had Tanith Low called Stephanie? A warrior? That was laughable. No matter what Tanith had thought she had seen in her, she was wrong. There was nothing warrior-like about her. She ran straight into trouble without thinking, without one moment of hesitation. Not because she was brave or heroic, but because she was *stupid*. Because she didn't want to be left out, because she didn't want to wait. She didn't have a plan, she didn't have a tactic, all she had was a penchant for raising Cain.

It came to her then. Her eyes widened and she stood up straight, a new strength coursing through her limbs.

And just like that, China's command over her was broken.

She needed Ghastly. She didn't really know where he lived so she needed his address, and there was only one way she could think of to get it. She left the restroom, passing the window, realising that it was morning already. She crossed the hall to China's apartment and knocked. No answer. She knocked again.

China wasn't in. Stephanie looked at the door. Nothing special about it. She hadn't noticed anything unusual about it on the other side either, no chains or bolts or extra locks. There could be a locking spell placed on it, and if there was then she'd be wasting her time, but she didn't think there was. Skulduggery had said a locking spell needed to be dismantled every time a door is opened, then cast again. She doubted China would have the patience to do that on a daily basis.

Stephanie took a step back. An ordinary door. An ordinary, flimsy door. It was possible; she knew it was possible. She was tall and strong. This door was all that stood between her and saving Skulduggery. She had strong legs. Her legs were muscled, a swimmer's legs. They were strong. The door was weak. She could do it. She had to do it. She had to save her friend.

Her boot slammed against the door. She kicked again... and again... and again... Her legs were strong. She couldn't fail. Desperation lent her strength. The door was weak and it burst open.

She hurried in, moving right for where she had seen the address book. It wasn't there. It wasn't on the small table. Where was it?

She looked around. China had moved it. Where? Why? Had she known Stephanie would be looking for it? No, there was no way she could have predicted that. Then she had moved it for some other reason, some other ordinary, average reason. She had put it away; she had put it back. Yes, she had put it back in its usual place.

Where would China keep an address book?

Stephanie went to the desk, opening the drawers and rifling through them. Papers, letters, no address book. She turned, eyes scouring the room, aware that China could walk through that broken door at any time. She went to the shelves: no address book. Where?

She moved into the bedroom. There, on the bedside table, the address book. She snatched it up, finding the B's, her finger moving down the page. Bespoke tailors. She memorised the address, dropped the book on the bed and turned to go.

"Hello, dear," China said. She walked in and Stephanie stepped back, wary.

"I saw your handiwork outside," China said. "What did my poor door ever do to you? Did you break anything else while you were here? A vase? A teacup perhaps?"

"Just the door."

"Ah, well, I suppose I should be thankful for small mercies. Did you find what you were looking for, child?"

Stephanie tightened her fist. "Don't call me that."

China laughed. "That look in your eye is almost scary."

"Have you done anything to help Skulduggery, or are you still too busy helping yourself?" asked Stephanie.

"He inspires loyalty, doesn't he?" China said, an eyebrow raised. "You can't be around our Mr Pleasant without liking him, without wanting to fight alongside him. You should have been there during the war, you know. You should have seen him then."

"I just can't understand how you'd betray him like this."

For the first time since she'd known her, China's eyes turned cold. "I haven't betrayed him, child. I may have failed him, but I haven't betrayed him. To betray is to act *against*. I just haven't acted at all."

"Whatever," Stephanie said.

"Not interested in semantics?" China asked, her smile returning. "But of course not. You're a straightforward kind of girl, aren't you?"

"I'm leaving now," Stephanie said as she headed for the door.

"Straightforward," China continued, "but not too bright. Stephanie, would you be a dear and stop?" Stephanie stopped.

"I admire your courage, child, I really do. But rallying a cavalry to go after Skulduggery is just too risky. Too much could

go wrong. Now sit in the corner there, like a good little girl."
Stephanie nodded and walked for the door.

"Stop," China ordered. "I said the corner."

Stephanie reached the door and looked back. China was frowning. "I don't understand. How are you able to do this? Stephanie, answer me!"

"I'm not Stephanie," Stephanie answered. "And if you want to keep me here, then you'd better be ready to kill me."

China's frown disappeared. "I don't want to kill you, my dear," she said and the hint of a smile appeared. "So you've finally chosen a name."

"Yeah. And I'm leaving. Right now."

"Maybe you stand some chance after all. Before you go, will you do me the honour of introducing yourself?"

"Of course," Stephanie said right before she walked out of the apartment. "My name is Valkyrie Cain."

Ghastly opened the door, saw Stephanie and nodded.

"I'm sorry if I upset you yesterday," he said. "I realise I have no right to tell you what you can and cannot do, but please believe that I was acting in your best—"

"They have Skulduggery," Stephanie said, interrupting him.

"What?"

"Serpine has him. Last night, he came in with his paper men and they attacked him and took him away with them. We need to tell the Elders."

Ghastly tried a smile to see if she'd return it, to see if she'd admit her joke. Stephanie didn't smile back.

"You don't know if I should be involved in any of this," she said. "That's fine. That's your opinion and that's fine. But let's forget about opinion. Let's look at facts. Serpine has Skulduggery. He's broken the Truce. He believes the Sceptre is real and he has proved that he's willing to kill to get to it. He has to be stopped and I need your help to stop him."

"You saw this? You actually saw Serpine do this?"

"I was there."

He looked at her and nodded. "Then I suppose it's a very good thing you decided to stick around."

Ghastly brought his car around and Stephanie told him exactly what had happened as they sped through the streets to the Sanctuary. The windows were heavily tinted, but even so he had a scarf wrapped around his face and a hat pulled low over his eyes.

The Waxworks Museum hadn't opened yet so they let themselves in the back and hurried through the darkness. Ghastly searched the darkened wall for the switch, found it and the wall parted. Stephanie was the first to reach the bottom of the stairs, and she strode into the Sanctuary. The Administrator hurried up to her, frowning.

"I'm sorry," he said, "you do not have an appointment."

"We're here to see Meritorious."

"The Elders cannot be disturbed," the Administrator insisted. "I must ask you to leave at once."

"It's an emergency," Ghastly said as he joined her, but the Administrator still shook his head.

"All requests to visit the Elders must go through the proper channels," he said, but Stephanie had heard enough. She barged past him, heading for the corridor. Suddenly there was a flash of grey and a Cleaver was before her, holding the blade of his scythe to her throat.

Stephanie froze. There was movement all around her, sound all around her, and the only still things in her world were herself and the Cleaver. She could hear Ghastly threatening the Administrator, threatening the Cleavers, and the Administrator protesting and insisting they leave. Ghastly's voice was rising, becoming angry, telling the Cleaver to lower the weapon, but the Cleaver was still and silent, a statue. Stephanie could see her burnished reflection in his visor. She didn't dare move.

Before the situation could spiral out of control, before

Stephanie's head became separated from her body, the Administrator gave in and agreed to ask Meritorious if he would receive visitors.

At a nod, the Cleaver stepped back and swung the scythe down by his side and behind him, making the mere sheathing of the weapon into an art form.

Stephanie backed off, moving slowly, but the Cleaver had gone back to his post like nothing had happened.

They stayed in the foyer while the Administrator hurried off, and presently they heard footsteps approaching. Eachan Meritorious entered and looked mildly surprised when he laid eyes on Ghastly.

"Mr Bespoke," he said, coming forward. "Will wonders never cease?"

"Grand Mage," Ghastly said as they shook hands. "You've already met Valkyrie Cain, I think."

"So you chose a name after all," Meritorious said with a slightly disapproving look. "I hope your Mr Pleasant knows what he's doing."

"Skulduggery's been captured," Stephanie blurted out. "Serpine has him."

"Not this again."

"It's true," Ghastly said.

Meritorious peered at him. "You saw it yourself?"

"Well," Ghastly said, hesitating, "no, but—"

Meritorious waved his hand. "Skulduggery Pleasant is an excellent detective, and we value his help and his expertise on many difficult cases. But when it comes to Nefarian Serpine, he does not have his usual detached perspective."

"Serpine has captured him!" Stephanie insisted.

"My dear, I like you. And I can see why Skulduggery likes you. You are a frighteningly upfront person and this is a quality to be admired. However, you are new to our culture and our ways, and you have heard a decidedly skewed version of our history. Serpine is not the villain he once was."

"I was there," Stephanie said, struggling to remain calm. "Serpine came with his paper creatures and they took him."

This made Meritorious pause. "Paper creatures?"

"Well, it *looked* like they were made out of paper."

He nodded slowly. "Hollow Men. Minions of Serpine. Terrible things, bloated by stink and evil."

"Now do you believe me? We need to get him back."

"Grand Mage," Ghastly said, "my friend is in danger. I know you don't want it to be true, but the Truce has been broken. Serpine and the sorcerers allied with him will waste no time in seizing power. The Elders must act *now*."

"On what authority?" Meritorious asked. "On the word of a girl I barely know?"

"I'm not lying," said Stephanie.

"But you may be mistaken."

"I'm not. Serpine wants the Sceptre and he thinks Skulduggery can get it for him."

"The Sceptre is a fairy tale—"

"The Sceptre is real," Stephanie said, cutting him off. "It's real enough that Serpine is after it, and he killed the two men you had spying on him so that you wouldn't find out about it until it was too late."

Meritorious hesitated for a moment. "Miss Cain, if you're wrong, and we move against Serpine now, then we are starting a war we are not ready for."

"I'm sorry," Stephanie said, seeing the trepidation in the Elder's eyes and speaking softly now. "But the war has already started."

The paper clip lay on the tabletop and didn't move. Stephanie focused, flexed her fingers and then thrust her palm towards it, trying to genuinely believe that thin air was nothing more than interlocking objects. The paper clip still didn't move. She nudged it, just to make sure it wasn't stuck or anything. Ghastly entered the room.

"We're ready to go," he said. "You're sure you want to do this?"

"Very sure." She put the paper clip in her pocket and nodded to the door behind him. "Is there an army out there?"

"Uh, not quite."

"How many?"

He hesitated. "Two."

"Two? He has an army of Cleavers and he gives us *two*?"

"Sending any more would arouse suspicion," Ghastly said. "Meritorious needs a little time to contact Morwenna Crow and Sagacious Tome and convince them that action is necessary, and until he does, this rescue mission is strictly unofficial."

"Please tell me they're as good as Skulduggery said they are?"

"Both their uniforms and their scythes can ward off the majority of magical attacks, and there aren't many deadlier in close combat."

"*Close* combat?" Stephanie said with a frown. "What about throwing fireballs and stuff? Are they Elementals or Adepts?"

Ghastly cleared his throat. "Neither, actually. Magic corrupts certain people, and Cleavers need to be seen as completely impartial, so..."

"So they're not magic? At all?"

"They have *some* magic, but it just adds to their combat abilities. They're quite strong and very fast."

"So what are they going to do? Run around Serpine until he gets dizzy and falls over?"

"If it all goes according to plan, Serpine won't even know we're there."

"And what are the chances of that happening?"

Ghastly looked at her and for a moment he held his ground. Then he looked away. "They're not great," he admitted.

"Exactly."

He looked up again. "But Mr Bliss has offered us his help."

"He's coming?" Stephanie asked nervously. She didn't like the idea of going anywhere with Mr Bliss.

"Not him," Ghastly said, "but he's sending someone. Five is a good number; we can sneak in, grab Skulduggery, sneak out. Simple."

The door opened behind them and Meritorious appeared. "I have arranged your transport," he said.

They followed him up out of the Sanctuary and exited the Waxworks from the back, where a large van was parked. As soon as Meritorious emerged into the sunlight, two Cleavers walked forward. They took the scythes from their sheaths before they climbed in. Stephanie hoped the van didn't go over any potholes or she'd be skewered before they even reached Serpine's castle.

Another person walked forward, a person she recognised from the library.

"Tanith Low," Meritorious said, "this is Ghastly Bespoke and Valkyrie Cain."

"We've met," Tanith said, giving Stephanie a polite nod. She carried a sword in a black scabbard, its lacquered surface criss-crossed with nicks and marks.

"Mr Bliss sent you?" Ghastly asked.

"He did. He thought I could be of use."

"That's quite a recommendation."

"He just wants this business to be over with as soon as possible," Tanith said. "I'm at your disposal for the duration."

"Then let's go."

Tanith climbed into the van and Ghastly got behind the wheel.

"Good luck," Meritorious said as Stephanie was about to join them.

"Thank you."

He shrugged. "You'll need it."

17

A FABULOUS RESCUE INDEED

The rescue team stood by the side of the road and looked up at the wall surrounding Serpine's land. It was maybe three times as tall as Stephanie. Beyond it lay woodland, and beyond that, the castle.

It occurred to Stephanie that if they didn't get Skulduggery back, it was all over. Serpine would get the Sceptre and the Faceless Ones would return. The fate of the entire planet rested on the shoulders of a skeleton, and the five people sent to rescue him.

"What if we *do* go up against Serpine?" Stephanie asked, fighting to keep the dread out of her voice. She had to remain strong. She couldn't let them see that she was just an ordinary twelve-year-old. "What if we can't just get in and get out without anyone noticing? Do we have a plan if we have to face him?"

"Oh," Ghastly said, considering it. "No, not really."

"I'm going to try and cut him with my sword," Tanith said helpfully.

"Right," Stephanie said. "Excellent. What about guards? Do you think they'll be expecting us?"

"Serpine is used to the Elders taking forever to make their calm, thought-out decisions," Tanith said. "So he won't be expecting anything as amazingly rash and reckless as this."

Ghastly nodded. "That'll teach him to underestimate stupid people."

"All right then," Stephanie said. "Just wanted to make sure we'd thought of everything. So let's go."

Without a word, the Cleavers ran forward and jumped, legs tucked beneath them, and cleared the top of the wall and disappeared from view.

"Show-offs," Ghastly muttered, sweeping both hands down by his sides. A gust of wind lifted him and swung him up towards the wall. He grabbed on and pulled himself to the top. Tanith turned to Stephanie.

"Want a boost?"

"If you wouldn't mind."

Tanith crouched, interlocked her fingers and Stephanie put one foot in her hands. On the count of three, Stephanie shot upwards. Tanith was strong, stronger than she looked, because Stephanie had no trouble catching the top of the wall. Ghastly helped her up, then dropped down the other side and turned to wait for her. She let herself hang down then released her grip, and her boots crunched on to dried leaves and brittle twigs. A moment later Tanith landed beside her.

The woodland was thick, and as they moved deeper into it, it became darker. The evening sun had difficulty filtering through the tall trees and it was cold enough to make Stephanie grateful for her coat. The Cleavers didn't seem to make a sound as they walked. The woodland was quiet, quieter than it had any right to be. No birds sang. Nothing rustled in the undergrowth. It was an eerie sensation.

They reached the tree line at the rear of the castle and ducked down. A small army of Hollow Men patrolled the grounds.

"Oh, joy," Ghastly said grimly. "How are we going to get by *them?*"

"We need a diversion," Tanith said.

"Any suggestions?" Tanith didn't answer, but after a moment she looked at the Cleavers. Ghastly understood immediately.

"But there are too many," he protested.

Tanith's tone was flat, but firm. "We don't have a choice."

The Cleavers tilted their heads towards her, and after a moment they nodded. They stole back among the trees and were gone. Stephanie waited with Tanith and Ghastly.

"They won't be able to hold them off for long," Ghastly said.

"Long enough for us to sneak in," Tanith said.

"That's not what I meant. You've just sent them to their deaths."

She didn't look at him. "They'll do their jobs. We'll do ours. Do you want your friend back or not?" Ghastly didn't answer.

"Look," Stephanie said.

The Hollow Men were moving fast, moving out of their field of vision.

"Let's go," Tanith said.

They broke from the trees, sprinting across the wide-open space towards the castle. Stephanie glanced to her right as she ran, saw the Cleavers standing back to back in the distance as the Hollow Men closed in.

They reached the castle. Tanith placed her hand flat on the lock and twisted her wrist. Stephanie heard the lock break within the door and Tanith pushed it open slowly. They crept in, closing the door behind them.

They kept to the outer corridors, staying away from the cold heart of the castle. They found a stairway leading down and Tanith went first, sword in her right hand, scabbard in her left. Stephanie followed a few paces behind, and Ghastly came last.

They reached the basement, although Stephanie thought that dungeon would probably be more accurate. Tanith held up her hand and they stopped and watched a Hollow Man clump ahead of them and pass out of sight.

They made their way forward. Tanith approached the first heavy iron door, and put her ear against it. After a moment, she pushed it open. The hinges groaned in protest, but the room was empty.

Ghastly went to the next door, listened, and opened it. Again, it was empty.

Tanith glanced at Ghastly and they shared a look, and Stephanie knew what it was about.

"We should split up," Stephanie whispered.

"No," said Tanith.

"No way," said Ghastly.

"If we waste time, the Hollow Men will be back outside the door and we won't be able to get away."

"Then you come with me," Ghastly whispered.

Stephanie shook her head. "I'll be fine. I'll listen at the doors. If I hear anything, I'll get you. If I meet a bad guy, you can be pretty sure you'll know about it. We don't have a choice."

They looked at her but didn't argue. Tanith went to the next door, Ghastly hurried down the length of the corridor and Stephanie turned back and rounded the corner. She came to another row of iron doors and listened intently at each one. She followed the maze of corridors wherever they took her. She found herself breathing through her mouth and tasted the foulness of the air on the back of her throat. There were puddles here, stagnant pools of water on the uneven stone floor. The doors were no longer made of iron, but of rotting wood. The flickering of the torches in the brackets made shadows dance on the walls.

She saw someone moving ahead and was about to duck back when she recognised Ghastly. He waved to her and she waved back, and started checking the doors closest to her. They were working their way towards each other when Stephanie came to a door and heard a low whistling. She frowned. Could Skulduggery whistle? He could *talk* without lips or breath, so she couldn't see a reason why he wouldn't be able to whistle. She didn't recognise the tune, however. She motioned to Ghastly and he crept forward. After listening for a moment, he nodded.

"That's 'The Girl From Ipanema'," he whispered. "That's him."

He held up three fingers, then two, then one and they burst into the room. Skulduggery looked up and stopped whistling. "Oh, hello," he said. "I know where the key to the caves is."

Stephanie closed the door as Ghastly hurried around behind him, stooping to examine the shackles.

"Quality workmanship," he said.

"I thought you'd appreciate it. There's a binding spell woven into the metal."

"Nice. It'll take me a moment."

"I'm not going anywhere."

"Are you OK?" Stephanie asked.

"I've been treated well," he answered with a nod. "Apart from all the torture. It's given me time to think, actually. I know where the key is."

"So you said."

Ghastly stood and the shackles fell. Skulduggery got to his

feet. "Is Meritorious here?" he asked.

"He's telling the other Elders what's going on," Ghastly said.

"Ah," Skulduggery said. "So you're doing this on your own?"

"Tanith Low is here, but basically, yes."

Skulduggery shrugged. "I must admit, it's going rather fabulously so far."

"The key," Stephanie said. "You didn't tell Serpine where it is, did you?"

"I couldn't have, even if I'd have wanted to. Just worked it out a few minutes ago. Simple really. It was right in front of us."

"We can talk about this later," Ghastly said. "We have to go."

"Will there be fighting?"

"I hope not."

"I'm in the mood for some fighting."

"If there is," Stephanie said, handing him his gun, "here's something you can use."

"Ah, bless. I've missed her. Do you have bullets?"

"Uh, no."

Skulduggery paused. "Excellent," he said, and tucked the gun away.

"Let's go," Ghastly said and stepped out of the door.

Stephanie and Skulduggery followed. They hurried down the corridor and turned a corner. A group of Hollow Men froze in mid-step and regarded them vacantly. Time stood still.

"Yes," Skulduggery said. "This is a fabulous rescue indeed."

The Hollow Men came at them, and Skulduggery and Ghastly went into action. Skulduggery worked with elbows and knees, wristlocks and armlocks. Ghastly deftly wove in and around attacks, firing out punches at whoever got close.

Beyond the silent Hollow Men, Stephanie saw Tanith sprinting forward, and then she ran up the wall and across the ceiling and continued running, upside down. Stephanie stared. She hadn't known Tanith could do that.

From the ceiling, Tanith joined the attack, swinging the sword and slicing through the tops of heads. Within a matter of moments, the Hollow Men were reduced to tatters and a foul smell.

Tanith jumped down, flipping to land on her feet. "There are more coming," she said, then added helpfully; "We should probably leave."

They reached the stairs without encountering any more opposition, but as they were running for the exit, two massive doors were kicked open ahead and the Hollow Men reinforcements arrived.

Skulduggery and Ghastly stepped up, clicking their fingers and hurling fireballs at the ground. Stephanie watched their hands move, manipulating the flames until there was a wall of fire keeping the Hollow Men back.

Tanith turned to Stephanie. "Coat."

"What?"

Without giving an explanation, Tanith gripped Stephanie's collar and pulled the coat off. She then ran for the window, covering her head with the coat, and jumped. She crashed through in an explosion of glass.

"Oh," Stephanie murmured.

She ran over, climbing through the window as Tanith got to her feet.

"Thanks," Tanith said, handing her back the coat.

"Watch out!" Ghastly shouted.

Stephanie dodged to one side as Ghastly and Skulduggery dived through the window – Ghastly lower down, Skulduggery above him – like two lunatic acrobats. They hit the grass and rolled, coming up at the same time.

"Flee," Skulduggery said.

As they ran for the trees, Stephanie saw one of the Cleavers who had accompanied them. Judging by the tattered paper strewn around him, the Cleavers had obviously put up an amazing fight, but the sheer numbers of Hollow Men had proven too much. He lay dead on the grass. She saw no sign of the other one.

And then they were in the trees and not slowing down, and Hollow Men were crashing through the undergrowth after them.

Ghastly reached the wall first, swept his hands beneath him and let the air lift him over the wall.

Tanith just kept running. Right before she was about to smack straight into it she gave a little jump and then she was running up the wall.

Before Stephanie could ask Skulduggery for a boost his arm wrapped around her waist and she found herself rushing upwards, the wind in her ears, and the top of the wall passing beneath her feet. They landed on the other side with such ease and gentleness that Stephanie almost laughed despite herself.

They got in the van and Ghastly turned the key and pulled out on to the road, and they left the castle behind them.

18

ON THE ROOF, AT NIGHT

Laughter drifted in the distance and Skulduggery looked towards it. They were standing on the roof of Ghastly's shop. Dublin City twinkled as it got ready for sleep. Stephanie could see over rooftops, over streets, down lanes. She could see the cars passing, and here and there people walking. When he turned back, he said, "So, Valkyrie Cain, eh?"

"You don't think it sounds silly, do you?"

"On the contrary, I think it sounds perfect. Valkyrie. Warrior women who guide the souls of the dead off the battlefield. A tad morbid, but then, who am I to judge? I'm technically dead."

Stephanie looked at him and took a moment before speaking again. "So was it bad? The torture?"

"It wasn't fun," he said. "I think after the first few hours he knew I had no idea where the key was. After that, he was torturing me purely for the sake of torturing me. Did I thank you for coming to my rescue, by the way?"

"Don't worry about it."

"Nonsense. Thank you."

She smiled. "You're welcome."

"Your friend Tanith seemed a bit quiet on the trip home."

"I think she regrets using the Cleavers as a diversion."

"I would have made the same decision," Skulduggery said. "The Cleavers have a job to do – let them do it."

"That's what she said."

"Ah, but it's one thing to understand that and quite another to accept it. Until that happens, she's going to have one or two nightmares about it. But she's a warrior. She'll make it."

"She's a good fighter."

"Indeed she is."

"If I started training now, would I be able to fight like her when I'm her age?"

"I don't see why not. Sixty years of good solid training is

enough to turn anyone into a tidy little scrapper."

"What?"

"What *what*?"

"Sixty years? How old is she?"

"I'd say seventy if she's a day."

Stephanie stared. "Right," she said firmly, "it's time for you to tell me how you people live so long."

"Diet and exercise."

"Skulduggery—"

"Clean healthy living."

"I swear..."

"Magic then."

She looked at him. "Do all sorcerers live forever?"

"Not forever, no. Not even close to forever. We do age, it's just we do it slower then the rest of humanity. The regular use of a certain amount of magic rejuvenates the body, keeps it young."

"So if I started learning magic now, I'd stay twelve?"

"It would take you a few years to reach the level where ageing slows, but yes, after that, you would stay young for a lot longer than is strictly fair. I know it's impolite to discuss a lady's age, but China is the same age as I am, and even I have to admit that she wears it better!" He laughed, then stopped and peered at her. "Because I'm a skeleton," he explained.

"Yes, I got it."

"You weren't laughing."

"I didn't think it was funny."

"Oh."

"So what are you going to do about her?"

"China? There is nothing *to* do. She behaved exactly as I expected her to behave. The scorpion stings the fox because that is its nature. You can't deny your nature."

"And what's *your* nature?"

His head tilted. "Odd question."

"China said some things about you. And Serpine. She said all you want is revenge."

"And you're wondering how far I'll go to *get* that revenge, is that it? You're wondering how much I'm willing to sacrifice in order to make him pay for killing me all those years ago."

"Yes."

He paused a moment then slipped his hands into his pockets and spoke. "What China didn't tell you, what *I* didn't tell you, is that I was not the only one caught in Serpine's trap." Stephanie didn't say anything. She waited for him to continue.

"The trap was exquisite. A thing of beauty, it really was. You see, Valkyrie, a successful trap needs one important quality, the same quality any trick or illusion needs. Misdirection. When your attention is focused on one thing, something else is happening behind your back.

"I didn't even realise it *was* a trap until it was sprung. Serpine knew me, you see, and he knew how I'd react to certain stimuli. He knew, for instance, that if he murdered my wife and child right in front of me, I'd never even suspect that the handle of the dagger I reached for was dipped in poison."

Stephanie stared at him, but Skulduggery just looked out over the city.

"I didn't use magic, you see, and he knew I wouldn't. He knew I'd be too angry, he knew my rage would fuel a *physical* attack, that I'd need to kill him up close and personal. And the moment my hand closed around that dagger, I realised my mistake. Of course, by then it was too late. I was helpless.

"It took him a few days to finally kill me. I died hating him, and when I came back, the hatred came back with me." He turned his head to her. "You asked me what is my nature? It is a dark and twisted thing."

"I don't know what to say," Stephanie said softly.

"Not much you *can* say to a story like that, is there?"

"Not really."

"Yep, I win on the ol' dramatic story front every time." They stood in silence for a while. Despite the warmth of the night it was chilly up there, but Stephanie didn't mind.

"What happens now?" she asked.

"The Elders go to war. They'll find the castle empty – Serpine wouldn't stay there after this – so they'll be looking for him. They'll also be tracking down his old allies to make sure they don't get the opportunity to organise."

"And what do we do?"

"We get to the Sceptre before Serpine."

"The key," she said, "where is it?"

He turned to her. "Gordon hid it. Clever man, your uncle. He didn't think anyone should have access to that weapon, but he hid the key in a place where if we *truly* needed to find it, if the situation got so dire that we *truly* needed the Sceptre, all it would take was a little detective work."

"So where is it?"

"The piece of advice he gave me, in the solicitor's office, do you remember what it was?"

"He said a storm is coming."

"And he also said that sometimes the key to safe harbour is hidden from us and sometimes it is right before our eyes."

"He was talking about the key, literally? It's right before our eyes?"

"It *was*, when those words were first spoken in the solicitor's office."

"Fedgewick has the key?"

"Not Fedgewick. He gave it away."

Stephanie frowned, remembering the reading of the will then the lock in the cellar, no bigger than Skulduggery's palm. She looked up at him. "Not the brooch?"

"The brooch."

"Gordon gave the key, the key to the most powerful weapon in existence, to Fergus and Beryl?" she asked incredulously. "Why would he do that?"

"Would you ever have thought to look for it with them?"

She let the notion sink in then started to smile. "They were left the most valuable possession Gordon had and they didn't even realise it."

"It's actually quite amusing."

"It actually is."

"So now all we have to do is get it."

Stephanie smiled again and nodded, then her smile dropped and she shook her head vehemently. "I'm not getting it."

"You're going to have to."

"No, I don't."

"Just pay them a visit—"

"Why can't you break in? You broke into the Vault."

"That was different."

"Yes, it had alarms and vampires – this'll be so much easier!"

"There are times when extreme measures are unnecessary."

"Extreme measures are *very* necessary here!"

"Valkyrie—"

"You can't ask me to visit them!"

"We don't have a choice."

"But I *never* visit! They'll suspect something!"

"Being a detective isn't all about torture and murder and monsters. Sometimes it gets truly unpleasant."

"But I don't *like* them!" she whined.

"The fate of the world may depend on whether or not you can bring yourself to visit your relatives."

She turned her head, looking at him out of the corner of her eye. "It *may* depend?"

"Valkyrie—"

"Fine, I'll go."

"Good girl." She crossed her arms and didn't respond.

"Are you sulking now?" he asked.

"Yes," she answered curtly.

"OK."

19

THE EXPERIMENT

The Cleaver lay strapped to the table. Fluids ran through the clear rubber tubes that pierced his skin, flowing into the quiet machine behind him. That which was unnecessary was removed, replaced with liquid darkness, with concoctions that mixed science with sorcery. The Cleaver's face was unremarkable and expressionless. He had stopped struggling over an hour ago. It was beginning to take effect.

Serpine stepped into the light and the Cleaver's eyes flickered to him. They were glassy and dull, without any of the fierceness that had met his gaze when the Hollow Men had brought the Cleaver to him and removed the helmet. Then, even as Skulduggery Pleasant made good his escape, Serpine had been given a new captive and he knew what he would do with him.

It was time. Serpine held up the dagger he was holding, let the Cleaver see it. No reaction. No wariness, no fear, no recognition. This man, this soldier, who had lived his entire life with blind obedience to others, was now about to enter into death, equally as blind. A pathetic existence. Serpine held the dagger in both hands and raised it above his head then brought it down, and the blade plunged into the Cleaver's chest and he died.

Serpine removed the blade, wiped it clean and put it to one side. If this worked some changes would obviously need to be made, some alterations, some improvements. The Cleaver was a test subject after all, no more then an experiment. If it worked, a little refinement would be in order. It wouldn't take long. An hour at most.

Serpine waited by the Cleaver's corpse. The warehouse was quiet. He'd had to abandon the castle, but he had been well prepared for that eventuality. Besides, it wouldn't be for long. In a matter of days, his enemies would be dead, and there would be no one left to fight him, and he would have everything he would need to usher in the Faceless Ones – a feat his old master Mevolent had never managed.

Serpine frowned. Had it been a trick of the light, or had the Cleaver moved? He looked closer, searching for the rise and fall of the chest, searching for a sign of life. But no, no sign of life. The Cleaver's pulse, when he checked it, was absent.

And then the Cleaver opened his eyes.

20

THE FAMILY CURSE

tephanie climbed through her bedroom window to find her reflection sitting on the bed in the darkness, waiting for her.

"Are you ready to resume your life?" it asked.

Stephanie, who was finding it very disconcerting to hold a conversation with herself, merely nodded. The reflection went to the mirror and stepped through, then turned and waited. Stephanie touched the glass and a day's worth of memory flooded into her mind. She watched the reflection change, the clothes Stephanie was wearing appearing on it.

And then it was nothing more then a reflected image in a mirror.

Stephanie woke the next morning, not happy with what she had to do. Dressed in jeans and T-shirt, she thought about calling on the reflection to imitate her again, then decided against it. The reflection gave her the creeps.

Realising that she could not put it off any longer, Stephanie trudged over to her aunt's house and knocked on the door. The sun was shining and the birds were singing and Stephanie forced a smile on to her face, but it wasn't a smile that was returned when the door opened and Crystal looked out at her.

"What do you want?" her cousin asked suspiciously.

"Just thought I'd call round," Stephanie said brightly. "See how you all are."

"We're fine," Crystal said. "We've got a stupid car and a stupid boat. How's your *house?*"

"Crystal," she said, "I know you're probably angry about the inheritance and everything, but I don't know why I was left all that either."

"It's because you were sucking up to him," Crystal sneered. "If we'd have known that all it took was just to be all smiles and have conversations with him, then we'd have done that stuff too."

"But I didn't know—"

"You cheated."

"I didn't cheat."

"You had an unfair advantage."

"How? How could I have even known he was going to die?"

"You knew," Crystal said. "You knew that sooner or later he was going to die, but you got in so early, the rest of us didn't stand a chance."

"Did you even like him?"

There was that sneer again. "You don't have to like someone to get something from them."

Stephanie resisted the urge to punch Crystal's smirking face long enough for Beryl to pass the doorway. She saw Stephanie and her eyes widened in surprise.

"Stephanie," she said, "what are you doing here?"

"She thought she'd call round," Crystal said, "to see how we are."

"Oh, that's very nice of you, dear."

Crystal took this opportunity to walk away without saying goodbye. Stephanie focused on Beryl.

"You're not wearing the brooch Gordon left you?"

"That horrid thing? No, I am not, and I don't think I ever will. It doesn't even sparkle for heaven's sake. People know something is cheap if it doesn't sparkle."

"That's a shame. It looked pretty, though, from where I was standing; it would have looked nice with one of your cardigans—"

"We saw you yesterday," Beryl interrupted.

"I'm sorry?"

"In a horrid yellow car, with that dreadful Skulduggery Pleasant."

Stephanie felt the instant flutters of panic in her belly, but she made herself frown and give a puzzled laugh. "Um, I think you may be mistaken. I was home all day yesterday."

"Nonsense. You passed right by us. We saw you quite clearly. We saw *him*, too, all covered up like last time."

"Nope, wasn't me."

Beryl smiled piously. "Lying is a sin, did you know that?"

"I'd heard the rumour..."

"Fergus!" Beryl shouted back into the house and a few moments later her husband walked out of the living room. He was at home every day now after suffering a "serious fall" at work. He was in the process of suing his employers, claiming that it was their negligence that resulted in his debilitating injuries. He didn't look too debilitated as he approached the door.

"Fergus, Stephanie here says she wasn't in the car with that awful Mr Pleasant."

Fergus scowled. "She's calling us liars?"

"No," Stephanie said with a half-laugh. "Just that it must have been somebody else."

"Stephanie," Beryl chided, "let's not play games. We know it was you. It's such a tragic thing to see, a dear sweet innocent child like you falling in with the wrong crowd."

"Wrong crowd?"

"Weirdos," Fergus said with a sneer. "I've seen their kind before. Gordon used to surround himself with people like that, people with... secrets."

"And why does he hide his face anyway?" Beryl asked. "Is he *deformed?*"

"I wouldn't know," Stephanie said, fighting to keep her voice even.

"You can't trust people like that," Fergus continued. "I've been around them my whole life, seen them coming and going. Never wanted anything to do with them. You never know who you're dealing with or what sordid little things they get up to."

"He seemed all right to me," Stephanie said as casually as

she could. "He seemed quite nice, actually."

Beryl shook her head sadly. "I don't expect you to understand. You're only a child."

Stephanie bristled. "You've never even spoken to him."

"Adults don't have to speak to other adults to know if they're bad news or not. One look, that's all we need."

"So anyone different from you is bad news?"

"Anyone different from *us*, dear."

"My parents always told me never to judge someone by how they look."

"Yes, well," Beryl said primly. "If they think they can afford to live in ignorance, then that's their mistake."

"My parents aren't ignorant."

"I never said they were, dear. I just said they *lived* in ignorance."

Stephanie couldn't take this any more. "I need to pee," she said suddenly.

Beryl blinked. "I'm sorry?"

"Pee. I need to pee. Can I use your bathroom?"

"I... I suppose..."

"Thanks."

Stephanie stepped in past them both and hurried up the stairs. She went into the bathroom, and when she was sure Beryl wasn't going to follow her up, she crept into the master bedroom and went straight to the jewellery box on the dresser. It was a massive thing, each of its compartments bulging with tacky trinkets that sparkled and twinkled and glittered. She found the brooch in a slide-out compartment at the base of the box, where it nestled with a single hoop earring and a pair of tweezers. She stuck it in her pocket, closed the jewellery box and left the room, then flushed the toilet in the bathroom and bounded down the stairs.

"Thank you," she said brightly, and Beryl opened her mouth to continue their conversation but Stephanie was already halfway down the garden path.

Stephanie sat on one of the boulders that sealed off the north end of the beach, waiting for Skulduggery. The weathermen had been predicting an end to the dry spell, but the morning sky was blue and cloud free. There was a shell on the boulder next to her, a pretty shell, a shell she suddenly found herself loving.

It moved. The air didn't do that cool rippling thing around her hand, but the shell still moved and it wasn't because of the breeze either. Stephanie's heart quickened but she didn't let herself celebrate. Not yet. It could have been a fluke. If she could do it a second time, then she could celebrate.

She concentrated on the shell. She held her hand up, seeing the space between her hand and the shell as a series of interlocking objects, waiting to be moved. Her fingers uncurled slightly and she felt it, she felt the air against her palm, solid somehow. She pushed against it and the shell shot off the boulder.

"Yes!" she exclaimed, sticking both arms up in the air. Magic! She'd done magic! She laughed in delight.

"You look happy."

Stephanie turned so suddenly she almost fell off the boulder, and her dad grinned as he approached. She blushed deeply, and dug her phone out of her pocket without him seeing, then held it up.

"Got a good text message," she said, "that's all."

"Ah," he said as he sat beside her. "Anything I should know about?"

"Probably not." She looked around as casually as she could, praying that she wouldn't see the Canary Car suddenly pull up. "Why aren't you at work?"

Her dad shrugged. "I have a big meeting this afternoon but I left the house without something important, so I thought I'd nip back during lunch."

"What did you forget? Architect's plans or something?"

"Something like that," he said with a nod. "Actually, nothing like that. I forgot my underwear."

She looked at him. "What?"

"When I was getting dressed my mind was on other things. It happens sometimes. Usually it wouldn't bother me but these trousers really *itch*—"

"Dad, ew, don't want to know!"

"Oh, right, sorry. Anyway, I saw you walking down here so I thought I'd say hi. You used to come down here all the time when you were younger, sit here and look out there, and I always wondered what was going through your mind..."

"Lots of clever little things," she responded automatically and he smiled.

"Your mother's worried about you," he said after a while.

She looked up at him, startled. "What? Why?"

He shrugged. "You just, you haven't been yourself lately." So they *had* noticed the difference between her and her reflection.

"I'm fine, Dad. Really. I've just, you know, I've been going through some moods."

"Yes, yep, I understand that, and your mother explained the whole thing to me, about young girls and their moods... But we still worry. Ever since Gordon died..."

Stephanie kept her frown to herself. So this wasn't just about the reflection.

"I know you were close," he continued. "And I know you got on so well, and I know that when he died, you lost a good friend."

"I suppose I did," she said quietly.

"And we don't want to stop you from growing up, even if we could. You're growing into a fine young woman and one that we're really proud of."

She smiled awkwardly and didn't meet his eyes. Gordon's death *had* changed her, but the change was far more drastic than even her parents realised. It had set her on the course she was on now, the course that had led to her becoming Valkyrie Cain, the course that would lead to whatever fate was waiting for her. It had changed her life – given it direction and purpose. It had also put her in more danger than she could have ever imagined.

"We just worry about you, that's all."

"You don't have to."

"It's a parent's job. You could be forty and we'd be stuck in the Old Folks' Home, and we'd still be worrying about you. It's a responsibility that never stops."

"Makes you wonder why anyone has kids."

He laughed softly. "You'd think that, yes. But there is nothing more wonderful then watching your child grow up, nothing more fulfilling. Of course, there's a certain age you wish they wouldn't go beyond, but there's not a whole lot you can do about that."

Not unless you have magic on your side, Stephanie thought to herself.

"Beryl called," her father said. "She said you'd just been to see her."

Stephanie nodded. She couldn't have noticed that the brooch was missing already, could she? "I felt like going around, seeing how everyone was. I think, you know, Gordon's death has made me value the family we have left, or something. I think it's important that we stay close."

He looked at her, a little startled. "Well, that's... that's a really lovely thing to be able to say, Steph, it really is. It's a beautiful sentiment." There was a brief pause. "I don't have to go round, do I?"

"No."

"Oh, thank God."

She didn't like lying to him. She had made it a point, years before, to be as honest as she could where her parents were involved. But things were different now. She had secrets. "So what else did Beryl say?"

"Well... she seems to think she saw you with Skulduggery Pleasant yesterday."

"Yeah," Stephanie said, as casually as she could, "she told me. That's weird."

"She thinks you've fallen in with the wrong crowd."

"You should hear her, Dad, the way she talks about him, and she doesn't even know him. She probably thinks I'm part of a cult or something..."

"And are you?"

She looked at him, appalled. "What?"

Her father sighed. "Beryl has good reason to think that."

"But it's insane!"

"Well, insanity runs in the family." She could see something in his eyes, a reluctance, but also a resignation.

"My grandfather," he said, "your great-grandfather, was a wonderful man – us kids loved him. Me, Fergus, Gordon, we'd sit around and he'd tell us all these fantastic stories. My father, however, didn't have a lot of time for him. All the stories he was telling us, he'd told my father when he was a kid. And when my dad grew up, he realised it was all nonsense, but my granddad refused to see it. My grandfather believed... He believed that we were magic."

Stephanie stared at him. "What?"

"He said it'd been passed down, this magic, generation to generation. He said we were descendants of a great sorcerer called the Last of the Ancients."

The sound of the sea faded to nothing, the sun dimmed and the beach vanished, and the only thing that existed in the world was her father, and the only sounds were the words he was speaking.

"These stories, this belief, has followed the family for centuries. I don't know how it began or when, but it seems like it's always been a part of us. And now and then, there have been members of our family who have chosen to believe it.

"Gordon believed. A rational man, an intelligent man, and yet he believed in magic and sorcery and people who never age. All the stuff he wrote about, he probably believed in most, if not *all*, of it.

"And because of this, he got involved in things that were... unhealthy. The people he mixed with, people who fed into his delusions, who shared his madness. Dangerous people. It's a sickness, Steph. My granddad had it, Gordon had it... and I don't want you to get it."

"I'm not mad."

"And I'm not saying you are. But I know how easy it is to be swept away by stories, by things that you wish were real. When

I was younger, I believed. I believed even more than Gordon did. But I stopped. I made a decision to live in the real world, to stop indulging this, this *curse* that has plagued us. Gordon introduced me to your mother and I fell in love. I put it all behind me."

"So you think Gordon was part of a cult?"

"For want of a better word, yes."

She remembered the look on her father's face the first time he had encountered Skulduggery, in Mr Fedgewick's office. It had been a look she had never seen before – suspicion, mistrust, hostility – and it had passed as quickly as it had appeared. Now she understood why.

"And you think, what, that I'm part of the cult now?"

He gave a gentle laugh. "No, I suppose I don't. Not really. But what Beryl was saying, it got me thinking. In the last few days, sometimes there's a distance in your eyes I haven't seen before. I don't know what it is. I look at you now and you're my little girl. But I've been getting the feeling that... I don't know. Recently, it seems like you're somewhere else."

Stephanie didn't dare respond.

"I just wish you'd talk to someone. You don't have to talk to *me* because you know how much I babble, but your mother... You could tell her, you could tell *us*, anything. And as long as you're honest with us, you know we'd help you in whatever way we can."

"I know, Dad."

He looked at her and for a moment she thought he was going to shed a tear, but then he wrapped an arm around her and kissed her forehead. "You're my little sweetheart, you know that?"

"I know."

"Good girl." He got off the boulder. "I better get back to work."

"See you later." He looked at her, gave her a smile and walked back off the beach.

Stephanie stayed where she was. If it was true, if the family legend was true, then this was, this was... Actually she didn't know what this was. It felt important, though. It felt big. She left the beach and waited by the road, and when Skulduggery arrived in the hideous Canary Car she told him everything her father had said.

Mr Bliss turned the brooch over in his hands. "Are you sure this is it?"

Mr Bliss was in black and Skulduggery was wearing a dark blue pinstriped suit that Ghastly had finished working on that very morning, along with a crisp white shirt and a blue tie. They were standing in the shade of the Martello tower, a centuries-old ruin that stood atop the grassy cliffs along Haggard's coast. Far below them, the sea whipped at the jagged rocks.

"I'm sure," Skulduggery said. "See how the pin folds back, actually becomes a makeshift handle? That's our key."

Stephanie tried her best not to be intimidated by Mr Bliss' presence, but whenever he glanced at her she looked away. She hadn't objected when Skulduggery told her that Mr Bliss would be accompanying them into the caves, but she hadn't exactly jumped for joy either.

"Thank you for calling me," Mr Bliss said, handing the brooch back to Stephanie.

"We need all the help we can get," Skulduggery admitted, "although I was surprised when you made yourself available."

"Serpine has become extremely powerful, much more so than anyone realises."

"You almost sound afraid of him."

Mr Bliss paused for a moment. "I don't feel fear," he said eventually. "When you no longer have hope, the fear evaporates. But I do respect his power. I respect what he can do."

"If he gets to the Sceptre before us, we're all going to *see* what he can do firsthand."

"I still don't get it," Stephanie said. "If he gets the Sceptre, OK, he's unstoppable, but how can he use it to bring back the Faceless Ones?"

"I don't know," Skulduggery replied. "In theory, the ritual could be known to no more than two people in the world – I wouldn't even know who to start threatening."

Mr Bliss shook his head. "He doesn't plan to threaten anyone. From what he has said, I think the Sceptre of the Ancients is merely a stepping stone, a toy that he needs to get what he wants."

"And what is that?" Mr Bliss looked out over the sea, but didn't answer.

"I don't understand," Skulduggery continued. "Were you talking to him?"

"This morning," Mr Bliss said. He had a resigned tone to his voice, and Stephanie narrowed her eyes. Something was wrong. Something was very wrong. She stepped back, but Skulduggery was too caught up in the conversation to notice.

"Did you see him?" Skulduggery said, moving closer to Bliss. "You saw him and you didn't take him down?"

"The reaches of his power were unknown to me and I do not start battles I cannot win. It was too dangerous."

"Where is he? The Elders are looking for him!"

"They don't need to. He will go to them when the time is right."

"Why did you meet him?"

"Serpine had something to say. I listened."

"What are you talking about?"

"He already knows about the caves. The only thing that had delayed him is the search for the key."

Skulduggery looked at Mr Bliss. Mr Bliss looked at Skulduggery. Stephanie realised that he was standing right on the edge of the cliff.

Mr Bliss put a hand on Skulduggery's chest and before Stephanie could even shout he shoved, and Skulduggery shot backward over the edge and disappeared from view. And then Mr Bliss turned to her.

21

THE CAVE

tephanie ran.

She glanced back but Bliss wasn't there, and then a shadow fell across her and he dropped from the sky. She ran straight into him and stumbled back. His hand moved like an attacking snake, snatching the brooch from her grasp. She landed on the seat of her jeans.

She looked to the edge of the cliff, expecting to see Skulduggery swoop up to save her. He didn't. Mr Bliss slipped the brooch into his jacket.

"You're going to give it to him," Stephanie said.

"I am."

"Why?"

"He's too powerful to fight."

"But you're stronger than anyone! If you *all* go after him—"

"I do not gamble, Miss Cain. If we went after him, we might beat him, or he might elude us and strike at us when we least expect it. It is far too unpredictable for my liking. War should be a delicate thing. It requires precision."

Stephanie frowned. Those words. Those eyes, the palest blue...

"China betrayed us too," she said, understanding. "It must run in the family."

"My sister's affairs, and her motivations, are her own."

"Is she siding with Serpine as well?"

"Not to my knowledge," Mr Bliss answered. "But then, I could be lying. That's the thing about allies and enemies – you're never quite sure which is which until the final move is made."

Stephanie got to her feet as he walked to his car, powerless to get the brooch back.

"We're going to stop him," she called out.

"Do what you must," Mr Bliss said without looking back. He got into his car and, without another glance at her, drove off down the dirt road away from the Martello tower, heading out of town. She watched the dust kick up in his wake then hurried down the narrow path to the bottom of the cliffs.

Please be all right, she repeated in her head. *Please be all right please be all right.*

When she finally reached the bottom of the path she looked over at the rocks, terrified that she might see him there. A fall like that would have smashed his bones to pieces. He wasn't on the rocks, however, so she turned her attention to the sea, just as Skulduggery's head broke the surface of the water.

"Skulduggery?" she called out, relief sweeping through her. "Are you all right?" He didn't answer immediately. Instead, he kept rising, rising straight up out of the sea until he was standing on the waves.

"I'm fine," he said curtly, walking to her. Stephanie had seen such peculiarities over the past few days that she was mildly surprised when anything struck her as odd any more, but Skulduggery walking on water definitely struck her as odd. He bobbed up and down with the waves but kept his balance perfectly, and when he stepped off the water on to the path, the vapour rose from his suit and dropped back into the sea. His clothes, she noticed, were undamaged by the fall.

"So that's why Serpine didn't send anyone after us," he said sourly. "He let us go so that we'd get the key, knowing he had someone on the inside to get the key *from* us. That's just... that's just cheating."

"Do you know anyone who *wouldn't* betray you?" Stephanie asked as they started walking back up the path.

"Hush now."

"And thanks for letting me know that Mr Bliss and China were brother and sister, by the way."

"You're welcome."

"If I'd have known that, I might have been able to warn you not to trust him."

"I must admit, China's treachery didn't come as a surprise, but Mr Bliss... He never does anything without due consideration."

"I suppose he thought Serpine was the winning side."

"Maybe."

"So what do we do now? We can't let Serpine find the Sceptre; he'll be unstoppable."

"What do you suggest?"

"I suggest I go get my work clothes, let my reflection out of the mirror, and we follow him into the caves and get the Sceptre before he does."

"That's a very good plan. We'll do that then."

*

They arrived at Gordon's estate to find a gleaming silver car parked outside and the front door once again lying in the hallway. Skulduggery led the way into the house, revolver in hand. Stephanie followed close behind, clad all in black. They gave the ground floor a cursory examination before moving downstairs into the cellar.

The key was in the lock and the door was revealed. A section of the floor was open, exposing stone steps descending into the earth. They followed these steps, sinking deeper into the gloom. They walked in near darkness for a few minutes until they came to the bottom, then walked through a narrow tunnel carved out of the rock. It was brighter down here, their way lit by dozens of small holes designed to catch the sunlight from above and cast it down into the depths.

They stepped out of the tunnel into a cave that split in two directions.

"Which way?" Stephanie whispered.

Skulduggery extended his arm and opened his hand. After a moment, he nodded. "A group of them, headed north."

"Are you reading the air?" Stephanie asked, frowning.

"Reading *disturbances* in the air, yes."

"So do we go after them?"

Skulduggery thought on this. "They don't know the exact

location of the Sceptre any more then we do. They chose that path as simply the place to start their search."

"So we should go the other way, hope we find it first?"

"If we can get it without Serpine even knowing we're here, we can seal the tunnel behind us, trap him here while we alert the Elders."

"Then why are we standing around looking pretty?"

They took the path to their left, moving quickly but quietly. The cave system soon proved itself to be enormous, but Skulduggery assured her he could find the way back without a problem. Here and there, the pinpricks of sunlight opened up to larger streams, which reflected off the rock walls and stabbed through the darkness. Strange plants and mushrooms grew, but Skulduggery warned her to stay away from them. Even the fungus was dangerous down here.

They had been walking for ten minutes when Stephanie saw something move ahead of them. She touched Skulduggery's arm and pointed, and they stepped back into the shadows to watch.

The thing that lumbered into view was magnificent in its awfulness. Standing well over two metres tall, its chest was broad and its arms were long, the forearms hugely distorted by bulging muscles. Its hands were the size of dinner plates, tipped with claws built for ripping. Its face was dog-like in appearance, like a Dobermann, and it had a dirty brown mane that ran from the back of its skull and joined the long matted hair on its shoulders.

"What is it?" Stephanie whispered.

"That, my dear Valkyrie, is what we call a monster."

She looked at Skulduggery. "You don't know what it is, do you?"

"I told you what it is – it's a horrible monster. Now shut up before it comes over here and eats us." They watched it disappear into an adjoining cave.

"Let's not go that way," Stephanie said.

"Good plan," Skulduggery agreed and they hurried forward.

Their path took them to the scene of a cave-in, so they doubled back and took another route, moving into a long tunnel. Things scuttled in the shadows beside them and fluttered in the shadows above, but as long as those things didn't jump out and bite them, Stephanie was OK with it. Skulduggery crouched, picking something up off the ground. A dusty chocolate-bar wrapper, or as he put it, "A clue."

Stephanie looked at him. "Gordon?"

"We're on the right track."

They set off again, scanning the ground for any further

evidence that Gordon had passed this way. Unfortunately, less then five minutes later Skulduggery stopped again and turned, hand out, reading the air.

"We're being followed," he whispered.

Precisely the words Stephanie did not want to hear. She looked back the way they had come. The tunnel was long and straight, and despite the gloom she could see a fair distance. She saw no one behind them.

"Are you sure?" she asked quietly.

Skulduggery didn't answer. He was holding both arms up – his left hand was reading the air, his right hand holding the gun.

"We should back away now," he said. They started backwards. She could hear something now, something echoing up to them.

"We should back away a little faster," he said.

They picked up their pace. Stephanie had to keep glancing at her feet to make sure she wasn't about to trip over anything, but Skulduggery seemed able to move as confidently backwards as he did forwards.

She realised the sound she could hear was bounding footsteps. She realised this because they belonged to the dog-faced creature that was now galloping towards them at a terrible pace.

"OK," Skulduggery said, "now I think we should run."

They turned and ran. Skulduggery fired six shots in quick succession, each one of them finding their mark, each one of them hitting the creature but not slowing it. Skulduggery reloaded on the run, dropping the empty shells and slipping fresh bullets into the chambers, snapping the gun shut with a flick of the wrist. The tunnel widened, the mouth just ahead.

"Keep going," Skulduggery ordered.

"What are you going to do?"

"I don't know," he answered, glancing behind them. "Probably something really brave."

He pulled up sharply and Stephanie shot past him, reaching the end of the tunnel and finding a vast cavern. Vines cascaded down from the darkness above, hanging over the yawning abyss before her.

She looked back just in time to see the beast collide with Skulduggery. The gun flew from his hand and he hit the ground hard and the creature closed its claws around his ankle. It stepped back and swung, lifting Skulduggery into the air and slamming him against the tunnel wall. He hit the ground with his shoulder but the creature wasn't finished swinging, and Stephanie watched as Skulduggery was thrown against the other wall. The creature roared and yanked and Skulduggery was flung back, deeper into the tunnel, and the creature was left holding one skeletal leg.

It snarled in confusion then snapped its head up, catching Stephanie's scent.

"Run!" Skulduggery yelled from the tunnel as the creature dropped the leg and came straight for her. Stephanie spun on her heel but there was nowhere else to run, so she sprinted for the edge and leaped upwards.

Her hands clutched at the slippery vines, desperately searching for a good grip as she started to drop. Her fingers closed around a thick vine and her whole body snapped up again, her momentum taking her forward. She glanced at the vast darkness below, felt the chilled, stale air that wafted up from the emptiness. She twisted as she swung back, just in time to raise her legs to avoid the beast's claws. It roared its displeasure at having being cheated out of its prey, swiping at her from the edge of the abyss. Her momentum took her away from it again.

Stephanie saw Skulduggery dragging himself along the tunnel floor and grabbing his limb, the shoe and sock still attached. He sat up, feeding the thighbone through his trouser leg until it met his hip, then twisted and tested it, bending it towards him. He snatched his gun from the ground beside him and got up, leaving the tunnel and moving up behind the creature as it continued to snarl and swipe at Stephanie. She was now just hanging there, swaying slightly on the vine, her heart no longer beating in her ears.

She kept eye contact, tried to keep its attention on her, but the closer Skulduggery crept, the harder it became, until one kicked pebble caused the creature to turn.

Skulduggery splayed his hand but nothing happened, and Stephanie remembered Mr Bliss saying that there were creatures in these caves who fed on magic. It looked like they'd just encountered one such creature.

"Damn," was all Skulduggery said and he charged, firing point-blank into the creature's chest and then cannoning into it, driving it back one step.

One more step and the creature would go over.

The beast slammed a huge fist down on to Skulduggery's shoulders and he dropped to one knee but was up again, swinging a punch as high as he could, his fist barely grazing the creature's chin. He ducked under another swipe, moving like a boxer, swinging the butt of the gun against its ribs, with little effect.

Stephanie frowned and glanced at the vine she was holding. Was she moving? She looked back across as Skulduggery grabbed a handful of mane with his left hand and jumped, straight up, bringing the butt of the gun down across the creature's face.

The creature bellowed and took a step back and its foot found nothing but emptiness. Skulduggery pushed away from it as it balanced there for a single moment, but there was nothing it could do to save itself. Skulduggery stumbled backwards as the beast fell into the abyss with a terrified howl.

"Right then," Skulduggery said as he dusted himself off. "That took care of that."

"I think I'm moving," Stephanie said as she felt herself being pulled gently up. Skulduggery stepped to the edge, his head jutting out slightly, curiously, then—

"Stephanie," he said, "that's not a vine."

"What?" Stephanie said, staring at the thing she was holding. "Then what is it?"

"Stephanie, swing towards me," he said, urgency in his voice. "Come on now, swing towards me. Hurry!"

She kicked out, starting the swing, forward and back, each arc bigger than the last, all the time being pulled gently upwards.

"Let go!" Skulduggery said, holding his arms out to catch her. She glanced below her as she swung, remembering the beast's howl as it fell, wondering if it had hit the bottom yet. When she was at the peak of her next swing she released her grip and was in the air, falling forward, falling towards Skulduggery.

But the vine snapped out like a whip, wrapping itself around her wrist and yanking her back painfully. Skulduggery made a grab for her but missed, and Stephanie was speeding upwards.

"Help me!" she screamed, feeling like her arm was about to be yanked from its socket. She heard Skulduggery curse, but she was moving too fast and there was nothing she could do to stop herself being pulled up, and Skulduggery could only watch her vanish into the darkness above.

22

THE SCEPTRE OF
THE ANCIENTS

Stephanie was pulled up to a ledge then dragged over it. She tried tearing the tentacle from her wrist, but more slithered from the gloom, wrapping tightly around her arm. She reached back with her free hand and grabbed on to the ledge, but it was no use. Her fingers couldn't take the strain and she had to let go, and she started sliding across the slimy rock.

There was something up ahead, a grey mass of flesh, a growth that had spread unchecked and unchallenged in this dark little corner. The tentacles were pulling her towards its centre, where a large mouth gaped hungrily, razor teeth dripping with viscous saliva.

Her free hand found a large stone and she grabbed it, holding the sharp edge as she would a dagger, and brought it down hard. The stone cut through the tentacles and she pulled her arm free and was up, running, but more tentacles flexed and shot out. They found her legs and Stephanie hit the ground. She tried to kick out but they tightened.

There were tentacles everywhere.

The thing, whatever it was, beat with a sickly pulse as it dragged her closer. She couldn't see any eyes. All it had was its tentacles and that mouth... Which meant it operated by its sense of touch.

Stephanie forced herself to stop struggling. Fighting against every instinct within her, she relaxed her body, and although the speed at which she was moving didn't change, she felt its grip on her loosen slightly. The other tentacles stopped their approach, but they were already too close. They'd be on her in an instant if she tried to pull away.

Stephanie lobbed the stone and it hit a tentacle and bounced away. Sensing another victim nearby, the remaining tentacles slithered after it, searching blindly through the shadows. Stephanie took a deep breath and reached for her ankles, waited until the grip was loosened further, and then grabbed the tentacles and ripped them away.

She got up, but instead of running *away*, she ran *forward*, towards the thing with the mouth. She leaped on to it, over its gaping maw, and her boot almost slipped on its wet, quivering flesh. She jumped, her hands catching the ledge overhead. She hauled herself up as the tentacles snapped and coiled below, their movements becoming more and more frenzied as the thing searched for its missing prey.

Stephanie didn't stop to rest. She got to her feet and hurried from the ledge into the gloom of the passage beyond. She fought off the sudden fear that she'd be lost down in these caves forever. *It won't be forever*, she chided herself. *If one of the monsters doesn't find me and kill me, I'll die of thirst anyway within a few days.*

Stephanie couldn't quite believe she'd just thought that.

Pushing all fears and doubts and pessimistic – though probably realistic – thoughts to the back of her mind, she slowed her pace and concentrated on finding a way back to Skulduggery. And then she saw a light.

She crept forward until she came to a balcony of rock, overlooking a small cavern. She peeked down to see a half-dozen Hollow Men, one of them holding a lantern. Mr Bliss didn't appear to have accompanied this little expedition.

Serpine was there, however, standing in front of a small boulder, its surface flat like a table. On this boulder was a wooden chest with a large lock. Her heart lurched. He'd found it.

She looked down. It wasn't that far to the cavern floor. A couple of metres. She didn't have a choice. She had to try.

The Hollow Men had their backs to her, so Stephanie eased herself over the edge without being noticed and dropped to the cavern floor. The light from the lantern didn't reach this far and the shadows enveloped her so that when one of the Hollow Men turned, its empty gaze passed right over the spot where she crouched. She waited until it had turned back before moving again.

The darkness along the edges of this cavern was so absolute, and her clothes so black, that she could creep up next to her enemies without being seen. She moved achingly slowly, taking only the barest of breaths. She was sure Serpine would hear her heart thundering against her ribcage, but he was preoccupied with the chest.

He tapped the lock with a skinless finger of his red right hand, and the mechanism rusted and snapped in an instant. He smiled as he pulled on his glove, opened the chest and lifted the Sceptre of the Ancients from within.

It was real. The ultimate weapon, the weapon with which the Ancients defeated their gods – it was real. The years hadn't dimmed its golden beauty, and it seemed to hum for a moment, acclimatising itself to its new owner. The ultimate weapon, in the hands of Serpine.

"At last," she heard him whisper.

A strange singing filled the chamber, and Stephanie realised it was coming from the black crystal in the Sceptre. Serpine turned as Skulduggery Pleasant stormed into the cavern.

Skulduggery waved his hand and the Hollow Men flew back off their feet. He crashed into Serpine and the Sceptre clattered to the ground. Serpine threw a punch and Skulduggery ducked under it and moved in close, his hand snaking up to Serpine's shoulder and his hip twisting into him. Serpine pitched over and hit the ground hard.

Stephanie crept through the murk, heading for the Sceptre. The Hollow Men were starting to get up, clumping back to fight at the centre of the cavern.

Skulduggery clicked his fingers and Serpine was too close to dodge the fireball. It hit him square in the chest and enveloped him completely. The Hollow Men froze as their master wheeled about, engulfed in flame. His foot hit the Sceptre and it skidded to the edge of the light…

… and closer to Stephanie.

Skulduggery splayed his hand and Serpine hit the far wall and collapsed to the floor. Skulduggery put out the flames with a casual wave. Serpine lay where he was, his clothes smouldering, his flesh charred and horribly burnt.

"It's over," Skulduggery said. "This is where your past catches up to you. This is where you die."

And then, impossibly, a laugh, and Serpine sat up.

"That," he said, "*hurt.*"

And as Stephanie watched, the burnt flesh started to heal itself and hair regrew along the blistered scalp, leaving not even a scar.

Serpine gathered purple vapour in his palm and threw it at Skulduggery, knocking him back. The vapour became a thin, snaking tendril that darted into the shadows, wrapping around the Sceptre and yanking it into Serpine's hand just as Stephanie reached for it. Skulduggery recovered, but he was too late to do anything. The sorcerer got to his feet, holding the Sceptre, and smiled.

"I'm in two minds," Serpine said as Stephanie moved, unseen, behind him. "Should I use this to destroy you, to reduce your worthless bones to ash, or should I just leave you down here in the darkness? Leaving you here would be more satisfying in the long term, I admit, but what can I say? I crave instant satisfaction. I'm shallow like that."

Stephanie lunged, slamming her shoulder into Serpine's back just as the Sceptre's crystal flashed. Black lightning zigzagged through the air, missing Skulduggery by centimetres and turning the rock behind him to dust. Serpine turned and grabbed her. Stephanie punched him with all of her strength but he just snarled, and then Skulduggery was there and the air rippled. Serpine went sliding across the cavern floor, but he was still clutching the Sceptre.

Skulduggery waved at the Hollow Men and they hurtled backwards, then Stephanie felt a gloved hand close around her wrist and she was dragged out of the cavern. Skulduggery sprinted so fast she just allowed herself to be carried along in his wake.

He knew exactly where he was going, and within minutes they were at the stone steps, hurrying up out of the caves. They reached the cellar and the key flew from the lock into his hand. The floor groaned and rumbled and closed up.

"Will that hold him?" Stephanie asked.

"He's got the Sceptre," Skulduggery said. "Nothing will hold him." As if to prove his point, the floor started to crack.

"Move!" Skulduggery shouted. They bolted up the stairs and Stephanie glanced back just as the floor vanished in a soft *whump* of dust and air.

They plunged out of the house into the bright sunlight, the Hollow Men right behind. Stephanie was three steps from the yellow car when one of the Hollow Men grabbed her.

Stephanie lashed out. Her fingers tore into its face and she ripped downwards and a blast of foul air escaped. The Hollow Man stumbled back, clutching at its head. Its entire body deflated, until it was nothing more than papery skin being trodden on by its brethren.

Another lunged at her and Skulduggery tackled it, rammed an elbow into the side of its neck and flipped it over his shoulder. There was movement to their right and Tanith Low ran towards them, her sword clearing its scabbard. She came in fast, the blade twirling and glinting in the sun, sending pieces of Hollow Men fluttering into the air like confetti.

Black lightning streaked from the doorway and the Canary Car crumbled to nothing. Serpine stalked out of the house. Stephanie felt heat flare beside her face as Skulduggery started hurling fireballs. Serpine waved the first one away and dodged back to avoid the others.

Stephanie was only aware of the other car when it screeched to a stop behind her. The door opened and Tanith sheathed her sword, pushed Stephanie into the car and jumped in after her, and the car was moving again.

Stephanie sat up in time to see Skulduggery hurl one last ball of fire and then turn and dive straight through the open window. He landed on top of her as the car swerved and she felt his elbow against her head. The car swerved again and they separated. Trees zipped past outside and she knew they were out of Serpine's line of fire.

They passed the huge gates that led out of Gordon's estate and Skulduggery righted himself. "Well," he said, "that was bracing."

A familiar voice came from the front seat. "One of these days I won't be around to get you out of trouble, you know."

Stephanie turned her head, saw the man in the bow tie behind the wheel and beside him, in the passenger seat, China Sorrows, poised and perfect.

"I don't know what you'd do without me, Skulduggery," China said. "I really don't."

23

THOUGHTS ON DYING HORRIBLY

The Elders were not happy.

Eachan Meritorious and Sagacious Tome spoke in hushed voices at the other end of the Sanctuary meeting room. Meritorious was calm but solemn. Tome was livid and panicking.

Stephanie sat beside Skulduggery. Across the table, Tanith was cleaning her sword. She had something in her hair.

"Tanith?" Stephanie whispered. Tanith looked up. "You have something..." She pointed to her own head as a hint. "It's a leaf or something."

"Oh, thanks," Tanith said and put her hand to her hair. She felt around until she found it and pulled it out. She examined it and frowned, looked closer, then her face contorted in disgust and she dropped it on the table. "Oh my God."

"What is it?"

"It's a piece of Hollow Man *skin*."

Stephanie blanched. "Oh, that's disgusting."

"It was in my *hair*," Tanith moaned, flicking the skin across the table.

Stephanie recoiled and flicked it back and Tanith started to laugh, but Skulduggery's hand came down, trapping it. He looked at them both.

"Four-year-olds," he said. "We're facing an unimaginable crisis and I'm dealing with four-year-olds."

"Sorry," said Stephanie.

"Sorry," said Tanith.

Morwenna Crow and China Sorrows walked in, followed seconds later by Ghastly Bespoke.

"Did they find anything?" Skulduggery asked, standing.

Morwenna answered. "The Cleavers have stormed every hideout and haunt we know of and they haven't found one trace of Serpine."

"The news about the Sceptre is spreading," China said.

"There are rumours that he is bringing his old allies in from the cold."

Meritorious and Tome joined them.

"If even one of the exiles returns," Meritorious said, "the balance of power will have shifted too much. We'll be overrun."

"We need to get that Sceptre from him," Tanith said, "see how *he* likes it."

"It wouldn't work," China said. "Even if we could get close to it without the crystal warning him that we're near, he owns it now and no one else can use it while he's alive."

"Then we kill him," Tome said.

Meritorious looked to Skulduggery, who nodded and spoke up. "Unfortunately, killing Serpine is not as easy as it may appear. He should be dead right now. I don't mean wounded, I don't mean dying, I mean dead. But he healed himself."

Stephanie frowned. "He can't be killed?"

"*Everyone* can be killed," Skulduggery said, turning his head to her slightly. "That's the one great assurance. I haven't encountered one thing on this planet that I haven't been able to kill, and I'm not going to let *him* be the exception to the rule."

"We need to strike *now*," Morwenna said, "before he can consolidate his power."

"How can we do that if we don't even know where he is?" Sagacious Tome asked impatiently.

"But we might know where he *was*," Skulduggery said. "Last night I received a call from a gentleman who supplies me with information from time to time. A distinctive silver car was seen on Denholm Street, near the docks. I made a call or two, established that almost every building on that street is being leased by a reputable firm. The one exception is a warehouse that has been leased to an individual, Mr Howard L. Craft."

Tome frowned. "So?"

"L. Craft. Lovecraft. Howard Philip Lovecraft wrote a series of stories commonly referred to as the Cthulhu Mythos, about dark gods who wanted to rule the earth. Some historians claim that Mr Lovecraft based his creations, in part, on legends he had heard about the Faceless Ones."

Tome made a face. "That's your only lead? A trick name Serpine *may* have used? We don't have time to waste on such vague half-clues; we've got to act on what we know!"

"Well what exactly do we know?" Morwenna asked. "We know he has a lunatic scheme to bring back the Faceless Ones, but we don't know how he intends to do it."

"Mr Bliss said the Sceptre was nothing more then a stepping stone," Stephanie offered.

"This is a grown-up conversation," Tome said, exasperated. "We don't need input from *you*, child."

Tanith and China spoke as one. "Don't call her child."

Clearly unused to admonitions from anyone who wasn't an Elder, Tome spluttered a bit and his face grew redder. Stephanie did her best to hide her grin behind a mask of serene indifference. Tanith caught her eye and winked.

"If the Sceptre is a stepping stone," Skulduggery said, ignoring Tome's indignation, "then he's going to use it to somehow retrieve the ritual he needs."

"Then it's our job to make sure that doesn't happen," Meritorious said. "Skulduggery, on behalf of the Council of Elders, I apologise for not involving you in this when we found Serpine's surveillance team dead. I also apologise for not listening to your warnings."

"Serpine would have had a back-up plan," Skulduggery said. "That's what makes him so dangerous."

"Maybe so. I'm afraid it's up to you and Miss Cain, and whoever else you might need, to try and find out what his next move is. I'm sorry for saddling you with that responsibility, but my fellow Elders and I are needed to prepare for all-out war."

Skulduggery bowed slightly. "In that case, we'll get right on it."

"Thank you."

Skulduggery wrapped the scarf around his face and put on his hat, then looked at the serious faces around him.

"Cheer up everyone," he said, a new brightness to his voice. "Since we're all going to die horribly anyway, what's there to be worried about?"

Stephanie very much feared she was going ever so slightly insane, because she found herself agreeing wholeheartedly with the living skeleton she was now following out of the room.

The Bentley was waiting for them when they left the Sanctuary. It gleamed like it was glad to be back to its former beauty. Stephanie got in and sank into the seat. The Bentley smelled nice. It smelled how beautiful cars ought to smell. The Canary Car hadn't smelled nice. It had just smelled *yellow*.

"It's good to have it back," Stephanie said when Skulduggery got in. "They worked miracles on it, they really did. Two days and it looks brand new."

Skulduggery nodded. "Cost me a fortune."

"It's worth it."

"Glad you think so. Also glad that I don't have to eat anytime soon. Or at all." She smiled and looked at him. He was looking out of the windscreen. Neither of them spoke for a few seconds.

"What is it?" she asked.

"I'm sorry?"

"You're thinking about something."

"I'm always thinking about something. Thinking is what I do. I'm very good at it."

"But you've just figured something out."

"And how did you know that?"

"You hold your head differently when you've just figured something out. So what is it?"

"It just occurred to me," he said. "In the cave, the Sceptre's crystal warned Serpine that I was close – but it didn't warn him that you were right there beside him."

She shrugged. "Maybe it didn't see me as a threat. It's not like I could have hurt him or anything."

"That's hardly the point," Skulduggery said. "We may have found a weakness in the ultimate weapon."

Stephanie frowned. "What?"

"Remember what Oisin, the nice man in the Echo Stone, said?" Skulduggery asked. "The black crystal sang to the gods whenever an enemy neared, but it was silent when the Ancients took it."

"So, what, it thinks I'm an Ancient?"

"Technically, according to your father at least, you might well be."

"Does that mean you're starting to believe that they were more than just legends and myths?"

"I'm... keeping an open mind about it. The thing I still don't understand, however, is why didn't Gordon tell me about your family history? We were friends for years, we had conversations about the Ancients and the Faceless Ones that went on for days, so why didn't he tell me?"

"Does it mean anything else? Being descended from the Ancients, I mean. What does it, what..."

"What does it signify?"

"Yes."

"It means you're special. It means you're meant to do this – you're meant to be involved in this world, in this life."

"I am?"

"You are."

"Then maybe that's why he didn't tell you. He wanted to write about it, from the outside, not be stuck in the middle of it all."

He cocked his head. "You're wise beyond your years, Valkyrie."

"Yes," she said. "Yes, I am."

24

PLANNING FOR MURDER

ister Bliss stood in the palm of the Grasping Rock and watched Serpine approach. The Grasping Rock was shaped like a massive upturned hand, jutting from the peak of the mountain, fingers curled, as if reaching for the sun in the blood-red sky.

Serpine climbed into the palm with ease and Bliss bowed slightly. Serpine, for his part, merely smiled.

"Do you have it?" Bliss asked.

"Luckily for you, yes."

"Luckily for me?"

"My dear Mr Bliss, if I had gone down to those caves and emerged without the Sceptre, where would that have left you? You would be standing in one of those cages in the Sanctuary's Gaol, powerless, awaiting judgement. Instead, you are here, standing with me, on the verge of a new world. Be thankful."

"You seem to forget that if you had emerged with nothing, you'd be in the cage next to me..."

Serpine looked at him. A short time ago they would have been equals. But not now.

"...my master," Bliss finished respectfully, inclining his head.

Serpine smiled again and turned his back to him, looking out through the curled fingers of the rock and down at the valley below them.

"Is it as powerful as the scholars have imagined?" Bliss asked.

"What the scholars have imagined pales in comparison to the reality. No one can stop us now."

"The Elders," Bliss said.

Serpine turned his head. "I have a plan to deal with the Elders. They are nothing if not predictable, and they will die because of it. Meritorious himself will crumble to dust. Nothing can stand in our way."

"The Elders may be predictable," Bliss responded, "but that is not a trait Skulduggery Pleasant shares with them. He's cunning, powerful, and very, very dangerous."

"Do not concern yourself with the detective. I also have a plan to deal with him."

"Oh?"

"Skulduggery Pleasant has always had one weakness – he forms attachments to people who are very easily killed. In the past, it was his wife and child. Now, it is this girl that is with him, this Valkyrie Cain. He is only a threat to us if he is thinking clearly. You know as well as I do that once he becomes angry, his judgement is clouded."

"So what are you going to do?"

"I have already done it, Bliss. I have sent someone to... cloud his judgement. In less than an hour, Valkyrie Cain will be dead and Skulduggery Pleasant will trouble us no longer."

25

THE WHITE CLEAVER

Day had been beaten back by the time they got to Denholm Street, and the night was soaking through the city. It was a long street, dirty and quiet. The Bentley pulled up outside the warehouse. Ghastly and Tanith were waiting for them when they got out.

"Anyone inside?" Skulduggery asked, checking that his gun was loaded.

"Not as far as we can tell," Ghastly said, "but they could be masking their presence. If Serpine is in there, or Bliss, we're going to need back-up."

"They aren't here," Skulduggery said.

"How do you know?" Stephanie asked.

"Serpine used this place for something, something big and strange enough to raise a few eyebrows. He'd know eyebrows were being raised, he'd know I'd hear about it, so he's already moved on."

"Then why are *we* here?"

"You can only anticipate what someone is going to do if you know exactly what that someone has just done."

They approached the single door, and Tanith put her ear against it and listened. After a moment she put her hand over the lock, but instead of the lock breaking, this time Stephanie heard it click.

"How come you can't do that?" Stephanie whispered to Skulduggery. "It's faster than picking a lock and quieter than blasting the door down."

He shook his head sadly. "A living skeleton isn't enough for you, is it? What does it take to impress young people these days?"

Stephanie grinned. Tanith pushed the door open and they went inside. The door led straight into the warehouse office, a dark, poky room with a desk and an empty corkboard. The place obviously hadn't been used by any reputable company for quite some time. The office had a door that opened out to the warehouse proper, and a grime-covered window that Stephanie peered through.

"Seems quiet enough," she said.

Skulduggery hit a few switches on the wall and lights flickered on. They walked out on to the warehouse floor. There were pigeons in the rafters, high above them, that cooed and hooted and fluttered from one perch to the next, startled by the sudden light. They walked to the middle of the warehouse, where an array of what appeared to be medical equipment was collected around an operating table. Stephanie looked at Skulduggery.

"Any ideas?" she asked.

He hesitated. "Let's get the obvious out of the way. A lot of these machines would suggest that some kind of transfusion took place here."

Tanith held up a tube, examining the residue within. "I'm not a doctor, but I don't think this is the result of medical research."

"Magic then," Ghastly said.

"You can *inject* magic?" Stephanie asked, frowning.

"You can inject fluids with magical properties," Skulduggery told her as he took the tube from Tanith. "Before we had wonderful machines like this, it was a far messier process, but the result was the same."

"And what was the result?"

"The patient came out of the operation a changed man. Or woman. Or... thing. The question here is, what was the object of the game? What changes was Serpine seeking?"

"And who was the patient?"

"Patients, actually."

"Sorry?"

"There are two sets of needles, two IV bags, two of everything – enough to take care of two separate operations. We'll take a sample back to the Sanctuary, break it down and try to find out what it does. But for right now, everyone take a look around."

"What are we looking for?" Stephanie asked.

"Clues."

Stephanie glanced at Tanith, saw her raise an eyebrow sceptically and managed to restrain her grin.

Skulduggery and Ghastly walked slowly, passing their gaze over every surface, examining every centimetre of the machines, the table and the surrounding area. Stephanie and Tanith found themselves side by side, looking straight down at the floor.

"What does a clue look like?" Tanith whispered.

Stephanie fought the giggle down and whispered back. "I'm not sure. I'm looking for a footprint or something."

"Have you found one yet?"

"No. But that's probably because I haven't moved from this spot."

"Maybe we should move, pretend we know what we're doing."

"That's a good idea."

They started to walk, very slowly, still looking straight down.

"How's the magic coming along?" Tanith asked, keeping her voice low.

"I moved a shell."

"Hey, congratulations!"

Stephanie shrugged modestly. "It was only a shell."

"Makes no difference. Well done."

"Thanks. What age were you when you first did magic?"

"I was born into it," Tanith answered. "Folks were sorcerers – my brother was always doing *something*. I grew up doing magic."

"I didn't know you had a brother."

"Oh, yeah, a big brother and all. You have any brothers?"

"I'm an only child."

Tanith shrugged. "I always wanted a little sister. My

brother's great, I love him to death, but I always wanted a little sister to talk to, to share my secrets with, you know?"

"I wouldn't mind a sister either."

"Any chance of that happening?"

"I can't see what would be in it for my parents. I mean, they have the perfect daughter already – what more could they want?"

Tanith laughed, then tried to cover it up with a cough.

"Found something?" Skulduggery asked from behind them.

Tanith turned, looking serious. "No, sorry. I thought I had, but, no, it turned out to be, uh... more floor."

Stephanie hugged herself, trying to stop her shoulders from shaking with laughter.

"OK," Skulduggery said. "Well, keep looking."

Tanith nodded, turned back and nudged Stephanie to get her to shut up. Stephanie clamped a hand over her mouth and had to look away when she saw Tanith's face, straining to hold her composure.

"Cow," Tanith muttered and that was it, the floodgates opened, and Stephanie doubled over with laughter that echoed throughout the warehouse. Tanith pointed at Stephanie and backed away. "Skulduggery, she's not being professional!"

Stephanie's laugh proved infectious and Tanith was soon on

her knees. Skulduggery and Ghastly just looked at them.

"What's going on?" Ghastly asked.

"I'm not entirely sure," Skulduggery answered.

They looked at Stephanie and Tanith and shook their heads. "Women," they said together.

Stephanie wiped the tears from her eyes and looked around at Skulduggery, and then something fell from the ceiling, and landed behind the detective without a sound. Her laughter vanished as she stood. "Behind you!" she yelled.

Skulduggery wheeled, gun in hand, and everyone froze. They looked at the man. His uniform, though identical in design to the Cleavers, was of startling white.

"Stand down," Ghastly said as Stephanie and Tanith ran up to join them. "We are working with the Elder Council. Stand down."

The White Cleaver didn't move.

"What do you want?" Skulduggery asked.

A moment dragged itself by, and then the White Cleaver raised his arm and pointed straight at Stephanie.

"That's all we need to know," Skulduggery said and fired, four shots to the chest and two to the head. The White Cleaver jerked with each impact, but it was clear that the bullets didn't penetrate his coat, and the two to the head ricocheted off the helmet, leaving dark scratches against the white.

"Damn," Skulduggery muttered.

Stephanie stayed back as Skulduggery, Tanith and Ghastly closed in on their new adversary. The helmet denied them any chance of knowing where he was looking, but Stephanie knew he was looking right into her eyes.

Tanith attacked first, feinting with a low kick then snapping it up high. The Cleaver didn't fall for the ruse and slapped the high kick away as Ghastly attacked from behind. The Cleaver spun with a kick of his own that caught Tanith in the gut, and he ducked under the punch that Ghastly sent his way. Ghastly's fists blurred but the Cleaver absorbed the blows and his hand shot out, catching Ghastly in the side of the neck. Ghastly staggered and Skulduggery thrust out his palm and the air rippled.

But instead of being pushed backwards, the Cleaver moved *through* the ripples without being affected. *The uniform,* Stephanie thought. Unfazed, Skulduggery threw a punch that the Cleaver caught.

Skulduggery was flipped over but when he landed he had reversed the grip. His foot sneaked out, striking the Cleaver's knee and now Skulduggery was the one doing the twisting, and the Cleaver was the one who flipped.

While he was in mid-flip, however, the Cleaver got his free hand to the ground to cartwheel back to his feet. A pause followed and Stephanie's three friends reappraised their opponent.

Tanith took her sword from beneath her coat and slid it from its scabbard. Ghastly let his jacket slip off and Skulduggery put away his pistol, freeing his hands.

"You don't have to do this," he said to the Cleaver. "Tell us where Serpine is –tell us what his plans are. We can help you. You are not going to lay one finger on Valkyrie Cain, but we *will* help you."

The Cleaver's answer was to reach behind him and draw his scythe. Skulduggery grunted in dissatisfaction.

The Cleaver darted towards them before anyone could react, using the scythe like a pole-vaulter to swing himself up, kicking both Skulduggery and Ghastly in the chest at the same time.

They went stumbling back and Tanith came in, sword flashing. The Cleaver dodged back, whirling his scythe to parry the blade.

Sparks flew as the metals clashed, sword against scythe, and such was the ferocity of Tanith's assault that the Cleaver didn't notice Ghastly until it was too late. Ghastly's strong arms wrapped around him, pinning his arms to his sides, making him drop the scythe.

Tanith moved in for the kill and the Cleaver's leg blurred in a crescent, his bootheel slamming into her wrist as she neared. She hissed in pain and dropped the sword, clutching her wrist.

The Cleaver rammed his heel into Ghastly's shin and whacked the back of his helmet against his nose. He then kicked both legs into the air and over his head, slipping out from under Ghastly's arms. His hands went to the ground and he continued the movement, sending both boots into Ghastly's face.

Ghastly fell back and the Cleaver held the handstand for a moment, then dropped back to his feet as Skulduggery came at him.

Skulduggery summoned fire and hurled two handfuls into the Cleaver. The flames didn't catch but they did throw him back, and Skulduggery threw a lightning-fast jab that he followed up with a right hook. He didn't seem to mind that he was hitting a helmet, and Stephanie noted with satisfaction the way their opponent was sent stumbling.

The Cleaver recovered quickly, however, and they started trading punches and kicks, elbows and knees, and she watched them block and lock and counter-lock, all the while moving around each other in an elaborate and brutal dance.

"Stephanie!" Skulduggery called out as he fought. "Get out of here!"

"I'm not leaving you!"

"You have to! I don't know how to stop him!"

Tanith snatched her sword off the ground and grabbed Stephanie's arm. "We have to go," she said firmly and Stephanie nodded.

They ran back the way they had come. As they were passing into the office, Stephanie glanced back, saw the Cleaver spin with a kick that sent Skulduggery to the floor. In one fluid movement, he got a toe under the staff of the scythe, flicked it up and caught it, and then he was running after her.

Stephanie burst into the dark alleyway and Tanith pressed her hand against the door as she closed it – Stephanie heard her mutter "Withstand" – and a polished sheen spread across its surface.

"That'll hold him for a minute," she said.

They ran for the Bentley. The Cleaver pounded on the door behind them, but it wouldn't open and it wouldn't break. The pounding stopped.

They reached the Bentley and Tanith looked at Stephanie. "Do you have the key?"

A window exploded, high up near the warehouse's roof, and

the White Cleaver dropped and landed in a crouch in the middle of the alley, shards of glass raining down with him. He straightened up, unfolded his arms and raised his head.

Tanith stood between the Cleaver and Stephanie, holding the sword in her left hand. She cradled her injured right arm by her side. The Cleaver twirled his scythe slowly.

Skulduggery and Ghastly leaped through the broken window. The Cleaver turned and Ghastly crashed into him.

"Start the car!" Ghastly yelled.

Skulduggery pressed the keyring and the locks sprang open with a *beep*, and they all jumped in. The engine roared to life.

"Ghastly!" Skulduggery shouted. "Let's go!"

Ghastly slammed a punch into the Cleaver and rolled to his feet but the Cleaver kicked out and Ghastly stumbled. The scythe flashed, the staff whacking against Ghastly's jaw. He dropped to his knees.

"Ghastly!" Stephanie screamed. Skulduggery opened his door, went to get out, but Ghastly raised his eyes, shook his head.

"We're not leaving you!" Skulduggery shouted.

The Cleaver stepped up to Ghastly, ready to swing the scythe.

"You've got to," Ghastly said, ever so softly.

He lowered his head and clenched his fists, his eyes closed.

As the Cleaver swung, the ground seemed to latch on to Ghastly's knees. It spread instantly, turning his legs to concrete, then his torso, his arms, his head, his entire body in the time it took the scythe to cross the space between them, and when the Cleaver tried to take his head, he could only chip at the neck. Stephanie instinctively knew what he'd done – this was the last Elemental power, earth, the power Skulduggery had described as purely defensive, and purely for use as a last resort.

The White Cleaver looked directly at Stephanie as Skulduggery put the car in gear. They left them there – the White Cleaver and Ghastly – and sped through the city streets.

26

THE LAST STAND OF...

Eachan Meritorious waited in the shadow of Dublin's Christ Church Cathedral, watching the world go about its business. There were times when he felt guilty about hiding magic from the masses, when he felt sure that they would embrace the wonder and the beauty if only they were given the opportunity. But then he'd come to his senses, and realise that humankind had enough things to be worrying about without a subculture that they might see as a threat to their very validity. As an Elder, it was his job to protect the outside world from truths they weren't yet ready to know.

Morwenna Crow walked up, her dark robes flowing over the grass. She was as clean and as elegant as the day he had first met her.

"It's not like Skulduggery Pleasant to be late," she remarked.

"Sagacious said he sounded urgent," Meritorious said. "He may have run into some difficulty."

Morwenna looked around the corner of the cathedral, to the busy street beyond the railing. The bright lights, amber and yellow, framed her face. She seemed almost angelic. "I don't like meeting out in the open like this. We're too exposed. He should know better."

"Skulduggery picked this place for a reason," Meritorious said gently. "I trust his judgement. He's earned that much at least."

They turned as Sagacious Tome appeared beside them, fading up from nothing.

"Sagacious," Morwenna said, "did Skulduggery say why he wanted to meet us here?"

Sagacious looked nervous as the materialisation completed and he became solid. "I'm sorry, Morwenna, he just told me to make sure both of you were outside the cathedral."

"This had better be good," she said. "We don't have a lot of time to spare these days. Serpine could strike anywhere, at any time."

Meritorious watched Sagacious smile sadly. "That's very true," Sagacious said. "And if I may, I just want to take this opportunity to let you both know, in the times when we were friends, they were great times indeed."

Morwenna laughed. "We're not dead yet, Sagacious."

And then he looked at her and the smile turned to something else. "Actually, Morwenna, you *are*."

The Hollow Men converged and Sagacious faded to nothing. Meritorious didn't even have time to register the betrayal before he saw Serpine, striding towards them, holding the Sceptre. He instinctively conjured a protective shield that made the air glimmer, but when the crystal flashed the black lightning came right through the shield like it wasn't even there and then there was—

Nothing.

*

The Administrator charged through a crowd outside the Olympia Theatre, drawing a chorus of angry shouts and curses. He stumbled but managed to stay up, managed to keep running. He glanced behind.

He couldn't see anyone pursuing him. He didn't think he had been seen, but he couldn't be sure. He had been standing by the car when Nefarian Serpine had appeared. He had seen Meritorious explode into dust and ash, saw the black lightning strike Morwenna Crow as she tried to rush her enemies.

He had ducked down, terrified. Tome betrayed them. Tome betrayed them all. The Administrator had abandoned the car and started running.

He had to get back to the Sanctuary. He had to warn the others.

27

NO CALM BEFORE
THE STORM

kulduggery had given her money and Stephanie had
gone in to pay while he refilled the Bentley's tank.
As she waited for her change she looked at the
chocolate bars on display and tried remembering the last
time she'd eaten chocolate. She always ate chocolate when
something bad happened, but these days chocolate just wasn't
enough.

Everything was going wrong. Tanith was injured, Ghastly
was nothing more than a statue and now they had the White
Cleaver to worry about. It was getting to the point where

Stephanie didn't know why they were bothering to fight any more, although she'd never say that to Skulduggery. He seemed to think she was like him – never give up, never surrender. But she wasn't. The only reason she didn't tell him this was because she liked the way he thought of her, and she didn't want to disappoint him. But the truth was, the Valkyrie Cain he thought he knew was a lot stronger than Stephanie Edgley could ever be.

She walked back outside. Skulduggery was slotting the petrol nozzle back into the pump. Tanith had gone to soak her hand in the same healing mixture she had given Stephanie.

Now that they were alone, Stephanie didn't quite know what to say. Skulduggery screwed the petrol cap shut and stood there, perfectly still. With his hat on and his scarf hiding his jaw, it could have been a mannequin standing there for all the difference it made.

"I'm sorry," Stephanie said. He looked at her.

"If it wasn't for me, Ghastly would be... he'd be with us. It's my fault he had to use the earth power." She fought to keep her voice from trembling. "How long will he stay like that, do you think?"

Skulduggery took a moment. "I sincerely don't know, Valkyrie. It's the most unpredictable power we have. He could be stuck as a statue for a day, a week, or a hundred years. There's no way of knowing."

"I've ruined everything."

"No—"

"That Cleaver was after *me*. Ghastly was forced to—"

"Ghastly wasn't *forced* to do anything," Skulduggery interrupted. "It was his choice. And it wasn't your fault. Serpine sent his assassin after *you* to hurt *me*. It's what he does."

"He sent him after me because he knew I wouldn't be able to defend myself. He knows you're looking after me, he knows I'm your weak spot."

Skulduggery tilted his head. "*Looking after* you? Is that how you see this? You think I'm babysitting you?"

"Well aren't you? I've got no magic; I can't fight; I can't throw fire or run on ceilings. What use am I to you? I'm weak."

Skulduggery shook his head. "No, you're not. You haven't trained in magic or combat, but you're not weak. Serpine underestimates you. Everyone underestimates you. You're stronger than they know. You're stronger than *you* know."

"I wish you were right."

"Of course I'm right. I'm me."

Stephanie heard a phone ring as Tanith walked into the light of the forecourt. She had wrapped a bandage around her wrist.

The magical properties of the healing mixture would already be working to reduce the swelling and mend the damage. Tanith held her phone to her ear. Stephanie didn't like the way her face seemed to slacken as she listened to whatever was being said.

She hung up without replying. "Skulduggery," she said softly. "You have your phone on?"

"Battery's low," he said.

"They've been trying to contact you. The Administrator, the Sanctuary."

"What's wrong?" Stephanie asked.

"The Elders," Tanith said, her voice empty. "Sagacious Tome betrayed them. The Elders are dead."

Stephanie's hand was at her mouth. "Oh, God."

"Tome's been working with Serpine all along. He's a traitor. Like Mr Bliss. They're all traitors. Skulduggery, what are we going to do?"

Stephanie looked to him, praying that he'd come up with a great new plan, a scheme to ensure victory and a happy ending. He didn't answer.

"Did you hear me?" Tanith continued, the emptiness in her voice giving way to sudden anger. "Are you even listening? Do you even *care*? Maybe you don't. Maybe you *want* to die again;

maybe you want to join your wife and child, but hey! *We* don't want to die, OK? I don't. Valkyrie doesn't."

Skulduggery stood there. A mannequin. Silent.

"Do you think we stand a chance against Serpine?" Tanith asked. "Tome? Bliss? That Cleaver? Do you really think we stand a chance against all of them?"

"What do you suggest we do?" Skulduggery said, his voice slow and steady. "Stand back and let Serpine grow stronger? Stand back and let him recruit more allies, let him open the door and let the Faceless Ones come through?"

"He's *winning*, OK? Serpine is winning this war!"

"No such thing."

"What?"

"There's no such thing as winning or losing. There is *won* and there is *lost*; there is *victory* and *defeat*. There are absolutes. Everything in between is still left to fight for. Serpine will have won only when there is no one left to stand against him. Until then, there is only the struggle, because tides do what tides do – they turn."

"This is insane—"

He turned to her so sharply Stephanie thought he might strike her.

"I've just seen a very dear friend turn into a *statue*, Tanith.

Meritorious and Crow, two of the few people in this world I respected, have been murdered. So yes, you're right when you say our allies are dropping like flies, but this was never going to be an easy fight. Casualties are to be expected. And you know what we do? We step over them and we move on because we don't have any other choice. Now I'm going to stop Serpine once and for all. Anyone who wants to come with me, they're welcome. Anyone who doesn't, it won't make a blind bit of difference. Serpine *will* be stopped and that's all there is to it."

He got into the Bentley and started the engine. Stephanie hesitated, then opened the passenger door and slid in. She glanced at Skulduggery as she buckled up but he was staring straight ahead. He waited three seconds, then put the car in gear and was about to drive off when Tanith got in behind them.

"No need to get all dramatic about it," she muttered and Stephanie managed to smile. Skulduggery pulled out on to the road, driving fast.

"Where are we going?" Stephanie asked.

"Weren't you listening?" Skulduggery responded, sounding like he was back to his old self. "We're going to stop Serpine. I just made a whole speech about it. It was very good."

Tanith leaned forward. "You know where he is?"

"Yes, I do. It came to me just there as I was filling the tank."

"What did?"

"The Sceptre. Why did Serpine go after the Sceptre?"

Stephanie frowned. "Because it's the ultimate weapon."

"And why did he want it?"

"To, you know, to retrieve the ritual he needs to bring the Faceless Ones back, to force whoever knows it to tell him."

"No."

"He *isn't* going to use it to retrieve the ritual?"

"The Sceptre's too clumsy, too unwieldy. If he threatens to kill the only person in the world who knows how to work the ritual – what if that person chooses death rather than hand it over? What's he supposed to do then? No. He used the Sceptre to kill the Elders. That's the only reason he wanted it. He knew he wasn't powerful enough to take them on without it."

"And so how does that help him retrieve the ritual?"

"This isn't just about the ritual any more. What do you get if you kill the Elders?"

"This sounds like a joke."

"Valkyrie—"

"I don't know."

"Yes, you do. Now think. What would killing the Elders result in?"

"Panic? Fear? Three empty parking spaces in the Sanctuary?"

Skulduggery looked at her and Stephanie's confusion lifted. "Oh, God," she said.

"He's after the Book," Skulduggery said. "He needed the Sceptre to kill Meritorious and Morwenna Crow in order to dismantle the spell protecting it. He doesn't have to force anyone to do anything; all he'll have to do is *ask*. He's been after the Book of Names all along."

28

CARNAGE

ublin City was quiet when they reached the Waxworks Museum, as if it was holding its breath. The stars were obscured by a veil of dark clouds, and as they left the Bentley and approached the rear entrance, the rain fell steadily. On the street beyond the gates, cars splashed through puddles and the occasional pedestrian hurried by with his head down. Skulduggery moved quickly but cautiously up to the open door, and Stephanie and Tanith followed.

Stephanie had expected to arrive in the middle of a pitched

battle – she expected to hear the sounds of fighting. But the Waxworks was silent. As they walked through the exhibits to the hidden door, Skulduggery slowed and eventually came to a complete stop.

"What's wrong?" Stephanie whispered.

He turned his head slowly, peering into the darkness. "I don't want to alarm anybody, but we're not alone."

That's when they came, the Hollow Men, detaching themselves from the shadows with only the faintest rasp of warning. In an instant they were surrounded by the mindless, heartless, soulless *things*.

Tanith waded through them, her sword strokes deliberate and devastating, every move claiming another un-life. Skulduggery clicked his fingers and a group of Hollow Men were suddenly alight. Stephanie shrank back as they wheeled around blindly. The flames ate through their skin and ignited the putrid gas trapped inside, and with a burst of fire and heat, the Hollow Men fell.

One of them avoided the flames and lunged at Stephanie and she punched it square in the face, her fist sinking into its head slightly. Its own fist swung at her and she ducked, then moved into it like she'd seen Skulduggery do, jammed her hip into it and twisted, and the Hollow Man hit the ground. It wasn't graceful and it wasn't pretty, but it worked. While it was down there she grabbed its wrist and stomped on its chest, and with a loud tear she pulled its arm off.

As the Hollow Man deflated beneath her, Stephanie realised everything had gone quiet again. She looked up at Skulduggery and Tanith, realised they'd been watching her.

"Not bad," Tanith said, an eyebrow raised.

"That's the last of them," Skulduggery said. "Now for the main event."

The hidden door to the Sanctuary hung open like a gaping wound. A dead Cleaver lay just inside. Stephanie hesitated for a moment, then stepped over the body and they followed the steps down.

The Sanctuary's foyer had witnessed most of the carnage. It was littered with the dead. There were no wounded here, there were no dying – there were only corpses. Some had been cut to ribbons, some were unmarked and there were places, spread across the floor, where there was only the dust of those who had fallen before the Sceptre. Stephanie tried to step without touching the remains, but they were piled so deep that this was impossible.

She passed the Administrator. His body was curled, his fingers hooked and frozen in death. His face was a mask of agony. A victim of Serpine's red right hand.

Skulduggery went to the doorway on their left and peered around, making sure the corridor was empty. Tanith passed, pressing herself against the wall and nodding to him. He moved forward, stopped, nodded back to her, and they continued like this as they stalked deeper into the Sanctuary.

No more walking straight into danger, Stephanie thought to herself. This was the only sign they gave that they might actually be afraid.

She followed along behind. Her palms were slick with sweat and her mouth was dry. She felt as if her legs weren't going to support her for very much longer. Her thoughts went to her parents, her loving parents. If she died here, if she died tonight, would they even notice? Her reflection would carry on with its empty masquerade and they'd gradually begin to realise that this thing, this thing they thought was their daughter, its affections weren't even real. They'd realise it was all an act, but they'd still think it was *her*. And they'd live out the rest of their days thinking that their own daughter didn't love them.

Stephanie didn't want to put them through that. She *was* going to die, she knew she was. She should turn now, and run, run away. This wasn't her business. This wasn't her world. It was like Ghastly said, the first time she met him – Gordon had already lost his life because of this nonsense. Was she so keen to join him?

She didn't hear him. She didn't hear his footsteps, not even when he was so close he could have reached out and stroked her hair. She didn't catch a glimpse out of the corner of her eye, and she didn't notice his shadow or see a reflection, because if he didn't want to be seen, he wouldn't be seen. But as he was moving behind her she felt his presence, she felt the air shift slightly and brush against the skin of her hands and she didn't even have to turn her head – she just *knew*.

She launched herself forward and Skulduggery and Tanith looked back as she rolled and came up.

The White Cleaver stood there, silent as a ghost, deadly as a plague.

Tanith turned to see Valkyrie coming up out of her roll and saw the White Cleaver standing behind her.

"Valkyrie," Tanith said, keeping her voice low and steady, "get behind me."

Stephanie moved backwards and the Cleaver attempted to stop her.

"I'll hold him off," Tanith said, not taking her eyes off her adversary. "You stop Serpine."

Tanith drew her sword, and she heard Skulduggery and

Stephanie hurry away. The White Cleaver reached over his shoulder and pulled out his scythe.

Tanith stepped towards him.

"I ordered you to distract the Hollow Men, didn't I?" she said. "You were one of the Cleavers assigned to us."

He didn't answer. He didn't even move.

"For whats it's worth," Tanith said, "I'm sorry about what happened to you. But it was necessary. And for what it's worth, I'm sorry for what is *going* to happen to you. But that's necessary too." He started twirling his scythe and she raised an eyebrow. "Come and have a go if you think you're hard enough."

He lunged and she blocked and sprang at him, her sword slicing through the air. He ducked back and blocked, spinning as the scythe whistled over Tanith's head. Her sword clashed with his blade and then the handle of the scythe, and his blade clashed with her sword and then the lacquered scabbard she still held in her left hand.

She ducked under his guard, staying in close, where she had the advantage, where he couldn't manoeuvre the scythe.

His blocks were lightning fast but he was on the defensive and one of her strikes would get through eventually. Her sword sliced through his side and he stumbled back, out of range. Tanith looked at the blood on his white coat and gave him a smile. Then the blood started to darken and a black stain moved over the red.

Her smile dropped and the bleeding stopped altogether.

She backed away. There was a door behind her and she waved it open as the Cleaver advanced.

The room she backed into was filled with cages, and in these cages, men and women stood and sat. She realised instantly where she was – the Sanctuary's Gaol. The people in these cages were the worst of the worst, criminals of such a sickening and grotesque order that they had to be held here, in the Sanctuary itself. The cages bound their powers while at the same time sustaining their bodies, keeping them healthy and nourished. It meant neither the Elders nor the Cleavers had to bring them food and water – these criminals only had themselves for company. And when the person in the cage next to each of them was as maniacal and as egotistical as they were, that was hell itself.

The Cleaver pursued her steadily down the steps, sparks flying as their blades clashed.

The prisoners watched, and for the first few moments, they were confused. The Cleavers were their jailers, yet this Cleaver wore white, and they recognised something within him, something that identified him as one of them. They started to shout and cheer as Tanith was forced back, enemies all around her.

She blocked a strike and her bruised wrist gave way. The Cleaver took full advantage, his blade passing along her belly, drawing blood. She grimaced in pain and retreated under the Cleaver's impossibly fast onslaught, barely managing to keep up her defence.

The prisoners laughed and jeered, reaching through the cage bars at her, pulling at her hair, trying to scratch her. One of them snagged her coat and she spun out of it, throwing her sword and scabbard into the air as she freed her arms from the sleeves and catching them again before the Cleaver could close the gap.

He swung and she blocked with the scabbard and flicked up with the sword but he was twisting the scythe, deflecting the strike and coming back with one of his own.

Tanith dodged back, lost her footing and went into a backwards roll as he brought the scythe down, the point of the blade striking the ground where she had just been.

The prisoners howled with laughter as she turned and ran to the wall, the Cleaver right behind her. She jumped to the wall and kept going till she was upside-down, and she crossed the ceiling, trading strikes with the Cleaver below her. He was forced to walk backwards, to defend and attack over his own head.

The Cleaver slashed and missed and she saw her chance and took it. She struck his left hand with her scabbard and his fingers opened. She dropped and flipped, landing before he could recover, and snatched the scythe from his grasp. She kicked out and he stumbled back and she drove her sword into him.

The prisoners stopped jeering. The Cleaver took a step back.

Tanith swung the scythe, burying the blade in his chest. He fell to his knees, black blood dripping on to the floor.

She looked down at him, felt his eyes through his visor, looking back at her. Then his weight fell back onto his haunches, his shoulders sagged and his head lolled forward.

The prisoners were muttering now, cheated out of seeing her die. Tanith gripped her sword and pulled it from the Cleaver's body, snatched up the scabbard and ran for the steps.

She heard a crash from elsewhere in the Sanctuary – the Repository – and urgency lent her speed. Just as she neared the top step, however, one of the prisoners laughed.

She turned and, to her horror, saw the White Cleaver standing, pulling the scythe from his chest. *He can't be stopped*, she said to herself. *Just like Serpine, he can't be stopped.* She ran the last few steps to the door and just as she reached it the breath went out of her.

She stopped, frowning, willing her body to move, but it wouldn't listen. She looked down, at the tip of the scythe that protruded through her chest.

She turned, cursing herself, saw the Cleaver walking up the steps toward her. That was some throw. She almost laughed. Her right arm was numb and her sword fell from her grip. He stepped up beside her and took hold of the scythe. He circled, moving her around, looking at her like he was observing her pain, remembering what it was like.

A twist of his hands and she was forced to her knees. She gasped when he removed the weapon, saw her own blood, deep red, mix with the black blood already on the blade. Her body was shutting down. She wasn't going to be able to defend herself.

He raised the scythe. Tanith looked up, ready to die, then realised that when he had circled her he had passed through the doorway, and was now standing out in the corridor.

She lunged, slamming the door in his visored face. She pressed her hand against it and whispered "Withstand." The sheen spread over the door just as the Cleaver began to pound on it from the other side.

She had failed. She had slowed him down but she hadn't stopped him, and now Serpine had his attack dog back.

Tanith tried standing but her body couldn't take any more.

She slumped to the ground. The prisoners watched from their cages with delighted eyes, and as her blood seeped through her tunic, they started whispering.

29

DEEP IN DUBLIN, DEATH

The White Cleaver stood there, silent as a ghost, deadly as a plague.

"Valkyrie," Tanith said. "Get behind me." Stephanie backed up until she was beside Skulduggery.

"I'll hold him off," Tanith said. "You stop Serpine." She drew her sword. The Cleaver drew his scythe.

Stephanie felt Skulduggery touch her arm and they moved off. "You're going to have to go after the Sceptre," Skulduggery whispered as they jogged through the corridor. "You can get close to it, I can't. It's not much of a plan, but sometimes simplicity is the way to go."

The Repository was just ahead. They slowed, and Skulduggery gripped both her arms and turned to her. "But you listen to me. If it goes wrong, if we lose the element of surprise, I want you to get out of here. No matter what happens to me, I want you to run, do you understand?"

Stephanie swallowed. "Yes."

He hesitated. "Serpine used my wife and child as a weapon against me. In order to do so, he had to kill them. He took my family's death and he made it about me. Valkyrie, when you die, it will be *your* death and yours alone. Let it come to you on your own terms." She nodded.

"Valkyrie Cain," he said, "it has been an absolute pleasure knowing you."

She looked back at him. "You too." If he'd had lips, she knew he'd be smiling.

They sneaked up to the doors. They were already open and Stephanie could see Serpine, the Sceptre in his hand and his back to them, taking slow, deliberate steps towards the Book of Names. Sagacious Tome was watching, but he too had his back to the doors.

"I can't see Mr Bliss," Stephanie whispered and Skulduggery shook his head – neither could he.

Stephanie hesitated, then passed into the Repository and crept to her left. She reached a heavy table laden with artefacts and peered around. Serpine had stopped walking, and for a moment she thought he knew she was there, but as she watched he turned and walked back, shaking his head.

"It's still too strong," he said.

"It's as weak as it's going to get," Sagacious Tome said. "I thought with Meritorious and Morwenna dead, the barrier wouldn't pose a problem. But I can't withdraw my contribution to the spell, not without the others joining me in the ceremony."

Serpine rejoined Tome, arching an eyebrow. "Then perhaps we shouldn't have killed them."

"*I* didn't kill them!" Tome said defensively. "You did!"

Stephanie stayed low as she crept from behind the table. Serpine laughed. "I may have been the one to turn them to dust, but you set them up, Sagacious, you drew them in. You betrayed them."

Tome spun on Serpine, jabbing at the space between them with his finger. "No, I didn't! It was their weakness that led to their downfall, their own shortcomings. They had all this power and they were satisfied to just, to just *sit* there and let it all go to waste."

"Until recently, I had never thought of you as ambitious..."

"No one had. *Sagacious Tome*, they said, *he's a non-entity. He's not the strongest, he's not the wisest... he's nothing.* That's what they said. I know it. For years, people have been underestimating me. It's time people recognised my power."

Stephanie got to her hands and knees and started crawling. She was in shadow and they weren't looking her way, but if either turned there was a chance they would see her. Stephanie wasn't in the mood to take any chances.

"I'm going to make them pay," Tome was saying. "Everyone who ever questioned me. The streets will run red with their blood."

"How dramatic," Serpine said and raised his hand. Stephanie saw the Book lift off its pedestal and hover there for a moment, then he grunted impatiently and let it drop again.

"I told you, that's not going to work!" Tome said. "It's how close you are to *getting* it. It doesn't have to be *physically* close; it isn't a *physical* barrier. It's a *mental* barrier!"

Stephanie held her breath. She was behind the pillar next to them. Serpine's voice was so close he could have been speaking right into her ear. "So with you, the final Elder, remaining, the barrier isn't sufficiently weakened to let me through, is that right?"

"Yes, but that's not my fault! I did what I could!"

"Yes, you did, yes, you did. And now there's one more thing you can do to help solve this little problem."

"What are you talking about?" Tome asked and then his tone changed suddenly, became afraid. "What are you doing? Point that thing somewhere else, Serpine. *I'm warning you, point that—*"

There was a black flash, and silence.

After a moment, she heard Serpine's footsteps move off again, and Stephanie took a peek. He was walking slowly, concentrating on the Book, his back to her. This was the only chance she was going to get.

She crept out from behind the pillar, ignoring the fresh pile of dust at her feet. There was no way she could close the distance without giving herself away. He'd hear her, sense her, whatever. But he was holding the Sceptre in his hand so *loosely...*

Stephanie narrowed her eyes and stepped forward.

He had heard her and was turning, but she didn't care. The Sceptre was coming up, the black crystal starting to glow. She flexed her fingers and splayed her hand, snapping open her palm and pushing at the air, and the space around her hand rippled and the Sceptre flew from Serpine's grasp, flew away from them both and hit the far wall.

Serpine hissed in anger and turned. They heard the Sceptre

start to sing as Skulduggery sprinted in. He dived into the air and the space around him shimmered as he shot forward. He covered the distance in the blink of an eye. He crashed into Serpine, taking him off his feet.

They hit the pedestal and it toppled, the Book falling as they sprawled on to the ground. Skulduggery was the first to stand and he hauled Serpine up, shoved him against a pillar and fired off a punch that jerked his head back.

Serpine lunged but Skulduggery snagged his wrist and stepped in and then *under* the arm. He turned and wrenched and Serpine yelled in pain as a loud *crack* echoed through the chamber.

Serpine tried gathering purple vapour in his hand but Skulduggery batted the hand away, chopped into the side of his neck. Serpine gagged and dropped back, and Skulduggery kicked his legs out from under him.

"You never could fight worth a damn," Skulduggery said, standing over him. "But then you didn't need to, did you? Not when you had lackeys to do the fighting for you. Where are your lackeys now, Nefarian?"

"I don't need them," Serpine muttered. "I don't need anyone. I'll crush you myself. Grind your bones to *dust*."

Skulduggery tilted his head. "Unless you've got an army

tucked away in that fancy coat of yours, I sincerely doubt it."

Serpine scrambled up and rushed at him, but Skulduggery drove in a kick and brought his closed fist down on to his shoulder, and Serpine fell to his knees.

Stephanie had to get to the Sceptre before Serpine recovered. She was pushing herself off the ground when she realised that the Book of Names was lying open right beside her. She glanced at the pages and the columns of names started to rearrange themselves before her eyes. She saw her own name written there, but she looked up when she heard Skulduggery grunt.

Serpine was on his knees but his lips were moving, and the wall behind Skulduggery came alive with hands that reached out and grabbed him. Skulduggery was pulled back and Serpine stood. There were a series of dull cracks and pops as Serpine's broken bones mended and realigned.

"Where are your oh-so-clever taunts *now*, detective?"

Skulduggery struggled against the grip of a dozen hands. "You've got big ears," he managed to say, before he was pulled even further back, *into the wall*, and then he was gone.

Serpine looked over, saw Stephanie, saw how close she was to the Sceptre.

He snapped out his hand and a thin purple tendril whipped towards the Sceptre. He pulled his arm back and the Sceptre flew off the ground but Stephanie lunged and managed to grab it.

She was jerked off her feet but her grip was strong and the tendril broke, becoming vapour, and she hit the floor. She heard a crash and looked around as a table hurtled straight at her. She tried to dive out of the way but she wasn't quick enough.

It hit her and she screamed, dropped the Sceptre and clutched at her broken leg. She shut her eyes against the tears of pain, and when she opened them again, Mr Bliss was walking into the room.

"Where have you been?" Serpine snapped.

"I was delayed," Mr Bliss answered. "But you seem to have done fine without me."

Serpine narrowed his eyes. "Indeed. Still, there's one more adversary to deal with."

Mr Bliss looked at Stephanie. "You're going to kill her?"

"Me? No. You are."

"I'm sorry?"

"If you want to reap the rewards of this night, you have to get your hands a little bloody."

"You want *me* to kill an unarmed child?" Mr Bliss asked doubtfully.

"Look on it as a test of your commitment to our lords and

masters. You don't have a problem with that, do you?"

Mr Bliss looked at him coolly. "Do you have a weapon for me, or do you just want me to beat her to death with a large stick?"

Serpine took a dagger from his coat and lobbed it over to him. Mr Bliss snatched it out of the air and held it, testing its weight. Stephanie felt her throat go dry.

Mr Bliss looked at her but didn't say anything. He just sighed and hurled the dagger, and Stephanie made a face and turned her head...

...and heard Serpine laugh.

She looked back. The dagger hadn't touched her. It hadn't even come close. It was in Serpine's hand. He had caught it before it had sliced into his glittering left eye.

"I thought as much," Serpine said.

Mr Bliss flung himself at Serpine, but Serpine ripped his glove off and raised his red right hand and Mr Bliss collapsed. Serpine listened to him scream for a few moments before dropping his hand, and Mr Bliss gasped.

"No doubt you want to kill me," Serpine said as he approached him. "No doubt you want to rip me limb from limb, and with your legendary strength, I know you could do it and not even exert yourself. But answer me this, Mr Bliss – what good is legendary strength when you can't get close enough to use it?"

Mr Bliss tried to stand, but his knees gave out and he hit the ground again.

"I'm curious," Serpine continued. "Why the pretence? Why go to all this trouble; why put yourself in this position? Why didn't you just stick with the detective?"

Mr Bliss managed to shake his head. "We mightn't have been able to stop you," he said. "I know you, Serpine... you always have plans to fall back on. You were too... dangerous... too unpredictable. I needed you to get the Sceptre."

Serpine smiled. "And why was that?"

Mr Bliss echoed that smile with one of his own, albeit a drained and sickly version. "Because once you had the Sceptre, I could predict your actions."

"So you predicted my invulnerability?" Serpine laughed. "Oh, well done."

"No one's invulnerable," Mr Bliss whispered.

"Yes, well," Serpine said with a shrug. "*You're* certainly not."

Stephanie watched in horror as Serpine again pointed his right hand and Mr Bliss contorted in agony. His screams reached new heights, and just when it seemed like he could take no more, Serpine picked him up and, with his hands pressed against him, gathered the purple vapour in his fists. Mr Bliss was blasted backwards through the air, into a group of shelves at the far side of the room. He didn't get up.

Serpine turned back to Stephanie.

"Sorry for the interruption," he said as he picked her up. His hands gripped the lapels of her coat and he lifted her off her feet, looking up at her as he spoke. Her right leg dangled uselessly, and that pain was all she felt. "How did you do it? How did you get so close without the Sceptre alerting me? Some magic I don't know about?" Stephanie didn't answer.

"Miss Cain, I know you're trying to hide it, but I can see the fear in your eyes. You don't want to die today, do you? Of course you don't. You have your whole life ahead of you. If only you'd kept out of all this, if only you'd left the death of your uncle alone, you wouldn't be here right now.

"Your uncle was a very stubborn man. If he had just given me the key when I asked, you wouldn't be in this predicament. He delayed my plans, you see, caused a lot of unnecessary stress and bother. A lot of people are dead now because of him."

Stephanie's face twisted. "Don't you *dare* blame my uncle for the people you've killed!"

"I didn't want this. I didn't want conflict. I just wanted to eliminate the Elders and take the Book. Do you see how simple that would have been? Instead, I had to wade through a river of corpses. Those deaths are on your uncle's head." Stephanie's hatred became a cold thing in her centre.

"But you don't have to join them, Miss Cain. You can survive this. You can *live*. I see something in you. I think you'd like the new world that's coming."

"I wouldn't bet on it," Stephanie said quietly.

Serpine smiled patiently and leaned his face in close to her. "You can survive... if you tell me how you got so close without the Sceptre alerting me."

With no weapons left, Stephanie spat on him. He sighed and threw her against a pillar. She smacked into it and her body twisted and she dropped on to her back.

Her eyes wouldn't focus. The pain was far away. She heard his voice like there was a wall separating them.

"No matter. I am about to make slaves of the entire population of this planet, and then there will be no more secrets. There will be no magic hidden from me. And when the Faceless Ones return, this world will be remade as a place of splendid darkness."

He passed her, a vague shape in the corner of her eye. She had to get up. She had to snap out of this. The pain. The pain from her broken leg, she had to let it in. It was nothing more than a sensation now – she had to allow it to flood her.

She focused on her leg. It was throbbing, the pain spiking, and with each new height it reached her mind sharpened a little more. Then the pain came at her, cascaded over her with its full force, and she had to bite her lip to stop from crying out.

She looked up. Serpine was approaching the Book. Stephanie gripped the edge of a table-top and pulled herself up on to her good leg. She grabbed the first thing she saw – a glass vial filled with green liquid – and threw it. It hit Serpine in the back and shattered, and the liquid turned to vapour and dissipated into the air. He spun round, angry.

"You, my dear, have proven yourself to be far too troublesome for your own good." He raised his red hand.

He raised his red hand, and from somewhere behind her she heard the Sceptre singing again. And then Skulduggery dropped through the ceiling, landing in a heap next to Serpine. The detective looked around.

"Ah," he said. "I'm back."

"You are," Serpine said, and Skulduggery looked up and saw him.

Serpine lashed a kick into Skulduggery's side and Skulduggery grunted. He tried to get up, but Serpine batted his hands away and grabbed his skull. He drove his knee into the side of Skulduggery's head and Skulduggery sprawled on to his back.

Serpine looked over to Stephanie and then to the ground behind her and she turned, saw the Sceptre. She lunged for it but a purple tendril wrapped itself around her waist and she was yanked back on to her broken leg. She cried out as the pain shot through her.

Serpine whipped the tendril to the Sceptre, yanked it into his left hand and whirled, the crystal flashing with a black light that streaked towards Skulduggery. The detective dived as a whole section of the wall behind him turned to dust. Skulduggery drew his gun and fired, hitting Serpine in the chest.

"Still with that little toy of yours," Serpine said, amused and unharmed. "How quaint."

Skulduggery circled him. Serpine held the Sceptre down by his side. "You'll be stopped," Skulduggery said. "You've always been stopped."

"Oh, my old foe, but this is different. Those days are gone. Who is there to rise up against me? Who is left? Remember when you were a man? A real man, I mean, not this mockery I see before me. Do you remember what it was like? You had an army on your side, you had people willing to fight and die for your cause. We wanted to bring the Faceless Ones back, to worship them as the gods that they are. You wanted to keep them out, so that this infestation of humanity, this celebration of the mundane, might be allowed to live and thrive. Well, they've lived, and they've thrived, and now their time is up."

Skulduggery's finger tightened on the trigger. Black blood sprayed from Serpine's chest, and the wound instantly healed. Serpine laughed.

"You have caused me so much trouble over the years, detective, it's almost a shame that I have to end it."

Skulduggery cocked his head. "You're surrendering?"

"I'm going to miss this," Serpine said. "If it makes it any easier, you can think of your imminent demise as a good thing. I don't think you'll much like the world once my lords and masters remake it."

"So how are you going to kill me?" Skulduggery asked, dropping his gun and holding his arms out. "With your toy? Or one of these new tricks you've learned?"

Serpine smiled. "I *have* been expanding my repertoire. So good of you to notice."

"And I see you've been playing around with necromancy again."

"Indeed. My very own pet Cleaver. Every home should have one."

"He's a tricky fellow to put down," Skulduggery said. "I tried everything I know – he just kept getting back up."

Serpine laughed. "There's an old Necromancer saying – you can't kill what's already dead."

Skulduggery cocked his head. "He's a zombie?"

"Oh, no, I wouldn't associate myself with those wretched things. He can repair, replenish, heal. A difficult process to master, but I am nothing if not accomplished."

"Of *course*," Skulduggery said, something new in his voice. "The medical equipment in the warehouse. The Cleaver was a test-run, to see if the process worked. Then you did it to yourself."

"Ah, the great detective finally figures something out."

"Bells and whistles aside, Nefarian, he's nothing but a zombie. And so are you."

Serpine shook his head. "Your last words are pathetic insults? I was hoping for more. Something profound, perhaps. Maybe a poem." He raised the Sceptre. "It will be a slightly less strange world without you, I just want you to know that."

Stephanie screamed his name as Skulduggery dived. Serpine laughed and the Sceptre sent out its bolt of black lightning but Skulduggery had seized the Book of Names and held it as a shield.

The black lightning hit the Book and it disappeared in a cloud of dust.

"NO!" Serpine screamed. "*NO!*"

Stephanie stared as the Book that the Elders couldn't destroy sifted through Skulduggery's fingers. He charged through the cloud, slamming into Serpine. The Sceptre fell and rolled away. Serpine's hands closed around Skulduggery's neck, forcing his head back.

"You ruined it!" he hissed. "You ruined it *all*, you pathetic creature!"

Skulduggery slammed a fist into Serpine's face and batted the hands away. He stepped in with a jab that rocked the sorcerer's head. Serpine blasted Skulduggery with purple vapour and Skulduggery was flung off his feet.

He landed on his side and rolled, coming up to his knees as Serpine whipped a tendril out for the Sceptre. It sped towards him but Skulduggery pushed outwards at the air, breaking the tendril and knocking the Sceptre off course.

Skulduggery gathered flame in his fist and threw it at Serpine, who barely managed to deflect it. It exploded on the wall behind him and Serpine hissed again, stumbling away before being launched backwards as the air rippled around him. He hit the wall and stayed there, high off the ground, held up by Skulduggery's outstretched hand from across the room.

"I'll destroy you," he snarled, his emerald eyes blazing with hatred. "I destroyed you once. I will do it again!"

He struggled to raise his right arm. Skulduggery pressed against him harder, drawing on his last reserves. But Serpine refused to be beaten. The fingers of his red hand pointed at Skulduggery.

"Die," Serpine whispered.

Skulduggery inclined his head a little to the right and didn't fall. Serpine's face contorted with rage.

"Die!" he screamed.

Skulduggery remained standing. "Looks like there's something that hand of yours can't kill after all."

A figure moved in the doorway. Serpine's laugh was one of spittle and gritted teeth as the White Cleaver appeared.

"So you have an immunity to my power... No matter. That scythe of his will shear through your bones. You'll be nothing but rubble when he's through with you. Cleaver, *attack!*"

But the Cleaver stayed where he was and Serpine's confidence started to ebb. "What are you doing? Kill him!"

The White Cleaver took another moment, and then walked away.

Serpine screamed his rage.

"You've lost, Nefarian," Skulduggery said. "Even your

henchman is abandoning you. Even he recognises your defeat. I'm placing you under arrest for murder, attempted murder, conspiracy to commit murder and, I don't know, possibly littering."

Serpine spat. "You will never beat me. I will *always* find a way to make you suffer." And then his green eyes flickered towards Stephanie, still lying on the ground.

"Don't," Skulduggery said, but Serpine was already moving his hand across his body. "Serpine, don't!"

Stephanie cried out as a pain more intense then anything she had ever felt scourged her body. Serpine twisted his fingers and the pain intensified, turning her cry into a scream, turning the scream to silent agony. She curled up, feeling something cold spread from her belly, a welcome numbness that cancelled the pain, that moved into her arms and legs, that wrapped itself around her heart and seeped into her mind. And now there was nothing, now there were just vague images, of Serpine and Skulduggery, a distant voice, Skulduggery calling out to her, but that too was fading. No pain now. No sound. Her eyelids fluttered. Serpine, with that grin. Skulduggery, holding his free hand out, and something moving through the air, everything moving so, so slowly.

The Sceptre, it was the Sceptre, and then it was in Skulduggery's gloved hand and his fingers were tightening around it. He was raising his arm and pointing, pointing the Sceptre at Serpine, and the little crystal started to glow. It glowed dark, a pretty little darkness, and then the air cracked.

The coldness had overtaken her now, the numbness was everywhere, and the last bits that made her who she was were gradually drifting away. She didn't care. She didn't mind at all. Let them go. She didn't have a care in the world.

Serpine's grinning face. His eyes. His smile. All those teeth. His skin, creased in savage pleasure. And now that skin was changing, and it was drying, and it was cracking, and the smile was fading, and the emerald green eyes were losing their gleam, clouding over, and Serpine turned to dust that fell to the floor.

And there was a ringing, a ringing in her ears, and her fingertips were tingling, and warmth was rushing back to her and her heart was beating again and her lungs sucked in air and Stephanie gasped.

Skulduggery ran over and kneeled beside her. "Are you all right?" he asked, but all she could do was shiver. Her leg twisted and she hissed in pain, but it was a bearable pain, it was a good pain.

"Come on," Skulduggery said, taking her arm gently. "Let's get you out of here."

She put her weight on him and he half carried her, half lifted her out of the chamber and into the corridor. They passed the gaol as the door opened and Tanith toppled out. She hit the ground and groaned. Stephanie looked down at her friend, at all that blood.

"Tanith?"

Tanith raised her head. "Oh, good," she muttered. "You're alive."

Skulduggery reached for her, pulled her carefully to her feet and, with an arm around each, he guided them both to the foyer. They climbed the stairs slowly and moved through the Waxworks. The rain had stopped and the ground was wet as they emerged into the night.

China Sorrows was standing beside her car, waiting for them. When they were close enough so Stephanie could see the delicate earrings China was wearing, she spoke. "You've all seen better days."

"Could have used your help," Skulduggery said as they came to a stop.

China shrugged her slender shoulders. "I knew you could do it without me. I had faith. Serpine?"

"Dust," Skulduggery said. "Too many plans, too many schemes. Sooner or later they'd cancel each other out. That was always his trouble."

"How did you manage it?"

"He wanted immortality, so he chose death on his own terms – a living death."

China smiled. "Aha. And because the Sceptre can only be wielded when its previous owner is dead, or in this case, when its owner is the *living* dead..."

"I took it and used it on *him*." He held up the Sceptre. "Something happened though. There's no power in it any more."

China took it from him, turning it over in her hands. "It was fuelled by his hate. Obviously, using it against him made it feed on itself. Congratulations, Skulduggery, you've managed to break the ultimate weapon. It's nothing but an ornament now."

"An ornament I'd like back," he said, holding out his hand. She smiled, turning her head slightly to look at him out of the corner of her eye.

"I'll buy it from you," she said.

"Why would you want it?" he asked. "It's worthless."

"Sentimental reasons. Besides, you know what an avid collector I am."

He sighed. "Fine, take it."

There it was, that smile again. "Thank you. Oh, and the Book?"

"Destroyed."

"How very like you to destroy the indestructible. You have quite an appetite for destruction, don't you?"

"China, these bones are weary..."

"Then I shall leave you."

"Bliss is still in there," Stephanie said. "I think he was working against Serpine the whole time. I don't know if he's alive though."

"That brother of mine is quite resilient. I've tried to kill him three times already and he just won't stay down." China got into her car, looked at them through the open window. "Oh, by the way, all three of you – congratulations on saving the world."

She gave them a beautiful smile and they watched her drive off. They stood there for a while. The sky was beginning to brighten, the first rays of the morning sun seeping into the black.

"You know," Tanith said weakly, "I still have a gigantic hole in my back."

"Sorry," Skulduggery said and helped them both towards the Bentley.

30

AN END, A BEGINNING

omewhere in Haggard, a dog was barking. Somewhere a driver beeped his horn and somewhere else people were laughing. It was a Friday night and music drifted to Stephanie's open window from the bars and pubs on Main Street, snatches of songs, piggybacking on the warm breeze.

Stephanie sat in her swivel chair, her foot resting on the bed. Skulduggery had taken her to a friend of his, a cantankerous old man who had mended her broken leg within an hour. It was still stiff and she couldn't walk on it, but the bruising had gone down and in another few days it would be like it had never been broken at all.

She didn't mind the recuperation period she had been advised to take. After the week she'd just had, a week in which she'd seen wonder and magic and death and destruction, she could do with a little holiday.

Skulduggery Pleasant sat on the windowsill and told her what was happening in the world outside her bedroom. The White Cleaver had vanished, and they still didn't know why, or even *how*, he had ignored his master's final command. Skulduggery had a suspicion that he was under orders from somebody else, but just who this mystery master was, he didn't yet know. Serpine's allies had resurfaced and struck, and then vanished again when the news of the sorcerer's demise had reached them. Serpine's grand scheme may have failed, but because of it, the Cleavers' numbers had been decimated, and their duties now stretched them thin.

"How's Tanith?" Stephanie asked. "Will she be OK?"

"She's lucky to be alive. The injury she took was severe, but she's strong. She'll pull through. I'll take you to see her when you're rested."

"And Ghastly? Any change?"

"I'm afraid not. They're keeping him safe, but... we don't

know how long he'll stay like that. Fortunately for him, the time will pass in the blink of an eye. The rest of us will have to wait. On the bright side, the Sanctuary has a new and interesting addition to their Hall of Statues."

"Do they *have* a Hall of Statues?"

"Well, no. But now that they've got a statue, maybe they'll start."

"What are they going to do about the Elder Council?"

"Meritorious was a good man and the most powerful Grand Mage we had seen in a long time. The other Councils in Europe are worried about who will fill the vacuum now that he's gone. The Americans are offering their support, the Japanese are sending delegates to help us wrest back some control, but..."

"It sounds like a lot of people are panicking."

"And they have a right to. Our systems of power, our systems of self-government, are delicate. If we topple, others will follow. We need a strong leader."

"Why don't you do it?"

He laughed. "Because I'm not well liked, and I'm not well trusted, and I already have a job. I'm a detective, remember?"

She gave her own little shrug. "Vaguely."

Another snippet of pub music drifted by the window, and Stephanie thought about the world she'd grown up in, and how different it was from the world she'd been introduced to, and yet how similar. There was joy and happiness in both, just as there was heartbreak and horror. There was good and evil and everything in between, and these qualities seemed to be shared equally in the worlds of the magical and the mundane. It was her life now. She couldn't imagine living without either one.

"How are you?" Skulduggery asked, his voice gentle.

"Me? I'm fine."

"Really? No nightmares?"

"Maybe one or two," she admitted.

"They'll always be there, reminding us of where we went wrong. If you pay attention to your bad dreams, they can help you."

"I'll be sure to keep that in mind next time I'm asleep."

"Good," said Skulduggery. "In any event, get well soon. We have mysteries to solve, and adventures to undertake, and I need my partner and student with me."

"Student?"

He shrugged. "Things are going to get a lot rougher from here on in, and I need someone to fight by my side. There's something about you, Valkyrie. I'm not quite sure what it is. I look at you and..."

"And you're reminded of yourself when you were my age?"

"Hmm? Oh, no, what I was going to say is there's something about you that is really annoying, and you never do what you're told, and sometimes I question your intelligence, but even so I'm going to train you, because I like having someone follow me around like a little puppy. It makes me feel good about myself."

She rolled her eyes. "You are such a moron."

"Don't be jealous of my genius."

"Can you get over yourself for just a moment?"

"If only that were possible."

"For a guy with no internal organs, you've got quite the ego."

"And for a girl who can't stand up without falling over, you're quite the critic."

"My leg will be fine."

"And my ego will flourish. What a pair we are."

She had to laugh. "Go on, get out. Mum'll be up soon to check on me."

"Before I go..."

"Yes?"

"Aren't you going to show me what you've been practising? You've been dying to show off from the moment I knocked on this window."

Stephanie looked at him and arched an eyebrow, but he

was right and he knew it. The other good thing about this recuperation period was that she had all the time she wanted to develop her powers, and she hadn't wasted the few days that had passed already.

She clicked her fingers, summoning a small flame into the palm of her hand. She watched it flicker and dance, then looked up at Skulduggery and grinned.

"Magic," he said.